(BRACKETS)

By Joanne K Jardine

"Dedicated to anyone who ever thought life didn't turn out quite as you planned"

Acknowledgments

I would like to thank everyone who has stood by me throughout the composition of my book, without who, I'm not sure it would within the covers it is today.

Thank you to SHN Publishing, who without, none of this would have been possible. And also to Andy Donnan for coming up with the cover idea, and Tracey Ramsey for bringing that idea to life.

Thank you to my Mum and Dad for always listening to me moan, groan and complain and for being the two people who have moulded me into the person I am today. Thank you for standing by my choices in life and leading me in the right direction towards these choices. And to Stuart for telling me every day you are never helping me with another thing but always being the first to offer support when I need it.

Thank you, to my best friend, Fiona Grant, the one person who for the last twenty-two years of my life has helped me to get through even the darkest day when I faced my own heart-breaking moments. Whether I see you every day or once a year, I know you are there every time I need you.

Thank you to Lisa Graham, my own tower of strength. I can turn to you even at the most difficult of times and know that you will say the right thing to make the smile come back to my face.

And finally, thank you to Chris Keltie, my very own Dale Brenton, only this one is all mine. Thank you for loving me through the good times and the bad, and for living my dreams with me every day.

"*Everyone has their soul-mate. That person they think of and smile, who gives them butterflies and they never have to struggle to put words together to make a conversation with. Everything around you relates to them and you are given constant reminders. Every song, every film, every word. When you find your soul-mate you get that kiss where everything around you goes hazy, the butterflies start again and you want that moment to last forever. You want to laugh and cry because you feel so lucky that you have found this person but so scared that they will go away at the same time. You want that person to be your first, your last, your everything, your every moment. You want every moment of your life to be spent with them. Everything you ever wanted to see you want them to be there with you just so you can look in their eyes, smile and create an image of the two of you together that will last a lifetime. Finding your soul-mate may happen at the best time or the worst time, but as long as you're willing to keep faith and hold on you will be with them one day and when that day comes it will last forever and your souls will be joined in this life, and the next*"

(Brackets)

First published in the United Kingdom 2011.

Copyright © Joanne K Jardine
All rights reserved.

A catalogue record of this book is available from the
British Library.

ISBN 978-1-907463-43-3

© Cover art by Tracey Ramsey

(Brackets)

Contents

CHAPTER ONE
August 11th, 2008
8.07am.

The nerves were starting to set in, and that wave of panic was easing slowly from my toes directly to my brain, so it became apparent this was all very real. Saying I was terrified didn't really cut it; if the world decided to open the ground and swallow me whole, it would've done me the biggest favour, ever.

"Ok, Kier, calm down." Looking in the mirror and talking to myself wasn't doing much to boost the fact that I was starting to think I was bordering on insanity. "You'll be fine. Just breathe."

You'll now be thinking I'm about to undergo some kind of major surgery, or some anxiety-stricken event that could destroy my whole world. Well, the surgery is a *no,* I'm fit and healthy, but the major event, well that's another matter altogether because I am about to face something so scary, so frightening that I can barely hold myself together. It was a no wonder I was becoming insane. You see, the thing is, I'm about to start a new...JOB.

Ok, I get it. I am ridiculous, in fact more than ridiculous; I'm positively stupid beyond belief. I mean, I was going to be starting possibly the most fantastic job imaginable, and I was going to be working for the same company I had been working with for the last eight years, just working in a different department. I had been recruited as one of the new designers for DB designs. That's right Dale Brenton, the most celebrated designer of the 21st century, and I was going to be allowed to have some of my designs be labelled under his illustrious name. I could hardly believe it. I had literally walked out of design school at Parson's in NYC and been offered an interview with one of the leading designers in the fashion world. To be offered an interview seemed an unbelievable success, but to actually be chosen, out of the hundred other people who had applied as one of the new designers, well, that was something all together more fantastic, amazing, wonderful, really just everything.

Having been doing mail room work for the company all the way through high school, and then design school, I knew every in and out of the company, and given that I was looking to become a designer, a few opportunities had arisen to allow me to show off my, I want to say talent, but I don't want to sound conceited. In actual fact, I had met Dale Brenton himself at a showcase event a few months previous. He was one of those people your eye instantly went to and he almost eluded power from his pores. He was simply breath-taking. Extremely good looking, with what seemed like a personality underneath, a hard thing to find in not only fashion designers, but men in general. There was evidently talk that he was as gay as every other major designer on the planet, but I was unconvinced. He didn't have the usual camp-ness, in fact, the opposite. He had this certain ruggedness that, to me, was irresistible. From the first moment I laid eyes on him I was under his spell. Unfortunately, me being me made some idiotic comment about being from the Bronx and then proceeded to babble about nothing that made any sense in any way. However, I obviously must have made an impression with my work, because it was he himself who scouted me for an interview, which is pretty unbelievable really, but very flattering at the same time. I hadn't stopped smiling since I got the call firstly about the interview, and then about the job offer, I honestly couldn't believe this was my life. Who actually ever gets their dream career? That's why I'm so nervous – I've got the dream and it terrifies me that I might do something to mess it up. I really do over think everything. If I learned to relax, life would be so much easier. I just have to keep telling myself that I got the job for a reason. They obviously have faith in me, so I should have it in myself.

08.23am

Ok, I am officially going to be late, which makes me more nervous. I'm going to have to sprint through Central Park, or more, skate really quickly given I'm never too far from my skateboard. God please don't let me be late.
One last look in the mirror. One last reassuring glance.

Smile. Good.

I had been planning my first day outfit since I heard I'd got the job; black skirt, white top with a black top over it, and a pair of killer knee high boots but I woke up this morning and decided that after having worked in the mail room for so long it would look suspicious if after having been a complete tom boy for the last eight years I suddenly showed up being girly. I wasn't exactly the best at dressing up so I went for my usual baggy Road denims, my favourite Batman T-Shirt, and a pair of white canvas tennis shoes. We'd been told to dress as we pleased; as dressed, or as casual as we liked. The 'we' in question is the four others I would be working with. The advertisement for the job had been for five new members of staff to work together on a new project. Although we would have our own thoughts and ideas we had been placed together to develop a new range of sport and active wear that DB Designs were hoping to launch in the New Year. We were still going to have every opportunity to design other types of clothing too, but they wanted people who had a sports background to be the soul creators. I wasn't sure who the other four were, or what their sporting backgrounds were, but mine lay in a variety. I had been a dancer since the age of twelve, been playing basketball for four years, and I had been skateboarding since I could walk. I've also played soccer, La Crosse, and had done numerous Triathlons, including one ironman. So as you can see, I'm pretty sporty.

I glanced in the mirror one last time and decided I was ready to go. I was ready to begin the first day of the rest of my life.

"Suranne Taylor. Great to meet you all."

The woman standing in front of me wasn't what you would expect from a design expert. I had known Suranne for years and never once seen her with any sort of personal style on show; she always seemed to wear the same style of black trousers, and black top everyday. I shouldn't make comments on her as she had given me a lot of opportunities when it came to showcasing my designs in different events that DB Designs were a part of. She was the manager for DB's Casual wear and was taking on the role as our "mentor" within the Sport and Active wear range, although mentor may be a strong word. Suranne was quite a dowdy character and obviously wasn't the most active person herself given she was a little "soft" round the edges. But, like I said, it's not my place to comment, I was sure Suranne was a fabulous designer and I had a feeling she had had a lot of input into me being hired, so I had a lot to thank her for.

"As you know, each of you has been brought here due to not only your talents in design, but due to the unique fact that you are all, or have all been involved in the sporting world at some point. Given the diverse nature of your sporting interests, you were all handpicked to create a range of clothing that can cover people within all areas of sport and leisure wear, allowing you all to propel DB Designs into a whole new vicinity of fashion."

Suranne looked like a proud mother on her kids' first day at school. I knew this wasn't her project idea, far from it, as she hadn't been too keen to go down the route of sportswear but her head had obviously been turned when it came to beginning the project, because she generally looked proud to be heading up such a vivacious venture.

"So I think introductions are in order. I already know Kier as she has been working in a different department of DB Designs for a few years now. Obviously none of the rest of you know her, and I don't really know any of the rest of you so let's start with you Kier. Just a brief intro, background etc." Suranne smiled over to me, and nodded her head to indicate for me to start talking.

I had been sitting almost in silence since I walked into the office. It's not that I'm shy but as soon as I viewed the other girls I almost wished I'd wore the skirt and boots. The four of them looked like they had just come off the runway, not about to design for one. They were possibly the most gorgeous group of girls that could've been placed in one room, ever. And me, well, I felt like a boy. I had topped off my outfit with my favourite baseball cap for luck and now I felt like an idiot. The only plus point was that I at least felt myself, so that was keeping me slightly calmer.

"Hi!" I instantly felt more relaxed when the words left my mouth. So I let my shoulders dropped, my smile return, and then I continued. "I'm Kier Scott. I just turned twenty-four and I graduated from Parson's School of Design in July. You'll be able to tell from the accent that I'm not American. I'm actually Scottish but I moved to NYC when I was twelve with my parents when my Dad got transferred for work, and for some reason, my Scottish twang is still easily recognisable. My background has been designing casual wear, although I won Young Designer of the Year for my range of Oscar-inspired dresses. Ok, so sports-wise, here we go. I've been a dancer for twelve years, been playing basketball for four years, and as you can probably tell from my outfit, and the fact my skateboard is attached to my bag, I'm a bit of a skater girl, too. I've been involved in a few other sports, in fact, pretty much most sports. I'm quite competitive so it was a good way to channel it. I've worked in the mail room here since high school and been lucky enough to have had the opportunity to take part in showcases where my work has been seen. I can't wait to get started within the design part of the company now having seen it from the background for so long." I meant what I said; I wasn't just trying to suck up or anything. This was my idea of a dream come true and I wanted Suranne to know how grateful I was that I was part of this project.

As I turned to sit down, I was suddenly aware of how big my smile had got and how I no longer felt that wave of panic that I'd had before. I was starting to calm down and I was just ready and raring to go. But of course, I had four co-workers to find out about. And without me realising it Suranne had already told the next girl to introduce herself.

"Hi, my name's Ashleigh Jenner, I'm twenty-nine, and you'll be able to see I'm all the way from Texas. Dallas to be exact. I graduated seven years ago from San Diego University, having studied textile design, and landed a job working in the wedding section of Vera Wang, which was wonderful, but not quite my idea of designing. I learned so much, but it was obviously quite restricting, being unable to use colour and design everyday clothing, so when I saw the advertisement for this job I was so determined to get it. I love DB Designs and the idea of designing or co-designing a whole new range is of course every designers' dream. My sporting background is in volleyball, played all through college, and I'm still part of a team here in New York where I get the chance to play as often as I want. Like Kier, I too feel completely ready to go, and I am so happy to be a part of such an amazing company."

Without Ashleigh saying a word you could've told she was a volleyball player. Tall, lean and a figure to die for. She had a mass of blonde hair, with platinum highlights and like I said before; looked like she should be modelling the clothes, not designing them. She seemed like your typical Texan, big smile and an even bigger personality. She seemed the type of girl I would definitely get on with and after hearing her speak my nerves were completely gone. She looked unbelievable in a brown and cream dress suit that, from the cut, I could tell was straight from YSL and teamed with some fabulous Christian Louboutin sling-backs, this girl was stunning.

"Thank you, Ashleigh. Ok, so who's next?"

The next girl in line stood up. She was tall, with a mass of brown curls and the most flawless tan you could imagine. She was wearing cream skinny jeans and a dressed up T-shirt and calf-high boots, all by Stella McCartney and all designs from Stella's latest fashion show, so this was either one very lucky, or very rich girl.

"Hey, I'm Sophie Kilean. I'm thirty-one and I graduated from the Fashion Institute five years ago and have been working as a designer for Stella McCartney for the last two years. Although I loved the job and being linked to such an amazing designer was incredible, I wasn't given the opportunity to expand and nurture my love of fashion. Obviously Stella has a very set design outlook whereas here at DB Designs, there are so many directions to go in and so many different areas to work within."

She explained how she had grown up in Colorado, and had a passion for skiing and was looking to do something different, so working for DB Designs allowed both her passions to be drawn together as one. She seemed nice enough and definitely didn't look thirty-one. She went on to describe how she got a rotator cuff injury and it had ruined any hope she had to have a career in downhill skiing. Although this girl seemed nice, as she went on about her skiing career and filled us on some more work she had done, I had to admit she seemed a little full of herself. I don't mean that in a bad way, but I'm not really used to people like this. I guess I shouldn't be judgemental; it's not my place, especially when I don't even know her as yet.

After Sophie, next up was Rhianne Coletta. A thirty-five year-old mum of two, who up until now had just been doing freelance design work. She had gone to NYU and had mainly been creating couture outfits for various companies. A New Yorker herself, she was mainly into running, having done the marathon four times, and still ran every morning at 5.30am before work. She was wearing a very simple black trouser suit, evidently by Ralph Lauren and a blood red top underneath and all of which were pulled together with a pair of blood red Jimmy Choo Mary Jane's. She looked great, and like Sophie, she didn't look her age, or like she had two kids.

And finally was Kimi Campbell who instantly described herself as, "authentically mod" and boy did she pull it off well. She looked very "Twiggy" in a sixties-inspired pink mini-dress, and gorgeous Miu Miu ballet pumps. "I love everything 60s. I'm totally crazy about the whole era, and everything that accompanies the style of that generation." She definitely looked like she'd just stepped out of a time machine, and with her bright red hair cut into a bob, with very prominent bangs across the front she was another who could've easily taken fashion week by storm as a "new face". I was shocked to learn she was thirty-two, having thought she was younger than me, or more, hoped she was, because I was suddenly aware I was the baby of the bunch. She informed us that she was from Boston and her main sport was horse riding, though she was partial to swimming, too. She had most recently worked with Bloomingdales as a fashion coordinator, but having gained her diploma from the Ivy League school, Brown, she felt she was wasting everything she had learned about design, so it was time to move on.

So that was us. The Fabulous Five (or maybe Fab Four, because compared to them I felt a little "meek"). I have to say I felt very intimidated surrounded by these "models" but I shook it off and just pushed forward, focussing on what Suranne was saying to us.

"So, as you know, each of you was picked specifically because of your sporting background as well as your talent for design as we want to propel DB Designs into a new area of style. And because each of you has such a diverse range of sports between you, Kier having pretty much taken part in every sport imaginable..." Suranne winked at me. I wasn't sure if she was 'bigging' me up, or just making me feel better because I was evidently out of each of these women's league when it came to personal style. "...We thought here at DB, that this would allow for a broader range of sporting fashion to be created as each of you will know different needs for different sports. Now please don't start to panic that we're throwing you in at the deep end as today is really going to be about getting to know people and more importantly, getting to know each other. Although you are a team I do want to make it clear you will be doing a lot of work alone. I want each of you to focus on the sports that you are most comfortable with and from start to finish, complete the necessary work for each design. We will also allow you to work on other projects for DB, including eveningwear, our wedding section and anything else you feel comfortable to design for. So girls, take the nervous looks of your faces." We all laughed tensely and then relaxed and as we looked at each other. I think we all realised we were in the same position and given that there were five of us it should make it a little easier, "...let's just go a walk around the office and you can meet whoever is around." Suranne stood up and walked towards the door, before turning and adding, "Oh and don't be put off by this but Dale is in the office somewhere today too, so hopefully we can introduce you all to him at some point, too."

With that my heart started to pound. I felt like an idiot. Here I was the youngest and dressed that way into the bargain. I hadn't even considered that we were going to be officially introduced to one of the most handsome men my eyes had ever seen and here I was looking like a 14-year-old and I probably looked even worse because I was surrounded by four supermodels. I just had to smile and get on with. I mean I was getting ahead of myself a little; I was acting like I wanted him to have the hots for me.

Believe it or not I actually have a boyfriend, who I'm pretty happy with. Aiden and I have been together for just short of two years and have a descent relationship. I have to stop being so stupid, he's just my new boss; my drop dead stunning new boss who I am completely attracted to. Yeah Kier, good one. Way to calm those nerves.

CHAPTER TWO

A s we walked down the corridor, we were introduced to the office girls that consisted of the manager, Arlene, and her two assistants, Louise and Sasha. I felt a bit more relaxed seeing Louise and Sasha; they were both around my age so I at least felt like less of the "baby". We were shown around some more offices too and met a lot of designers, the accountants, the business managers and a few others who I'm sure I would get to know over time. As we walked through the last set of double doors, my heart stopped as I came face to face with Dale, standing with another man, drinking coffee and watching the Knicks games from the weekend.

When he saw us, he instantly turned and put an amazing grin on his face as he introduced himself.

"Hi, I'm Dale Brenton. You must be my new dream team?" He looked directly at each of us and I melted. He was unbelievable. He had the most gorgeous chocolate brown eyes, and a smile that made me grin like nothing else. Ok, so maybe I has a tiny a crush happening. "So how are all you girls doing?"

The other four started talking at once and Dale tried to keep up by smiling, nodding and laughing at all the right times, before turning to me, "You must be the quiet one?" "Me?" I was slightly taken a back, and I didn't want to seem rude or like an idiot, so all I could think to say was, "You'll wish I was quiet when you get to know me." I smiled and I'll admit, a little flirtatiously. "Sorry, I was just having a quick glance at the game, I was so busy over the weekend I missed the whole thing. I didn't even catch the scores. Don't tell me the result, what are we 3rd quarter, Knicks up 21?" Yes I was that sad. I still managed to keep up with my love of sport whilst standing in front of an extremely gorgeous man.

"Basketball fan?" He smiled again, and I had to use every bit of will power in my body to stay standing upright.

"Of course. Impressed with the Knicks this season they have been awesome." Sport means everything to me, almost as much as fashion so by focussing on this I was unaware of my nerves, unaware of how much this man was making my heart race. I somehow managed to force myself to concentrate on the ball game. "Deonesci has been one hell of a point guard this season. He is like...wow! I mean I know it's not about one person making the team but with him playing how could the Knicks lose, ever? Some of those 3 pointers hit, and his jump shot, and when he matches up with Deangelo, well it's inspiring." I babbled on and on, rambling away and didn't realise I had been talking for a solid three or four minutes without taking a breath and the whole time I had been staring directly into Dale's eyes. Snapping myself back to reality I didn't know what to say except, "Oh, sorry. Me and sport, you get me started, it's tough to stop."

"Not at all. It's good to see, or more, hear that there is a voice in there." He laughed and again I melted into those chocolaty eyes of his. "I have never heard anyone in the fashion world having such a keen interest on sport, well me aside I mean. Anything else you're into?" He leaned against the door frame and I swear I almost fell into his arms. I couldn't believe we were having an actual conversation, one on one, surrounded by so many other people.

"Everything. Football...Chargers Fan, not New York, I know but never liked the Giants. Baseball, Yankees all the way. Soccer, though only international, even though Scotland isn't too great at playing against...."

And with that I was interrupted.

"Thought I recognised the accent. Let me guess, somewhere near Glasgow?" Dale moved closer to me and almost seemed to block everyone else out of the conversation.

"Yeah, how did you know?" I was in shock, no one ever guessed the accent, let alone know where in Scotland it's from.

"West of Scotland, myself. Stirling actually. Though that was many years ago." He looked almost happy at the suggestion of his home town and for some strange reason I felt instantly close to him, simply because of our Scottish connection.

"No way." I grinned and could feel the excitement pouring out of me, "I stayed in Cumbernauld. This is amazing. I didn't know you were Scottish, though you do have a very difficult accent to place." I couldn't believe this. Couldn't believe how easy it was to chat away to one of the most successful designers in the world and discover he used to live fifteen miles away from where I use to stay.

"Yeah, eighteen years in New York and anyone would lose their accent. Yours still sounds amazing." He smiled again, this time flashing some pearly white teeth and making my knees shake a little. I had to distract myself with the Knicks to keep composure, though they had just made a bad move and my knee jerk "Jock Girl" reactions came out.

"Jesus Rodrigo sucks, what is he, a girl?" My outburst was probably a dead giveaway that I was thinking about more than Dale being Scottish, but I continued on anyway. "That guy needs to learn the net's for the ball to go into." I kind of half smiled, whilst pretending to be annoyed at the game.

"Feisty this one isn't she." Dale signalled to Suranne, who looked less than impressed by the conversation we had been engrossed in for the last ten minutes which had also included completely blocking out the rest of the girls.

"Yes. Quite." Man, oh man, did she sound annoyed. I didn't know how to play it, I mean he's the boss, am I supposed to ignore him.

"I like her." He winked at me again. "And if she's a big sports fan, she can hang around the office everyday, in fact, are you into Starbucks?" He turned back to me and signalled towards a private Starbucks at the opposite end of the office.

Well if I say my eyes lit up like a kid on Christmas morning that wouldn't even cover my happiness at that moment. I have been an avid lover of Starbucks since the minute I arrived in New York and tasted my first latte at JFK Airport. My tastes have changed over the years but a Grande Sugar Free Hazelnut Soya Latte lights up my world and turns me to jelly. Aiden never got my love of Starbucks saying at $4 a coffee, it was an expense that shouldn't be indulged in all the time. He was a bit, well, tight with money and me not caring and spending money like it was going out of fashion wasn't his favourite part of me.

"We have a private Starbucks? I think I've died and gone to heaven. Can someone check my pulse because no way is this happening when I'm alive?" I laughed and as I did Dale leaned over and put his hand on my neck and said,

"No, you've still got a pulse." Then he leaned in towards me and said, "Still breathing too."

I breathed deeply, smelling what I guessed was Davidoff Coolwaters, looked between the TV screen and Starbucks and tried to avoid the fact that I was pretty sure I had just fallen for him.

"Yeah, good, I think. Em, well, yeah, Starbucks and the Knicks games on in the office, I could live here. Yeah, just live here, in this office, here." I realised again that I was babbling, and not making even a little sense. But my body was on shut down, and my mouth seemed to be only half functioning, while my brain was complete mush.

"Not just the Knicks, we've got all sports." He was so calm, so cool, so everything, and me, I was a riot. "And if I remember your designs as much as I think I do, with your talent, and your obvious bonus quality of loving sport and coffee, you're going to fit in great here. Looking forward to seeing you around. It's Kier, isn't it?" Then obviously realising that he had pretty much ignored the other girls, including Suranne, he added, "In fact, looking forward to seeing all of you girls around. We certainly needed some talent in this office, and I don't just mean your design." He laughed, as did I. Obviously being called "talent" was lost on Americans, given it was a very West of Scotland way to call someone good looking. "But seriously girls, Starbucks is free, the TV is always showing some form of sport and my door is always open if you need to talk. Suranne can vouch for that, right?" He grinned over at her, and she put on a false smile to hide her annoyance at him speaking to me and simply said, "Always." Before turning to us and saying, "Anyway, enough messing around girls it's time to get on with some actual work." She seemed annoyed, really annoyed but I brushed it off and proceeded to follow on behind the other girls. As I walked away I couldn't help looking over my shoulder and caught another glance of Dale as he yet again flashed me a smile and, given the extreme high I was on at the moment, I couldn't help but grin back, before hurrying forward and falling in behind the other girls.

CHAPTER THREE

Working at DB Designs was proving to be much more than I thought it would be. Two months into the job and we were full steam ahead with our design ideas. I worked on my own ideas, baggy clothing for skating, basketball and dancing, whereas Kimi and Rhianne seemed to stick together, maybe because they were a little older or just because they actually had similar tastes in sporting style; clean cut lines and tight fight fashions, which for me was part of another world but they definitely impressed Suranne. Sophie was very much into high-end apparel and was designing a range of "ski-couture" that I had to admit looked fabulous. She and I got on decently well but I was right when I said she had a high opinion of herself. Turns out she came from a very wealthy background and even if she hadn't worked a day in her life it wouldn't have mattered. She went on a lot about her failed career as a skier too. She could've been in the Olympics but after her injury, that was ruined. Her dad hired every medical expert he could but nothing could repair the damage so she decided to pursue her next love of fashion and I have to say, she was talented. Her ski range was gorgeous, although a little over the top for sport. I wasn't sure how it would fit in with the rest of our designs.

Ashleigh was lovely and the one I probably got on with most. She was very down to earth and kept herself to herself mostly. Her designs were very focussed around similar ideas to Nike or the new lines by McKenzie; young, fresh and, without sounding like an idiot, hip. In fact her ideas mimicked mine in the sense of being very up to date, although mine were a little more street and Ashleigh's were slightly more urban, with a bit more of a "glamour" edge. But when we were together we got on really well. To be honest none of us really spent any great deal of time together. When we weren't in the work room drawing or putting together samples, we had to meet with different clients and pitch how great our designs would be in their stores, shows, everything. In fact, I had even managed to get myself meetings with three rap groups and a few singers that were up-and-coming in the hip-hop/ R&B world and thought given the street side of my work, it would be perfect for them to wear them in videos, on tour, anything at all that would get DB Designs out there in the new light that Suranne had spoken about. The first two months had flown by and I could hardly believe I had already put together my first eight outfits for sample shows. I was inspired to create bigger, better and bolder designs that I'd ever done before; my mind was working in overtime. And as much as it pains me to say, my apparent "just attraction" to Dale had turned into a full on crush. I would make stupid excuses to walk past his office and I'd taken to drinking five coffees a day just because I could look straight into his office from the Starbucks Stand. And, as sad as it sounds, I'd almost got it to a tee when he would go for lunch so I could make sure I was there at the same time. I had never felt like this before and every time I saw him I couldn't stop smiling. I loved even spending the odd five minutes here and there talking to him. And every time we did speak, I discovered more things we had in common. Aside from our love of sport, and Starbucks, we both hated to lose, no matter what we were doing, we both loved stupid things like smoked salmon on bagels, peanut butter and banana sandwiches, and we both got driven crazy by petty jealousy from other people, which when you love to win competitions of any kind, and it would seem in both our cases we did win, people tended to get the green eyed look around you a lot.

One Wednesday morning, I was grabbing my second latte of the day, when Dale came up behind me.

"Hey Kier, how you doing? You hit this caffeine stand more than me. Not working you too hard are we?" He placed his hand on my shoulder and I couldn't help getting a dreamy eyed stare across my face. Even him touching my shoulder made me weak.

"No, not at all. Just love coffee." I gazed up at him, and continued to speak. "Anyway, I'd happily spend most of my days here. Honestly, I love every second of it."

"God you're actually my number one employee." He

almost ran his hand down my back slightly, as he took his hand off my shoulder. "I'm impressed with your work; everything you do is so new, so now. You have all these wild ideas, and I love the whole skater meets sports star style."

I couldn't stop grinning, and my dreamy eyed look had been replaced with a wide eyed, I'm so happy right now face. He said he was impressed, with me, or my work at least. God, what was he doing to me? Every time I was near him I had to resist stroking his arm, or fight the urge to run my fingers through his hair. I had to constantly remind myself of a little person called Aiden, who was very much, still my boyfriend.

"Thank you, I appreciate that, more than you'll know. I mean you're one of the best designers I've ever come across and I feel so lucky that I get to work under you." Realising what I said I back tracked. "Underneath you, I mean, oh God." My face was scarlet and Dale was laughing so hard he was struggling to catch his breathe. He has the most amazing laugh ever that you can't help but join in with, so my embarrassment turned to a school girl like giggle.

"You're very good at making me laugh Kier and maybe the working under me will come later." He winked, picked up his coffee and walked away, before a quick glance over his shoulder and one of those amazing Dale Brenton grins.

My face froze. My whole body froze and I just stared into space, unable to move from the one spot. Did he just say that? To me? Was that flirtatious, was he flirting with me? I didn't want to get too excited; I mean he was probably like that with everyone. Anyway, I had recently found out he was married, probably very happily, and had two boys too, so I doubted he meant anything by that statement.

I was in a daze walking back to the work room. I still couldn't believe that Dale had said that. To me he said, "We'll see about you working under me later." What did he mean by that? Am I just doing my usual Kier thing; over thinking every situation and coming up with an outcome that is so far from the truth? I have a tendency of over thinking everything. I didn't used to be like this, I used to be quite calm and collected, your typical skater-girl but things happen that make you doubt the smallest thing.

(Brackets)

When I was nineteen I got engaged to, who at the time, I thought was the most fantastic man ever. He was my first boyfriend, the "love of my life" or so I thought. But, he met the love of his life, and I got pushed aside. I had given everything to him, never over thought our relationship, was just happy knowing I had him and put every bit of trust I had into the two of us, so for it to fall apart, to say my confidence was dented is an understatement. My life became a car crash. I stopped eating right, dropped loads of weight, started doing various drugs, and just became a different person. If it hadn't been for my best friend at the time, Marcus, I don't know how my life would've ended up. He made me realise that life wasn't about a boy, or about ruining myself because of a boy, so I got help, spoke to an amazing councillor called Julianne Carraway, who became one of my closest friends. Unfortunately, Marcus is no longer in my life; he met the man of his dreams too and forgot about me too. But by having met Julianne, I realised that sometimes when you move on in life you have to leave things behind to get to somewhere better and, well, I'm living proof that I'm living a dream life. Well if you can push aside that I'm pretty sure I'm falling in love with my boss and I know that sounds extreme but I cannot get him out of my head. Over the last two months, every time I've spent with Aiden, I've found myself thinking about Dale. Thinking what it would be like to be lying in bed with him, kissing him, being with him. I mean is that normal? I've never really had a crush before, or if I have nothing that has attracted such strong feelings as I have just now. I hardly know Dale, aside from our little conversations we have every now and again. How can I have fallen for him? Or am I just caught up admiring someone because he is where I want to be? But if it's just an admiration for him, then why do I get so annoyed when I come into work and he's not in? Why is it every time I see a slate grey Range Rover, I double take at the licence plate to see if it's his, and why, when I see that plate "DB 1", does my heart race and I just want to be near him?

I was now standing in the restroom, just off the workroom, staring in the mirror, and doing what I do best...talking to myself.

"It's just a crush, Kier. That's why you hear things that aren't really what they are. He probably didn't even say that about you being under him, you just thought he did because that's what you wanted to hear. You have boyfriend who, for all intents and purposes, you love. You do. You love Aiden. You wouldn't have been with him for two years if you didn't. Aiden is your life; he's the one you go to when you finish. Kier, get it into your daft head...you love Dale." As the words escaped my mouth, I hoped no one was around. Here I had been babbling on and on about how Aiden was the one and at crunch time, Dale's name just slipped out. OMG, this wasn't good.

"Pull yourself together Miss Scott, focus. You have a job to do and it does not include sleeping with your b....."

"Kier, what are you doing?" Ashleigh looked confused and slightly worried, as she walked through the restroom door.

"Oh, you know, giving myself a pep talk." I laughed nervously. "I can be a little strange sometimes. So subject change, how you doing?" I wanted to get the topic away from the fact I must've looked a complete weirdo. Good one, Kier, make your co-workers see you're a complete loon.

"Don't worry about it, I do that too. Usually when I drive. Never used a bathroom mirror before, but we all have our little quirks." She smiled and continued towards the sink and proceeded to wash her hands. "I'm doing well. I'm having a little trouble with the tracksuit I'm working on. I want it to be chic but without looking like it should never be worn. Am I making sense?" Ashleigh squinted up her face and I had to laugh.

"You're crazy. I can have a look if you like, as an outside view and well, we are still part of a team, even though we probably all only see each other for about a minute a week." I laughed again; I was really forcing the conversation now just in case Ashleigh did still think I was actually insane. Though to be honest most designers are so maybe I should've just kept up the pretence.

"Are you sure? That would be great. I mean we seem to have a similar view when it comes to fashion design and I think maybe we could work together on a few pieces, make things a bit cohesive if you want? I mean, if you don't mind?" Ashleigh was getting a little excited, so I went along with it. I thought if nothing else she could keep me distracted from the stupid thoughts I was having about Dale.

"Sounds like a plan. Just let me finish talking to myself first." As I turned towards the mirror again, she looked over a little confused and said,

"Ok, I'll get you in the workroom then?"

I burst out laughing, "Ashleigh, I'm kidding?" As she joined in laughing too she still looked a little confused at my attempt at a joke she obviously didn't quite get.

Half an hour later we were messing around over designs and were shocked to discover that our designs linked together, even though we hadn't shown each other anything.

"This is amazing, I can't believe how much this looks like a collection, even though it's been created by two different people." It really didn't take much for Ashleigh to get excited but to be honest, it was catching. In the last half hour I had gotten to know her a bit better and we definitely had similar personalities, though I think I was a little "tamer" than she was.

"I know. I love the colours. Red and black always look phenomenal together and they work for everything. Did I show you the jacket I have been working on over the last four days?" I indicated towards a mannequin on the other side of the room. It was a Black basketball style jacket, made from jersey material, with red designs integrated into the fabric. I had just started working on it but I really wanted to make it to be the show piece of my skate collection.

"WOW!" Ashleigh looked impressed. "You made that in the last four days? It's incredible. I mean the detail is so intricate and I know it's meant to be aimed within your skate collection but I swear to God that could be dressed up or down. Oh my God, Kier. That's what I call talent." She sounded completely blown away which made me get a rush of excitement pulsing through my veins. "Has Suranne seen this yet?"

"No, haven't shown anyone except you. I wanted to get the rest of the outfit together first." I loved the attention drawn from something I made. And Ashleigh's opinion meant a lot to me, she had an eye for design and her everyday style was amazing. Take today for instance, she done power dressing like no-one else. She has on another fabulous YSL dress suit, this time in a dusky pink colour, teamed with cream Manolo's. I had given up even thinking about dressing that way. I had on my baggy skater cut-off jeans, a cerise pink NYC T-shirt and my favourite multi-coloured Nike basketball boots. This was pretty much my everyday style, though occasionally I had basketball shorts on and a Knicks top, sometimes just jeans and a FDNY grey hooded jumper. To me being comfortable helped me to design, and looking around the office, there were plenty of dressed up people to pull inspiration from.

"Well you should get her down here. She will be beyond impressed. God you honestly have the best style ever. Wish I could come into the office dressed like you. You always look so cool, so funky and fab."

I was awestruck. I couldn't believe I had just been given a compliment in relation to my style. Especially when I've spent two months debating if I should buy some trouser suits. "You know, I thought I should've been dressing more like you guys, wearing suits, looking like a designer instead of someone who runs out for the bagels." I had a cheeky grin across my face, that when teamed alongside my baseball cap and jeans probably made me look like a kid.

"You're kidding. You look unbelievable everyday. I think that's why Dale feels so comfortable talking to you all the time."

I looked dead at her and felt my expression freeze. "What do you mean?" I quizzed her, but tried to remain calm.

"Well, I mean come on, we all get a *"hi"* or a *"hello"* or a *"how you doing?"* Whereas he talks to you, he takes an interest in you because you're different and evidently you don't seem to get panicked around him like the rest of us which he probably finds as a relief. Having worked here over the last two months you see things, like no-one else ever speaks to him really, well except Arlene but she's his assistant, I'm sure he'd prefer not hearing from her." Ashleigh laughed and looked quite proud of herself for having made a joke. "But I'm being genuine when I say this, I would love to show up in jeans but I feel a little, I don't know, like I have to do this now every day now or else I wouldn't feel like I fit in." I didn't hear the last sentence she said, my whole body had been taken over and consumed by the idea Dale showed me attention, treated me different. Me.

I couldn't believe she had said that. So she noticed that Dale spoke to me too. Did that mean something? Did that mean he was in fact taking a special interest in me, or was it just that I spoke to him and he felt comfortable that I wasn't scared of his "power status"?

"Yeah Dale's cool. He's into sport and stuff so that's all we ever really communicate about. He's pretty easy to speak to when you start." I was being very calm and collected. I couldn't act excited or anything and I definitely didn't want to give away that I had a crush on him, or that I practically stalked him so I could 'accidently' bump into him and we could engage in those conversations that makes me lose control of myself. "Just start watching ESPN and you'll find loads to talk to him about." I was really pushing that we just spoke about sport purely because I didn't want to give away that we communicated about everything from our favourite foods, to our favourite movies. We had become pretty friendly over the last two months but I didn't think it was right to tell someone else in the office about that.

"Maybe. And maybe I'll even pull on a pair of jeans tomorrow too." Ashleigh smiled, and then laughed. "I must sound ridiculous worrying about wearing jeans to work especially in a place where we've been told we can wear what we like and you show up looking like something from Sports Illustrated in your basketball gear."

"Shut up. First to be in Sports Illustrated I'd have to look like a model and secondly, I'd love to be able to pull off what you wear but I'd probably look like a man in drag."

"You're crazy. You look amazing. Anyway, let's just say you're an inspiration to me."

"Well you are to me too, so let's inspire each other to create the most amazing collection of sportswear this planet has ever seen."

"Deal." We shook hands, and then continued looking over each other's work.

CHAPTER FOUR

We had been messing about for about two hours when Suranne unexpectedly showed up and wanted to have a look at what progress we had made with our individual designs. I was pretty excited about showing her my jacket and the boarder shorts I had been working on so I shouted her over straight away.

"So, as you can see the jacket can be teamed with anything. It's a basketball style with a skater edge, and the boarders are in this incredible heavy duty satin like material, so they could be crossed over for skating or basketball, anything really. In fact, I think they'd be pretty comfy to wear doing most sports, light-weight, but durable, with an edgy style that it is so different from anything out there." I smiled, allowing my excitement to take over, and waited for her response.

"No, no, no, no, no. I hate it. All of it. This is not the Kier Scott design show. Come on Kier, maybe you would be happy dressing down in these, but DB Designs is about style, about fashion. This looks like something you could buy in Wal-Mart. I am not happy Kier. You have been here for two months now, get your head screwed on and start designing like Dale Brenton wants you to. This really is a let-down. We don't do cheap here, we do class, and we do something that everyone wants, not just what you want. Think about that Kier; think about it long and hard."

And with that Suranne stormed out of the work room without even looking over at Ashleigh. I was so embarrassed. Here I was getting all excited because of what Ashleigh had said and now Suranne had completely destroyed all of that. My designs look cheap? I couldn't understand what had just happened. I was so proud of my collection, beyond proud and now here was my "mentor" telling me I was designing for myself not DB Designs. I thought that was the idea of our job, design clothes we would wear. Was that not the reason behind hiring us all for our different sports? I kept replaying her words over in

28

my head and each time it broke me down more and more. My whole body was shaking and I was about to break down. I ran into the bathroom and instantly tears fell from my eyes as I grabbed onto the sink. Before I could do anything else, I felt Ashleigh wrap her arms around me.

"It's ok, don't cry Kier. Please don't cry."

"Did you hear her?" I struggled to talk, but kept going, forcing out every word. "She slated me. Completely slated me. She didn't even say anything to guide me on where to go from here. Are my designs that bad? She called them cheap? Is that true?" I was searching Ashleigh's face for answers, at the same time terrified of what those answers would be.

"Are you nuts? Kier, I told you, your designs are amazing. In fact, I'm actually wondering what just happened in there myself. Honestly, I would love to have your talent for creation. Suranne is obviously having a bad day and you've been the one to take the brunt of it. I bet she'll come down and apologise soon enough and if you're concerned you're going in the wrong direction then call Dale down. It's his company so really it's only his opinion that matters."

"Is that not going behind Suranne's back though?" I didn't want to annoy her. After my first day conversation with Dale she had become a little off with me but nothing like today.

"Not at all. We can just cover it by saying we were flying through designs and we were just interested in his opinion. Come on, you're his buddy." She did quote fingers when she said "Buddy", "I bet he'll run down here if you ask him to." She smiled and I have to admit she was making me feel better.

I smiled back. She was great and I thought if nothing else, at least I'd get to have a look at Dale, which would no doubt make me smile, though there is the worry he'll hate what I've been doing too. But I decided to suck it up. If he tells me he hates everything I've done then I can get his advice on how to sort it, and I'm sure he will be more constructive than Suranne had just been.

"Ok, that sounds like a plan. I'll ring him through when I'm done here and see if he's free. I just have to wash my stupid tear stained face." I laughed, "I don't want him thinking I'm some kind of bumbling loser." I also didn't want to look any less attractive, though I couldn't say that out loud to Ashleigh. I already had a feeling she could tell I had a crush on him even though I was sure I was doing a good job at hiding it.

I tidied myself up and touched up the little amount of make-up I wore and walked back into the work room, and finally relaxed enough to allow myself to get excited about seeing him. Ok Kier, calm down. Remember he is your boss, he is married and, more importantly, you have a boyfriend. Seriously, get a grip of your life Miss Scott. I had been doing this a lot lately, talking to myself I mean, but even my pep talk to myself couldn't stop the nerves coursing through my veins as I picked up the phone.

"Hi Dale, its Kier." I tried to sound upbeat and happy.

"Hi Kier, how's my star employee doing? Gorgeous as ever?" He sounded happy and I could tell he was smiling. And he called me gorgeous. WOW!

"I'm doing well thanks and looking like a skater, as always." I laughed, nervously. "Anyway, Ashleigh and I have been doing some work and we were wondering if we could maybe pick your brain and get your opinion on it? We know you're probably really busy, but if you could we'd really appreciate it." My fingers were crossed tightly, willing him to say yes.

"For you Kier, anything. I'll be down in five, just finishing off an email and I'll come straight through. Oh and get that smile on for me and give me a reason to have my day brightened." He laughed as he said goodbye but I wasn't sure if he was being serious or not about the brightening his day thing, but I have to admit, it certainly started the butterflies going in my stomach. I composed myself and turned back to Ashleigh.

"Ok, he's finishing an email and then he's heading down. I'm really nervous, I mean, what if he has the same opinion as Suranne. I think I'll just quit." I stared at the floor and messed about kicking a ball of material.

"Kier, cheer up. Dale will love your designs; it's me who should be worrying. Bet he'll think mine are a pile of crap and that's me being polite." Ashleigh suddenly lost her excited spark that was usually vibrantly glowing. After how great she had been with me I had to say something.

"Are you completely insane? It's me that's supposed to be the crazy one; I talk to myself in mirrors." I grinned before continuing. "You are an amazing designer Ashleigh, a complete inspiration to me and the other girls too I'm sure. So put that smile back on and let's impress the life out of Mr Brenton."

We didn't have to wait long because within seconds Dale was standing in front of us in a light grey pinstripe suit and black shirt. It had to be Prada and it fit him like a glove and I shouldn't say it but his bum looked unbelievable in the pants. As soon as he came in he kind of high fived me and made a comment about the sports scores; there were some tennis tournaments drawing to a close, and we were both rooting on Andy Murray, a young guy from just outside where Dale is originally from, in a small town called Dunblane. We chatted for a minute or so and with that out the way we got on with the business side of things.

"So what pleasure do I owe for getting to come down and visit two of the dream team; my favourite two of course." And he winked. My God was he gorgeous, stunning, and ridiculously good looking.

"Ok, we just wanted your opinion on what we've been doing for you slaving in the workroom day and night." I was trying to keep it light and not let on that Suranne has already been down and tore a path of destructive comments through my designs. "Obviously we've been here for two months and our collections are really starting to come together so we thought this was the perfect time to get your expert opinion." I tried to make it seem like I wasn't secretly drooling over him as well as hide the fact that I could barely contain my smile just because he was standing in front of me.

"Great." He turned to Ashleigh first. "Well Ashleigh, let me have a look at what you've been doing. You're our volleyball girl, am I right?"

"Yeah, that's right." She sounded a little nervous but I was sure they would fade when she started talking so I walked over to my work unit and left them to it. "Although obviously volleyball players wear shorts and vests pretty much all the time I have tended to go for what I like wearing when I'm between training or going to training/ competitions etc. I think I've created a collection so far that is very Urban Chic and almost captivates the very essence of New York or at least in my eyes it does." She actually said the whole sentence in about five seconds, obviously feeling the nerves of the main man himself standing in front of her.

"Ok, I picked up a little of that but let me see the designs and I'll draw my own conclusions." He was talking so calmly, obviously picking up on Ashleigh nerves and trying to relax her.

He walked over and examined her sketches, some fabric samples and had a good look at what she had started to create. He literally mulled over everything for easily fifteen minutes before he even spoke.

"Very ingenious Ashleigh." He smiled, still looking over her sketches, "You have definitely taken the spirit of Urban Chic and turned it to sport. I just need more now. Obviously you are comfortable doing tops and over-tops but what I need now is jackets, pants, shorts. Everything. Maybe even look at doing a few pieces like a volleyball player would wear during competitions but switch it up. I like the direction you are heading in though, so keep it up." He turned round and started walking towards me at the opposite end of the room. "Ok my Star-Girl, let's see what you have."

I was overcome with excitement. I wasn't really sure why he had called me Star-Girl, maybe because I have a star tattooed on my wrist but by adding "my" beforehand it threw me. I still couldn't suss this out. Was he just flirty? I wish I had listened in on what he said to Ashleigh but I didn't want to be rude hanging over her shoulder.

"Ok, I have to admit, I've targeted my designs around my own personal style because I thought that was our brief. I thought we had been chosen because of our individual sporting passions, so I've kept to that, creating a smash between clothes that are hard-wearing enough for skating but still have that almost "pretty" edge for dance but again are comfortable enough to slam some hoops in. So I have a lot of samples, and also some that I have made up for you to have a look at. Ready?" I was a little panicked, I wanted to impress him so much and Suranne's earlier comments had knocked my confidence. If Dale hated what I was designing did I really have a career here?

Dale examined everything with a fine toothcomb and I mean everything. He looked at every one of my sketches and every sample of fabric that has gone with it and then all of the clothing I had made up. He had them on and off the mannequins and then kept looking at the piece and referring back to the sketch that accompanied it.

"Well, Miss Scott..." OMG he sounded angry and I really wasn't prepared for this, I felt my shoulders tense and my face scrunch up, "I am so impressed." I let out a breath and felt my shoulders instantly ease off, and I was aware of my wide eyed, mouth open expression. I was in shock. Dale obviously sensed this and just like before placed his hand on my shoulder. "You have quite a talent, don't you? I mean, some of these designs are beyond even me. So creative, so different and the fabric, WOW. Kier this is fantastic work. I certainly landed lucky getting you as an employee. You're what age, twenty-two?"

"Me, no, I'm twenty-four." I hoped that didn't sound really young, Dale himself, by my guessing was thirty-seven or there about, but to my surprise he just smiled and with a wink he added, "Even better." Before continuing on with complimenting my work. "I love the jacket and I love the fact that for the main part everything is unisex, am I right?"

"To be honest, I didn't actually plan them that way. I'm sure you can see from the sketches everything was designed around, well, me. But as I started to sew and put pieces together, I realised if I changed the fit slightly then I could make them unisex and I thought well why not. But if you want I can go into more separate styles, just for men, or just for women. My every wish is your command." I felt a bit stupid saying the last part but when I heard Dale's next comment, I was glad I did.

"Well some things I'd wish for from you may be unavailable, so I better keep my mouth shut and go back to talking about your designs." He has a cheeky grin on his face and once again my whole body felt as though it had melted into the floor. This was full on flirting; there was no denying it this time.

So I decided to flirt back a little now, "Well, sometimes the things you think are unavailable are the ones that turn out the best." I moved a little closer, stared him in the eye and this time I added a wink myself, and just in case I'd assessed the situation wrong, I added on, "I mean, when I was saving for my first skateboard, I was so convinced that I wouldn't get it, I was set to take up handball...I mean imagine if I'd been designing handball wear instead of skate wear, doesn't have the same ring to it does it?" I smiled, still flirtatiously and kind of patted him on the shoulder, "So, sometimes, you just have to go with your instincts."

"Well my instincts are telling me that what I want is you around for a bit; with a smile like yours and the fact you are going to make me a lot of money with ideas like that, I never want you to leave." He squeezed my hand, and then just before walking away added, "Seriously Kier, you're amazing."

I swear I felt like I was flying. Amazing. Did he just say that? I couldn't believe this was happening. I couldn't believe that Dale Brenton just called me amazing. Me; dowdy, skater girl Kier Scott. Me. I was about to go full swing into a fantasy thinking about Dale and I when Ashleigh jumped over.

"So, what did he think? He was impressed with my work. He said I just have to go into a bit more, sort out creating different pieces and not be so focussed on the one area. But he seemed to like it and was happy for me to continue as I have been. I'm in heaven. Dale Brenton liked my designs. How great is that? What did he say about you?"

I had to control myself, if I let on exactly what he had just said Ashleigh would maybe have something to say about that.

"He liked most of it actually. He was impressed with how I'd made everything unisex and that it was well designed and put together. Suranne must've just been in a bad mood, either that or maybe my designs just aren't her style. I'm just happy that Dale liked it, and at least I haven't wasted two months of my life designing something that would end up on the scrap heap."

"Well, you don't have to worry about that. Come on, let's get on. We have a vision to create." She gave me a quick hug, and smiled.

As she walked back to her station, and I sat down at my desk, I got lost in my own thoughts. Amazing. The word replayed over and over in my head. He called me amazing. My crush on Dale Brenton was in overdrive. In fact, honestly, I was crazy about him.

CHAPTER FIVE
"CRRRAAAASSSSHHHHHHH!!!!!!"

It was Thursday night and I was lying on the couch watching Die Hard for the 20th time. Aiden has a big passion for action films and after the way I had been thinking over the last two months, I thought I should indulge his passion and try to focus my attention back on him.

"Pop Quiz hot shot..." Aiden insisted on talking alongside Bruce Willis and given he had seen it more times than I've had hot meals, he played the part just as well. I stared up at him and remembered why I loved him. He wasn't the most outgoing guy and to be honest he was a little dull but at the same time he could be sweet when he wanted to. Like tonight he came round with the biggest jar of Jelly Beans just because I have a huge passion for them and he wanted to congratulate me on doing so well at work. The guilt of my crush was getting to me and I felt like I was forcing myself to pay Aiden attention because I was too busy thinking about Dale every second of the day.

The rest of the week at work included him saying I had a movie star name to go with my movie star good looks, telling me I was like super girl, and when he saw me messing about on my skateboard at lunchtime one day he said I could be a female James Bond. He also felt the need to put his hand on my shoulder or high five me whenever he saw me in the office or the workroom. And he also made comments about how gorgeous I looked because I wore my hair down one day after I had it cut and coloured. He said he loved the jet black colour and it made him go a little weak at the knees. He also made comment about how he wouldn't be able to concentrate on his board meeting because he came into the workroom when I had my basketball shorts on and a skimpy sports top after a lunchtime sessions with some of the other guys in the office. Think he was shocked to see I had quite a descent body underneath all my baggy clothes.

Anyway, here I was lying with my boyfriend, the guy who

only two months ago I was convinced was the man I was going to marry and I couldn't even spend longer than thirty seconds thinking about him because my attention was constantly elsewhere. Why had this happened? Why had I suddenly developed this stupid crush? I had never even looked at another man when I had been with Aiden and now the only man I wanted to look at was Dale Brenton.

"You look tired babe. You overworked?" Aiden knew I hated being called babe but insisted on it all the time. He had become annoyed with me because I was working 12-hour days and I was constantly yawning when I was with him. He was convinced I was being overworked, though of course the real reason I stayed late was because so did Dale and I liked the idea of being alone in the office with him. Not that it happened that often. Suranne was often hanging around, as well as another girl Paula, who dealt with getting DB Designs into all the stores seemed to stay around late too. Sasha, one of the office girls, said there was a rumour that Dale and Paula had an affair and were probably still screwing each other's brains out. Sasha and I had become quite close lately. She was twenty and looking to work her way up the career ladder and guessed starting small in a big company was a good way to go. She was the most fun loving person I had ever met and it turned out she had a similar crush to mine. Not on Dale but on Harry Devin, one of the business managers that she worked directly for. Like Dale and I, there was a fairly big age gap, eleven years to be exact. Harry was thirty-one and also married to some uptight lawyer called Layla, who, no offense to her, reminded me a lot of my mum. Sasha and Harry were pretty good friends, much to the annoyance of most people at DB Designs and when she confided in me that she had feelings for him I almost spilled the beans about how I felt about Dale but thought it was best to keep it under wraps. It wasn't that I didn't trust her, it was just I didn't think I was ready to tell anyone anything. It did help however talking about her situation, knowing anything she said could just be relayed back into my own thoughts and feelings. She had questioned me about what I thought about Dale, only once, and I said truthfully that he was attractive and we had a lot in common, which lead her to tell me she was sure I was on his "list", which to be honest made me feel like crap. But, she did make a comment on how she had never seen Dale speak to anyone in the way he spoke to me and then added, "Maybe you're not on the list, perhaps he just sees you as one of the guys." Don't get me wrong, I was happy she hadn't sussed out just how much I liked him, but it was hard hearing I could just be a notch on the bedpost, or worse again, a "friend".

Anyway, I realised I had zoned out a bit, and Aiden was staring at me waiting on an answer.

"Working, yeah. Just trying to finish the majority of the collection, and get as much as possible made up before fashion week. I know we're not launching until March next year but this is such a massive opportunity and I don't want to let Dale down." The words left my mouth as quickly as I tried to resolve it, "I mean, well it's his company and I want him to see even though I'm young I deserve to be there."

"Just don't kill yourself babe. I need you in tip-top shape." He ran his hand down my chest before saying, "How about Die Hard gets put on pause and we have a bit of duvet time." He leaned down and kissed me and as soon as he did a wave of panic came over me that I couldn't control, so I done the only thing I could...

"Can we maybe leave it tonight? Like you said, I've been working a lot and maybe I should just try and get some decent amount of sleep for a change. Is that ok?" I felt horrible lying and even worse because Aiden had been really attentive since I got the job. In the past he tended to put everything else before me. Monday night football, his work, doing overtime at work, everything. Last Christmas things didn't go too well for us when I hardly saw him for the whole two weeks of the holidays and I somehow got blamed for being annoyed that he had to work or he had to do other things that didn't involve me. But lately, since I haven't been craving to be with him as much as I use to, he's turned things around. He is now the one calling me to get together, wanting to come over every night and doing all the stuff that I wanted two months ago. It's strange how things turn out, because now, my mind was so consumed with thoughts of Dale, I was almost wishing Aiden did just act how he used to. At least then I wouldn't be struggling to keep up the pretence of the perfect girlfriend.

"Of course. Just thought it would help you to unwind a bit. You know, we've not really done anything like that since you started the job. But I understand you can't focus on everything and once you get this line together then we can have a full weekend of uninterrupted fun time." He laughed and kissed me hard on the mouth. This was so difficult. Here I had a great guy, a guy who was finally making me his world and I couldn't focus on him because I was slowly, what felt like, falling in love with someone else.

Lying in bed that night, I stared at the ceiling for what seemed like forever. Aiden was staying over, and casually snoring away beside me. Why was this happening? Why now did I suddenly not want to be with Aiden when he was turning into someone who I did want, the type of guy who I could see myself marrying? The only thing going through my mind, the only thing that has been going through my mind for the last eight weeks was Dale Brenton. I was starting to crave seeing him. It was like I was addicted. When he wasn't around the office I would go into a mood and lock myself away in the workroom but when I knew he was in, I felt like my whole aura was brighter and I just wanted to shine for him. He had this knack of looking at me and flashing me a smile that I never saw him give to anyone else at work. Being near him I had this uncontrollable urge to touch him, to just be closer to him, to just feel skin on skin with him, so I would nonchalantly high five him, or offhandedly touch his arm. He was like no one I had ever met in my life. I had known him for a little over eight weeks and yet I felt so comfortable talking to him. I felt so happy having him anywhere around me. I had never experienced anything like this in my life, never had such a draw to someone that they dominated every thought I had. It was completely mad but I don't think a minute passed that he wasn't somewhere in my thoughts. And trying to control my feelings, trying to stay away from speaking to him proved impossible. He somehow searched me out. He found me and we would engage in these conversations that seemed to last forever. It was killing me trying to work out what he was thinking, what he was feeling. I knew this was wrong of me even wanting him to like me. I knew he was married, I knew he was older than me (turns out he was forty) and more importantly I knew he had kids but I couldn't help but just want him. I fantasised about even spending one night with him, one night of complete passion, where I could just take in every inch of him and lose myself in how fantastic I know it would be. I dreamt every second about what it would be like to kiss him, even once. I kept coming up with all these stupid fantasies in my head, about him coming into the workroom late one night and just throwing me on my work bench and us having the most amazing sex ever. I have never done this before. When I got together with Aiden, we met in a bar, I asked him to dinner and from there that was it. I never had any type of fantasies about sleeping with him or anything like that. It just happened and before I knew it we were a couple. "The Perfect Couple" as so many people pointed out. Little did they know I had been through the works with him, just like I had been with every other boyfriend I had had. There were times he made me feel like I was worth nothing, so many times I would wait for hours for a phone call, a text message, anything. There were so many times where I cried myself to sleep, and was left feeling like I had no one in the world to turn to because I wanted people to believe he was the perfect boyfriend that they all thought he was. And now, here he was, putting the effort in, being that person, and doing what he could to make me feel special, talking about taking me away for weekends to Vegas, or LA, or Vermont. He was doing and saying all the things I wanted little over eight weeks ago and by some cruel twist of fate I was struggling to get interested at all. I was struggling to even find the time to be with him. How bad a person did this make me? I know I hadn't cheated on him, but it certainly felt like I had. I hardly knew Dale and yet the feelings I had for him were so much stronger than any feelings I had before. Even for Damien, the guy I was engaged to. Dale was so different. From the minute I first laid eyes on him, I felt this instant attraction, this instant surge of just wanting him. It was like even though I had never spent any real one on one time with him, I already knew he was special. He was someone who could be special. I couldn't really describe it, all I knew was I was completely hung up on him and if I didn't work out how or why I was feeling this way soon, I was going to find myself without a boyfriend.

CHAPTER SIX

It took me hours to fall asleep that night. I tried to push Dale out my head. I even tried to hug into Aiden to feel some kind of closeness to him but as soon as I closed my eyes all I could do was imagine it was Dale I was wrapped around.

Aiden left pretty early for work. He was a stockbroker and liked to be on Wall Street before too much of a rush set in with everyone else. I kissed him goodbye, told him I loved him and watched him leave as I sank into a state of guilt. Why could I not shake this? Why could I not just forget Dale and go on with loving Aiden? I was sure I did love him, maybe not 100% like before but about 90% or maybe 80%. I kept trying to tell myself I was only caught up in my thoughts of Dale because it was new, it was exciting and he was someone who I suppose I had a huge amount of admiration for so maybe that was why I felt like I had such strong feelings for him. I honestly didn't know. There was no one I could talk to about this either, no one I felt close enough to that I could divulge that type of information too. Of course I had close friends but the thought of opening up to them about this, I suppose, would make it real and I wasn't ready to admit that to myself, never mind anyone else. But at the same time it was eating me alive knowing I felt this way and I couldn't just let it out. None of my friends would understand or they would make a joke out of it. Sasha was amazing but I wasn't comfortable confiding in someone I had only known for a little over a month. Talk about spaghetti head. I was caught between a rock and a hard place because if I spoke to someone maybe they could help me realise it was just a stupid crush and it would pass or they would make me realise I shouldn't be with Aiden if I felt this way. Making matters worse was the fact that I was meeting one of the rap groups today regarding them wearing my designs and when Dale heard about it he insisted on coming to meet them too because he wanted to assess what types of people would be displaying his name. So it was going to me and Dale, alone. We were meeting the band at their hotel and then Dale had suggested going to one of my favourite restaurants on the Upper East Side called Puccini's, quite a quaint little Italian place that would allow us to round up the meeting and discuss a plan of action if needed. As much as I was looking forward to that part, I was also completely terrified at the same time. It was going to be me and Dale, no one else, no other interruptions, and I was scared. I had thought about this scenario so many times, thought about what I would do, what I would say if we were ever alone together and now it was actually going to happen. I wasn't sure if my nerves could take it, I wasn't sure if my brain could stay focussed throughout the whole of the meeting? I would just have to try and focus on my love of fashion and sport, and forgot about Dale, worry about the lunch when it happened. Dale had told me to take the morning off before we met the group at 12 noon, preparation time and what not. Yeah preparation for me to get my head screwed on properly and realise that this was a married man, who valued me as an employee. JUST AN EMPLOYEE.

It was 8am, so I had four hours to get myself straightened out, straightened up and ready to get my clothes on a group who are set to be the next big thing. This whole thing with Dale was at least distracting me away from worrying about presenting my designs to people who I hoped to pull in as clients. This was going to be my chance to show Suranne that my designs were worth it, that I was going in the right direction to meet the needs of my job. Since last week she had been completely off with me, and both Rhianne and Kimi asked Ashleigh and I why we had presented designs to Dale without Suranne's permission. Luckily Dale had agreed to say he was only down having a nosey, hoping to catch all five of us together at the one time, which we thought was great of him. The other three girls weren't ever in our work room. They tended to work at the other workshop, where Suranne was based. Something to do with closer to home etc. but it was also tiny and miles from a fabric store. Aside from the day we met Rihanne and Kimi in the main office and they commented about Dale, I had only seen them about five times since we started. And Sophie, well I had seen her once. She seemed to do the great disappearing act to God only knows where. It was a no wonder Ashleigh and I had gotten to be close friends, we were in the work room for sometimes six hours at a time together and this did nothing to help with the Suranne issue. She seemed to almost have a guard up against Ashleigh and me and would do anything to get at us. The incident with my designs wasn't the first or last. She was also annoyed at me for setting up a meeting without consulting her first, for buying fabric without discussing it with her and pretty much anything else she could find. And she was taking it in turns to make my life a misery one day and Ashleigh's a misery the next. It was hard work walking into the office and praying I didn't see Suranne's cheap little convertible in the parking garage and when I did a wave of panic would come over me and it would be like my first day at work all over again. It was horrible. She made me feel so uncomfortable. To be honest if it wasn't for the fact that I had my "friendship" with Dale, I think I would struggle to get by in there. I hated to say this, because it made me seem like I was 'bigging' myself up, but I didn't know if Suranne was slightly jealous of Ashleigh and I and this is where her problem dwelled from. We were younger and although Suranne started off as a nice person, her attitude towards us made her quite an unattractive person to me. She always found a way to make comment on how I dressed or spoke or anything she could to try to bring me down. Luckily I was quite a strong person and after the first day of tears I no longer allowed her to affect me too much

Anyway, getting this account with the rap group would hopefully show Suranne that my designs were definitely the way forward and even if she wasn't a fan, the high-end clients we needed were. And anyway, Dale had complete faith in me which meant more to me than anything that Suranne could say.

Getting ready was tough. I knew I couldn't get dressed in my usual attire, I think basketball shorts and a trucker hat might not go down as me being a serious business girl, so I had decided to go all out and wear a very Ashleigh inspired outfit or maybe that should be more Miss Moneypenny inspired outfit. I had a black pencil shirt, white blouse and a short black dress jacket as well as some serious heels to top off the outfit. I was slightly nervous about this side of things too because I hadn't mentioned to Dale that I wasn't going to be the usual skater sports girl I am at the office but fingers crossed he would approve. It was too late now anyway, it was fast approaching 11.30am and I had to be at the Plaza by noon so I had to get a jet on.

Walking into the Plaza, I felt a rush of power. I felt good dressed in my new attire and I was ready with my portfolio and Dale was bringing along the jacket to show them how things looked when they were put together, more because it can be hard to tell how something is just from a sketch. I arrived at the Plaza just before 12:00pm and couldn't see Dale anywhere so I just hung about in the reception area and hoped he wasn't going to be too late. My nerves would start to grow the later he was and I don't think my heart could take that. Luckily I didn't have to wait too long, though it was funny because Dale was obviously looking for me dressed in jeans or shorts, and walked straight past me. I had to literally shout to him to show I was there.

"Kier, you look incredible. I didn't realise you had a pair of legs like that hidden under your baggy shorts and jeans." It felt amazing standing there with him, because, without an exaggeration, he was staring at me, just staring. "And here I was thinking you looked gorgeous around the workshop and now you have blown me away by being completely stunning." He was gushing away, and I loved every second of it. "You could've warned me. This is going to be a hard meeting to get through with you looking like that. Seriously, you look like a model. You could try and sell these guys a bin sack and they'd snap it up. Good shot Miss Scott." He laughed at his little rhyme and then, putting his hand on my lower back ushered me forward towards the reception desk so we could be taken to the groups' room. At that moment though, anything could've been going on and all I could think was how I could feel electricity coming through his fingers into my body. How someone's touch, just a simple touch, could feel that way, I just couldn't understand it.

The group we met were called Keep Me Cupid and after hearing a few of their songs I could see why they were tipped as the next big thing. I'm not a massive fan of rap, I prefer Paramore, Evanescence and 30 Seconds to Mars, the usual "skater music" but I could appreciate that these guys were good. After the initial introductions, we sat down and I explained everything about my designs and showed them what I had been working on. Thank God Dale had remembered the jacket, it was definitely my showcase item and my sketch really didn't do it justice at all.

"....So as you can see, although the range has that sport feel, I have managed to combine it with street fashion to create a comfortable and casual air to it, with a look that I feel will be very much sought after. Any of these styles can be changed in colour to suit whatever you desire for yourselves and as you can see from the jacket the fit can be tailored to be a slimmer fit or looser. So, what do you think?" I wasn't sure if that was right way to end my speech but I had been talking for what seemed forever and I just wanted to know their verdict.

"To be honest..." Great, this didn't sound good, "Your stuff is off the hook. Straight-up."

I breathed, smiled and without thinking leaned in towards Dale and kind of sideways hugged him. Thankfully he hugged back and looked pleased with how things were going.

"You really like it? Honestly?" I was in shock and wasn't sure if I had actually heard them properly.

"Honestly. And you're only twenty-four? And you designed all of these and made them yourself?" One of the guys, Tag, looked more in shock than me.

My smile was growing by the second. "Yeah, I was lucky enough to go to Parson's School of Design, so I've had the best tutors imaginable, so it's really them I have to thank." Before I could add any more, Dale cut in.

"She's just being modest. Kier has only worked for me since August and in that short time has become my star employee. She is a fantastic designer with the most innovative designs I've seen in a long time and I think you guys are making a good choice if you go with her." Dale was amazing. I couldn't believe how fantastic he made me feel and this was him only talking about my work.

"I think I can vouch for all the guys when I say we agree.

We want to not only impress people with our music but we want to look amazing doing it. And not just like the usual rap groups, we want to look styled and it think Kier's designs do that and of course DB Designs is an amazing company for us to be associated with. Obviously we have to talk this over with our manager but we are more than happy to work on a deal to go ahead with production for after the holidays, sometime in January?"

Dale was grinning as much as I was, as he stood up to shake each of the guys' hands. "Thank you. You have no idea how happy I am that you're impressed with not only my newest designer but with DB Designs in general. Thanks again. I will get one of my business managers to contact your manager and we can go from there, see if we can draft up some kind of deal and get you guys suited and booted as soon as possible." He was talking a mile a minute, obviously excited at the prospect of getting new clients.

"Great, Fred, our manager, will be waiting for your call. It was great to meet you Mr Brenton, and Kier, keep up the amazing work. You're going to be responsible for making us look slammin'"

We finished shaking hands, said our goodbyes and Dale lead me through the Hotel and out to the street.

As soon as we got outside, Dale gave me a little hug, and gushed, "Well Kier, how does it feel to have your designs being snapped up?"

"Honestly Dale, I feel on top of the world. I don't know how to thank you; none of this would've happened if it wasn't for the amazing opportunity you have given me." Ok, so I sounded like a suck up, but I meant every word of what I was saying. And although I had my "feelings" for Dale, I also respected that I would never have anything like this happen if it wasn't for his company. I couldn't get the grin off my face.

"Don't thank me; it should be the other way round. You are an amazing designer and if you hadn't designed that clothing, we would've never had clients like those guys. I mean rap groups? I've been dressing actresses, princesses and socialites forever. Fresh blood is really going to lead us in the new direction that we hoped for and that's all down to you. You're completely amazing." He squeezed my shoulders and lead me towards the chauffeured driven car parked awaiting us. "Let's get lunch, we can discuss this in more detail over some food. I don't know about you but I'm famished."

I had to admit I was pretty hungry myself, but I was getting nervous realising it was just going to be me and him. I have to admit, I felt a million times sexier dressed in my new clothes and definitely more attractive but that didn't mean anything was going to happen. I was getting completely ahead of myself. Dale hadn't said anything out of the usual. He simply complimented me on how good I looked, but why wouldn't he, I was dressed completely different from my usual apparel; anyone would've given me a compliment. I had to calm down and realise this was just the debrief of our meeting and this would give us the chance to begin sorting out what needed to be done.

The drive to the restaurant was pretty quiet, Dale had some calls to catch up on and I messed about answering some emails on my Blackberry. As we stepped out onto Park Avenue, again Dale placed his hand on my lower back again and led me into Puccini's. He had requested a quiet booth at the back, obviously hoping we could get on with discussing the contract with Keep Me Cupid and start to draw together some time limits and the other details that would be a concern at this early stage.

Given that Dale was starving, we decided on a full three course lunch. And as we worked our way through bruschetta, antipasti, Bolognese, pesto pasta, and numerous other side dishes, we talked and discussed what would be expected of me now and what the company would be doing to help me along the way. I realised how stupid I had been even thinking Dale was going to have some big heart to heart with me about his feelings but at least I had something to look forward to with my designs and maybe now I could focus on Aiden and actually get it into my head how great a guy he is and that maybe I should focus the same level of attention on my feelings for him as I do on my feelings for Dale. I had to realise, that to Dale, I was an employee and that is all he had probably ever seen me as.

This was a business lunch, nothing more.

Since we had already managed to eat our weight in food we decided to skip dessert and just have some coffee to finish off.

"So things are going to fall into place pretty quickly." Dale was just finishing off his Latte, and as I looked up from my own coffee, I noticed he had foam across his top lip creating a moustache.

I couldn't help but laugh, "You have a little..." I tried to signal using my own mouth but he missed the point and looked lost. "Here, let me." I reached over and rubbed my thumb across his top lip. Before I could retract my hand, he took it in his and stared into my eyes.

"Kier, I'm crazy about you."

CHAPTER SEVEN

I couldn't believe what I had just heard. I couldn't believe those words had just come out of Dale's mouth. Those words that I had longed to hear and now, here he was, holding my hand, staring straight into my eyes and telling me exactly what I had wanted to hear for the last eight weeks.

"You are an incredible woman, Kier. I noticed it straight away at the showcase you done with us back in May. You have this amazing personality that drives me crazy, in a good way of course. And when I see you in the office I'm just drawn towards you and I just want to be near you, talk to you, whatever. To be honest, I have had this massive thing for you from day one and as strange as it is to admit it, you have completely taken over my thoughts."

I just started into his eyes and gripped his hand tighter. I was trying to find words, anything, but in the end I just decided to tell the truth and with a deep breath I let go of everything I had been holding in for the last two months.

"I feel exactly the same. I have had this huge, well I suppose crush on you since the first moment I laid eyes on you. The first time I spoke to you I was under your spell and the same thing happened, I couldn't stop thinking about you. You have completely dominated my thoughts for weeks. I didn't have a clue that you felt the same. I thought you were just a flirty person and obviously there are all the rumours round the office so I tried not to think into how you acted around me too much." I couldn't believe I was holding his hand and it felt completely right, like I was always supposed to hold his hand. This was completely surreal; people don't just hold hands that have only really just gotten to know one another.

"I know about the rumours but I swear I have never slept with Paula, or Arlene, or anyone else in that office. I kept trying to feel out whether you liked me or not but I'm a boy, I don't have a clue how to read feelings so that's why I decided to come to this meeting today, I wanted to get time on my own with you and just tell you how I'd been feeling.

The whole thing has been eating me alive. I've wanted to say something for so long." He placed his other hand on top of the one he was holding and stroked it gently.

"I can't believe this is happening. I have thought about this for so long that I'm still wondering if I'm dreaming or not." I realised how young I must've sounded or more how much like a girl I must've sounded.

Dale just stared straight at me and flashed that amazing smile that made me fall for him more and more every time I saw it. "Well, it's definitely real, which is the scary part." He obviously sensed I wasn't sure what he meant by that statement and explained himself further, "I don't know where this all came from and obviously you know I'm married and I have kids. And believe me, until you came along I was completely happily married. I hate to admit that I have strayed a few times, but it didn't mean anything, just lapses in judgement, bad judgement at that. And can I just say again, never with a member of staff. But then you showed up, and from the moment I laid eyes on you there was some spark in my brain that made me want to be close to you, have contact with you, just be with you whether that was standing at the Starbucks counter or watching you in the work room. This has all come as a shock to the system for me but for the first time in my life I can't disguise these feelings. I'm just so attracted to you. And it's not just the fact you're completely stunning." I blushed and looked down at the table. As I did Dale put his hand under my chin and lifted my head up so I was looking straight at him again. "Seriously, Kier, I know you think you're just an A-typical Skater Girl but to me you are incredible. You are the most attractive woman I've ever seen and that's without trying, so you can imagine my delight today when you showed up looking like you had just walked out of Bryant Park. And then, into the bargain you have this massive personality that I can't get enough of. You have this way of just, well, babbling on and on when you get excited and I can't do anything but smile at you. I get this wave of just, I don't know, happiness that makes me want to stay looking at you for as long as possible."

This was beyond a dream; this was beyond any fantasy I had ever had about him. He was telling me that he was attracted to me, crazy about me. My brain was struggling to process all this and my heart wasn't helping because it was pounding so loudly that I couldn't think straight.

"I know you're married, yes, and well, I have a boyfriend too who I've been with for nearly two years. But since meeting you I've been struggling to concentrate on him at all. I just get lost in thinking about you, all the time." These words were coming out of my mouth; I was having a hard time grasping that. I was telling him the complete and total truth, hiding nothing. For me this was a big step, not because I'm a compulsive liar or anything like that, but I find it difficult to put my trust in people given my past, so I tend to just keep a guard up a lot of the time.

"Same. I love my wife, my family but something about you has just taken over my senses and all I can think about is you. It's strange but you have become like an addiction but a good addiction. I feel like over the last few weeks I've always needed a little "Kier fix" and then my day just brightens and I feel like I can do anything."

"I can't believe you said that, I feel the exact same way. And this is a little embarrassing but when I'm in the office and you aren't in I go into like a little mood and I just lock myself in the workroom. God, I'll be putting you off me now because I'm so sad." I cringed at what I was saying, hoping I wasn't coming across as a complete dork.

He looked at me, and gave me the most amazing smile ever. He just stared into my eyes, and said, "Ditto."

I had to laugh. It was a hard concept to grasp that he has been feeling the same way as me all this time. He had wanted to see me just as much as I had wanted to see him. This was beyond incredible, beyond amazing, just beyond real life. But it was real life and I had to know what now. I had to know if he was telling me this because he wanted to make it clear that we were going to have to hide our feelings and get over each other or if he wanted something to happen. I had to know.

"I don't want to sound pushy or like I'm putting pressure on you but where do we go from here? I mean, I have a boyfriend, who I'm pretty sure is only a few steps away from asking to marry me and well, you are already married. Are we crazy?" I suddenly realised what I was saying. He was married, and I did have Aiden. What was I doing? What were we doing?

Dale obviously sensed my mind had switched into overtime and before I could say anymore, he spoke.

"It's ok, you're right to want an answer but let's be adults about this. Ok? Let's not rush into something just yet. We have obviously established we have a mutual attraction towards each, or as it seems, it's a bit more than just an attraction. So I think it's best not to act on this just yet." My face dropped, I wasn't sure where Dale was going with this, but I wasn't ready to be rejected after just finding out he felt the same as me. "As you probably know, I'm going on vacation next week with my family and I don't think us barricading ourselves in a hotel room tearing every desire we have apart will really help matters. So, maybe, we take a week out, a week to process exactly what we're feeling and how we want to go forward with this now we know how each other are feeling."

"Is this your get out clause?" I smiled a cheeky grin, "A week away and you'll come back forgetting me?" I tried to look as serious as I could.

"No, it's not that, it's just...." Dale was getting flustered, so I decided not to leave him out on a loop anymore.

"I'm kidding Dale. I understand completely where you're coming from." I giggled a little, and felt the grip, which had gone a little strong round my hand, loosen off and turn back to the gentle touch I had been feeling for the last hour.

"This is something I have thought about so many times but never thought I would have to actually deal with what would happen if you ever felt the same. This is a lot to take on board and believe me when I say I have never had such strong feelings for someone after knowing them for such a short period of time; in fact, we don't even really know each other, aside from out little snatched conversations at the Starbucks counter. All I know for definite is anything that I do know about you, I'm crazy about. The smallest things we speak about we seem to have in common and that doesn't happen very often with me. You have somehow managed to sweep me off my feet and that was before you told me anything that you just have in the last hour and honestly Dale, if you think after mulling this over for a week I'm going to suddenly realise I don't actually have an attraction towards you, or have any feelings for you, well your mistaken. I'm going to feel the exact way that I do now, only possibly worse, because I know you feel the same, so it's actually ok for me to be thinking about you." These words escaping my mouth were coming from nowhere and there was some force letting my brain to allow this to happen, allowing me to spill out what my heart was feeling. "Just thought you should know that."

"Thanks." And I melted again as he continued stroking my hand, "and honestly, don't think for a second it's not the same for me. No one has ever kept my mind this occupied before. I'm famous for being Mr Work Work Work, spending every waking hour focussed on DB Designs and now suddenly there is you and I get a rush of excitement every time I hear you singing as you walk down the corridor. And when you flash your smile into my office at me like I said before, it's like a drug, and once I get that fix I feel like I can do anything. There is something special about you Kier and I guess I just need a week to suss out what is actually going on in my head. Time to process what is going to materialise from our revelations in the last hour."

"I get it, honestly I do. And you're right. We should think some more, especially now we know we've been feeling the same for the last eight weeks." I was using every shred of will power I had to make these words come out. I wanted to grab him, to kiss him, anything, but he was probably right, a week wasn't going to make a difference to what I was feeling but if it did to what he felt then I guess someone was telling me this wasn't meant to be.

"You do realise if something happens between us then this is going to get complicated." He looked deep into my eyes and looked totally serious.

I wasn't sure if he was saying this because we work together, or because I have a boyfriend and he has a wife, or because he is my boss. Or if he was saying this because this was something he hadn't experienced. Maybe he had deeper feelings for me than he has expected to have and he was worried about what that meant. I have to admit when we started out this conversation I thought we would have an afternoon of passion, maybe meet a few times, you know have a fling but having listened to everything he has said and heard him, well I suppose, pour his heart out to me it made my opinion change. I couldn't be sure but I think he was having the same strong feelings that I had for him and given the position he is in it had undoubtedly scared him and I don't mean just because of the position he was in with having a family but at the end of the day he was my boss and if it got out in the office it would cause controversy beyond compare with so many people putting their own spin on things, which could completely discredit my work. Instead of looking to believe that anything good that happened to me was because of my designs, it would now be down to the fact I was sleeping with the boss. When I thought about it that way I wasn't too sure myself what I thought should happen. I wanted to be a recognised designer, I wanted to be seen as something special within this industry, not just seen as the girl who has an affair with her boss and gets to the top that way. Never in the whole time that I had been crushing on Dale and developing these feelings for him did I ever think that it would progress my career in anyway. It was him I liked, not where he could take me. Take away the fact he owned one of the most successful fashion brands in the world, I wouldn't care. I had fallen for this man who made me smile just using his smile, a man who made me feel completely amazing because of his reactions towards me and a man who just got me. He didn't care that I didn't walk around in the latest Ralph Lauren designs with a brand new pair of Manolo Blahniks on my feet. To him I was just as good in my regular clothes; baggy jeans, cartoon T-shirts and baseball caps. He was something special and it was tough to think this would be as far as it would go with us, but of course I had to understand why he was feeling like this. There was a lot more to factor in than just how he and I were feeling.

"So, let's just give it a week. And we can meet on that first Monday when I get back if that works for you?" He was still stroking my hand, and staring into my eyes, and suddenly the words escaped his mouth, "But do you know what, maybe one kiss wouldn't hurt."

My heart started to pound again and I braced myself for something I had wanted so much over the last eight weeks. As Dale moved himself over to my side of the booth, I stopped fantasising about how good this moment was going to be and just prepared myself to take in every second of the moment that was about to happen. As he leaned in towards me and placed his hand on my cheek I felt the biggest rush of electricity just before our lips met and then everything around me melted away. The butterflies were going into overtime in my stomach, my whole body was tingling and I couldn't believe this was happening. I couldn't believe I was kissing Dale Brenton and he was kissing me. Even in my dreams I could never have pictured this being this amazing, feeling this fantastic. He had just taken over my entire being for the whole time our lips were together. I no longer thought I had fallen in love with him; I knew I was in love with him. Not that I would tell him that, but surely he could feel this too. Surely he could feel that wave of excitement and sheer passion that was pouring out from just a kiss.

As he pulled away, he rubbed his nose off mine and moved to lay a gentle kiss upon my forehead. And with his hand still on my cheek, he stayed close to my face and whispered, "That was definitely something special."

"Ditto." Now it was Dale's turn to laugh.

"Ok, Miss Scott, let's get going. We both have a lot to think about over the next week. Just keep working through those fantastic designs of yours, and we'll discuss everything else when I get back. Does that sound ok?" He was still holding my hand and almost reassuring me that we would still talk regardless of what way we felt in a weeks' time.

"Deal. I'll make you proud. And anyway, like I said, when you're not around in work, I just lock myself in the workroom and the ideas flow." I tried to make it seem like I was half joking, even though I think he knew I wasn't.

"Good. A week without me in there you'll have designed a whole new collection to show me." He winked, and continued, "Come on and I'll drop you off wherever you want to go."

"Actually, is it ok if I just walk? I don't stay too far from here and I've got a lot to think about as I'm sure you do too." I wasn't lying; being in a car with him would be a massive temptation that I didn't think I would be able to resist.

"Totally understandable. As long as you'll be ok on your own." He stood up and helped me into my jacket. "And in nine days we can meet again and see where we go from there."

Before I could answer, he again kissed me lightly on the lips, and added, "But regardless, you are definitely an amazing girl, Kier. Keep that in mind."

We walked out and he got into the car and waved goodbye. I turned to head towards Greenwich Village where my apartment was. I couldn't believe the last few hours had just happened. I couldn't stop the urge to keep touching my lips. They still felt numb from the excitement that they had been engaged in only half an hour ago. Those kisses had made me feel more alive, more feminine, more wanted than I had in a long time. Aiden was a wonderful person, there was no denying that but there was a missing spark, a missing piece of zest that we had never had. But after one kiss, well technically two kisses with Dale, he had me feeling whole. Is that stupid? Feeling complete with someone after just a kiss? I was confused by the whole situation to be honest. Maybe I had felt that way before with Aiden but after two years, passion fades. Dale was new and exciting and maybe that was why it felt so amazing. All I knew was I had a week to think about what was going to happen, assess every outcome and do what I thought was best. And all at the same time, keep my fingers crossed that he would come back from his vacation and feel the exact same way as what he had just described to me. All I knew was that today, Friday Oct 17th was going to be a day I would remember for a long time.

CHAPTER EIGHT

Six days had passed since Dale had spoken up and said he was "crazy about me". I was dying on my feet and I didn't know what was going to happen when he came back. I didn't know if he was coming back to tell me that he wanted something more or if he would have woken up and realised I'm a baggy jean wearing idiot who he really doesn't want to look twice at. It was driving me bananas and I just seemed to float around the office in a daze. My days were filled with skateboarding, designing, shooting hoops and dancing around just trying to pass the time. Ashleigh had already made comment on the amount of work I had done in such a short period of time but little did she know that was purely because I had been working fifteen hour days and aside from a few hours of sport and very little sleeping, I wasn't doing much else. I think this was mostly because focussing on work, as strange as it sounded, was the only thing that distracted me from Dale. When I got lost in designing, sculpting material, sewing and putting together my creations I felt better about the whole "situation". Of course he was still on my mind but if I focussed on work at least I wasn't obsessing over what was going to happen when he got back, I just became more concerned with doing the job that he expected of me and doing it to the ability that he wanted me too.

"So, you have seriously completed fourteen pieces?" Ashleigh was eyeing up the rack of clothing that I had put together.

"Yeah, I've been in the zone this week I guess. Don't know where my inspiration is coming from but I've not left the workroom before 10pm and every time I look at the clock I can't believe it's that late. Everything is clicking into place and with Dale being away, I need to get as much done as possible before he gets back so at least then the group we met will have plenty to choose from and some basis for a contract to be drawn up or at least I hope it can." In the midst of everything that happened with Dale I had forgotten to worry about the group changing their mind or deciding they actually hated my ideas, or maybe their manager would decide against the whole idea all together. Now, I was panicking; my brain was ping-ponging back and forth between worrying about my designs, to Dale, to Dale and my designs. I would've continued to panic but Ashleigh started talking again.

"Oh, God, I completely forgot you had that meeting last week. How did it go? I can't believe I didn't remember." She looked like she was telling me she had just killed someone. I had to laugh, well on the inside anyway.

"Don't be daft, you. I know you're just as busy as me. Anyway, it went really well. The group seemed impressed and they had been searching for something a bit different to launch their "personal style" and my designs fitted the bill. I'm still trying not to get too excited, you know, just in case but the interest was there. But they want to speak on Monday when Dale gets back from his vacation. I suppose that's why I've been working in overtime...getting the work done I mean, not because Dales on vacation, I mean why would I care that Dale's on vacation." I laughed, nervously, realising how ridiculous I must've just sounded.

"Oh no I get what you mean, in both respects actually." I couldn't breathe. Did Ashleigh know how I felt? Could she have picked up on it especially since we had been working quite closely of late? But I panicked a little too soon, "Obviously with Dale away you can focus on just designing without the worry of him coming down and making changes here and there. Believe me, I feel the same. He is a fantastic guy but when I know he's in the office I find it a little intimidating. Obviously with Suranne, if she hates what we design we both have the frame of mind that she isn't really the boss, so I think neither of us worry too much about her, but with Dale, well that's top of the chain. If he hates it there is no way to rectify it. It's not that he has ever completely slated my work, just minor comments, but it still throws me. I'm sure you know where I'm coming from."

Well, actually Ashleigh, I was thinking more about the fact that I kissed Dale six days ago and he told me he's crazy about me, yes me, Kier Scott. And he has never made comment on my designs because he thinks I'm amazing and I am keeping every body part I have crossed in the vain hope that he will come back on Monday and tell me he wants to kiss me again, he wants to wrap his whole self around me and he wants to show me what it is that has been missing from my life.

Ok, I was dreaming and I would never say that out loud, especially not to anyone who actually knew Dale, so I had to use the cover that I also replayed in my mind just for a time like this.

"I know, tell me about it. He has come down here a few times before and I've been coming to the end of a design and had to change it." I was lying completely. Dale had only ever commented on how unsullied my designs were and he couldn't have done a better job himself. I have to admit though I did worry that he was only saying that now because of how he had been feeling about me. But he was a professional and no way would he allow anything to be designed for his company that wasn't completely perfect in his eyes. I had to keep that thought at the forefront of mind or I would drive myself insane with worry, even more so than I had been already and to be honest I didn't need anything else to worry about this week.

"I think a lot of people in this place assume I get to create exactly what I want and Dale ok's it because we talk and are quite friendly but that's not the case at all." It was true. The office gossip about Dale and I had started already and according to Sasha, had been floating around since day one of me arriving there. Evidently our "friendship" had caused some split decisions in the office. Lots of people saw that we had a lot in common and that was it, they were happy to see it as only that. But of course there were the "haters" who just wanted to gossip. Nothing really nasty, just that we had a thing for each other, although I suppose to give them credit they were right but that didn't give them any right to be spreading rumours. "Dale is just as hard on me as everyone else." I wanted to steer the conversation away from this so I decided to talk about the other girls. "Did you hear he gave Sophie and Kimi a hard time for not having enough done? I think between them they had five finished designs. They have been in here a lot this week working the same kind of hours as me."

It was true. He had gotten a hold of them early on last

week at the other studio and felt they were lacking in what he expected of them. They had been in a panic all week in the work room, though I have to say, their rushed designs weren't exactly something that I would be proud to show him. And when I tried to point this out in as nice a way as possible, Sophie was less than impressed.

"Well what can I say, the designs I have done already were works of art, which is what I see fashion as, but of course to his highness Mr Brenton, that wasn't good enough. If he wants quick designs and lots of them he'll have to deal with them not being as strongly designed and crafted. We can't be expected to do everything." Sophie just ranted on and on. I was annoyed at the way she was bringing down Dale. Of course he wants amazing creations; this is his company, his life. How could she even let these words come out of her mouth, was she really that self-involved that she couldn't realise what she was saying? I didn't even see the point in showing her the amount of work I had managed to complete. It seemed pointless and I was already aware that she was one of the ones who were involved in the office rumours, which to me was absurd because she was hardly ever even in the office. If I had shown her everything I had done she would twist it round that Dale had helped me or he had other people helping me because I was his "favourite" and I couldn't deal with that. Not now. Not when I was worrying about everything else that was going on. I decided to take the moral high road and not let someone like Sophie get under my skin.

"Just don't sell yourself short Sophie. I'm sure there is a way to do well-structured designs, just a little quicker. Ashleigh has a fabulous line going on and I'm doing ok myself." I gave her what was possibly my falsest smile ever, not on purpose, I was trying to smile but this girl was impossible. She was so self-obsessed, self-absorbed and hated anything to take the lime light away from the Sophie Kilean Show. "I've seen the earlier work you done, so don't just throw something together for the sake of getting it done." That pretty much finished the conversation, nothing much else was said after that. I just had to listen to more of Sophie complaining and Kimi going on about her creativity was being stifled by an overbearing idiot who wouldn't know style if it was thrown into his face (yes that was Dale, and yes it annoyed the life out of me).

After relaying the story to Ashleigh she went into work-overdrive, obviously getting slightly alarmed at hearing how harsh Dale could actually be when he wasn't Mr Nice Guy like he was to the two of us. At least it had gotten her away from talking about him. As much as I hated to admit it I missed him and I was having a hard enough time trying to get through the day without having to speak about him too. This was harder than I thought it would be. I was used to not seeing him for two and three days but after six days I would've given anything to hear his voice, see his face. Anything. I think if I didn't know everything we had spoken about on Friday I would be ok about having not seen him but I was constantly replaying the conversation over and over in my head. I had analysed every detail of what we had spoken about, taken the good and bad from it and tried to sort out some kind of outcome that was going to come from it all. Half the time I thought he had gone to the effort of telling me how he felt and if he didn't want something to happen why would he have told me anything? But then on the other side I thought maybe he would regret having said anything after having spent a week with his family. He would realise that was where he belonged and that would be the end of it. This was driving me insane. I just had to focus on work and realise I was lucky enough to have experienced what it was like to have kissed him even just that once so if nothing else come from it then I just have to put my faith in God that he had planned this to happen for some reason and I would see that reason one day. It was just difficult to imagine how fantastic it felt on Friday even just holding his hand and all I keep thinking is that could be it. Full stop.

22.34pm

I couldn't believe how late it was. I was still hauled up in the workroom trying to create designs that would make Dale go wild with excitement. In the last six days I had managed to put together four new creations and without bragging too much, I had produced some of my most awe-inspiring work. I wanted to keep going, to keep creating the most wonderful pieces I could so that I would still impress him, regardless of what he decides. In a way I thought this week would have made me realise I can't do this. I can't be the girl who wants to be with a married man, the girl who is even contemplating it because deep down I know how strong my feelings are for him and if his are half as strong then that could possibly make me a home wrecker. Did I really want to be that girl? I honestly didn't know. I was trying to be the better person. I was praying so hard for my own answer to this but all I could think about was that I was almost sure I was falling in love with this man and there was some force pushing me towards him that I couldn't shake off and for now I had no clear answer. To make matters even worse, I had practically ignored Aiden all week too. Every time he sent a text message or called I just fed him some nonsense about having a late meeting or a works dinner or some other lie because my brain couldn't process giving him the love and attention he wanted, as well as try to sort out my feelings for Dale. In my mind if I wasn't seeing Dale, I shouldn't see Aiden either because that would just confuse things. I needed to stay away from Aiden too so I could see if I missed him in the same way that I missed Dale. And truthfully, so far, I hadn't missed Aiden at all. I didn't know if it was because I didn't have enough energy to focus on missing him, missing Dale and being able to concentrate on work, or if maybe I wasn't allowing myself to put my attention towards Aiden because I knew he would be there regardless, which I suppose makes me a horrible person because I am playing with Aiden's emotions so that I don't have to face up to my own. But horrible person or not, this is just what I have to do to keep my own sanity if nothing else.

It was just leaving 23:30 when I decided to pack up and head home. I had heard my phone beep to alert a text message about half an hour ago but had just ignored it. I'm good at doing that these days, ignoring my phone, my boyfriend, my friends; everyone. I picked up my Blackberry and almost dropped it straight away. I couldn't believe what I was staring down at: 1 message received from Dale. Dale had text me. Dale had text me. DALE HAD TEXT ME!!

My hand was shaking and my whole body felt like it was fighting against itself to go in different directions and this was before I had even opened the text. Ok Kier, calm down, breathe.

"K, catch up next week to go over those fabric samples. D"

What the FRANCE! I didn't understand what I was looking down at. He was texting me about fabric samples. FABRIC SAMPLES. I had been waiting for five days to hear anything from this man and he talks about fabric samples. I couldn't understand what was going on, couldn't get my head to switch on to what this meant. Was he just sending me anything so I knew he was thinking about me but obviously being with his wife he didn't want to write anything that would give that away? Was this his way of telling me I was still on his mind and we would be getting together next week to discuss that? Or was this his way of saying, yes we'll get together but I just want to set you up to realise it is purely in a work capacity, nothing more. I honestly didn't know. My head had been like mush before, but now it was even worse. I had another four days to get through before he was even back and I had this new factor to try and work into the equation, another factor to consider, to tear apart, to completely mess up my brain even further. This was ridiculous. Why do I have this pre-set mind that feels the need to analyse every single detail of a situation to the point where I drive myself insane. I had to just stop thinking about this, I had to find some way to get through the next four days and stop thinking about what was going to come of this. If Dale didn't want anything more too happen then I should just realise that is probably for the best. I can't expect a married man to just decide to pursue an affair with me. An Affair. That's what it would be. I would be like some dirty mistress. Me, Kier Scott, the skater girl, as someone's Dirty Mistress. I hadn't considered it in that way before and I don't think that was a role I was really prepared to play. But on the other side I was struggling to imagine not taking his hand again or not kissing him again, even after that one time. This whole situation was wearing me out and at this moment I would just be happy to have any answer so I could get some normality back to my brain. As I continued to re-read the message for the hundredth time I realised I hadn't even bothered to consider a reply back to him. Did I reply? Was he expecting me to respond so he would know if I was thinking about him? Quickly typing, "No problem, next week sounds good. See you then. K" I hit send before I could analyse the situation even more and left it at that. Monday was only four days away and until then I wouldn't know anything more than I do now so I had to stop worrying about it. Anyway, it was Sasha's 21st this weekend so I at least had that to look forward to and hopefully it would be a welcome distraction from everything else.

CHAPTER NINE

It was Saturday afternoon and I was practically knocked out lying face down feeling unable to move. Everything around me seemed hazy, and I couldn't really focus on anything. No, I hadn't just been attacked; I was lying in the Ola Conelia Health Spa, getting possibly the most amazing massage ever. My brain was switched off and I felt like I was drifting in and out of reality. Every negative thought I had been having over the last week had gone and for the first time since the 17th of October I was focusing on myself. The masseur had been working on my shoulders and back for twenty minutes and I could feel myself fall into a deep relaxation with every stroke. This was exactly what I needed to get rid of all the tension I had been building up over the last week.

It was the day of Sasha's 21st and there were six of us spending the day at the spa before heading out later for dinner and cocktails. I had never been to a spa before but if today was anything to go by then I was hooked. I had already had an intense facial, a cocoa butter body scrub and now a massage, I was in heaven. Dale, Aiden, work, in fact everything were a distant memory. I was so relaxed that nothing negative was getting in, not today. And I still had a leisurely swim and steam to look forward to and Sasha's parents had rented her a room in the Waldorf Astoria, so we planned to go there and get ourselves ready after our monster pampering session.

I had been introduced to Sasha's friends, Heather and Susie, as well as her two cousins Lisa and Victoria. I'm not too great usually when it comes to being friends with girls but this lot were great. They were all up for a good time and they didn't seem hung-up on the usual superficial matters that most girls do. Having been a tom-boy my whole life I didn't get the deal with worrying about if my make-up looked good or if I had a hair out of place. My make-up consisted of some black eyeliner and natural coloured lip-gloss, so not much to worry about there and as for my hair; I own sixteen baseball caps, so generally my hair is hidden

underneath one of them. I had made an effort for tonight
though and had borrowed a Red and Black DB dress from
the office (it was last season's so no one really minded us
borrowing things) and I had purchased a pair of black
Manolo Blahniks sling backs that were unbelievable. And
when we got back to the hotel I planned to curl my hair,
team the outfit with my red FCUK bag and I would be good
to go. Some of the other people from the office were meeting
us later, including Ashleigh and Harry, much to Sasha's
delight. She had spoken to me earlier about how crazy she
was about him and it killed her to know he had a wife
because she was almost positive he felt something for her
too. I had to agree. Whenever he arrived in the office he
made a beeline for her desk and they had lunch together
almost every day. I had also taken note of the way he stared
at her just that little bit longer than would be normal before
he walked away from her but who was I to judge. I was so
hung on Dale that I could barely keep a smile off my face
when he was around and I was the one who had spent last
Friday afternoon staring into his eyes and finished the
afternoon with a kiss. Having spent all afternoon being
pampered though, all of those thoughts seemed to have
disappeared from my mind and all I was looking forward
to was the meal we were going to have at Nobu and then
onto Bed for cocktails.

As my massage came to an end, I pulled the oversized
fluffy dressing robe on and walked towards the pool, where
Sasha and the rest of the girls were sitting enjoying some
fruit smoothies and handmade sushi.

"Kier, how was the massage?" Heather shouted from one
end of the pool to the other. This girl had the biggest,
brightest personality I had come across in a while and I
couldn't help but think how much I liked her.

"I swear if heaven is like this then I want to be there now.
I have never felt so relaxed in all my life. It was amazing.
How have all your days been?" I had now reached the table
they were sitting at and started to eye up some of the
California rolls and Unagi that was sitting in front of us.
As I reached to take some, the girls filled me in on the
treatments they had been trying out, including honey
wraps, berry body blitz's and I had to grimace when Sasha

told me about her all over body wax.

"Honestly, Kier, it was amazing. You would love it. And as much as you think it's going to hurt its nothing at all. The first few strips maybe a slight ouch, but after that it's easy. You just woosed out on me. I have to say though you do look a lot more chilled than you have this week at work, so maybe the pampering is just what you needed." Sasha had already commented on how tired I had been looking and how I'd spent the week looking like a zombie, just going through the motions of life but not really taking anything in. And she was right. I had been but I couldn't bring myself to tell Sasha anything about Dale, in fact I couldn't even bring myself to tell her I had feelings for him, it just didn't seem right, not when she worked with him everyday and I doubt very much he would be pleased at me spilling the beans to another employee. But, without even trying Sasha had made me feel better than I had in over a week just by inviting me along today. She was such a great girl and she was finally getting the chance to do work behind the scenes for the Walkerton Show, getting all the designers working together, liaising with Dale and the rest of the Senior Management Team and working to pull everything together. This was the first time she had been asked to do anything that was so heavily involved in the fashion side of the company, instead of just the usual clerical work she had been doing. This was what she wanted. She told me her dream was to become a show co-ordinator so this was a step in the right direction. I had a feeling that Harry was the one who had recommended using her but to be honest I couldn't think of anyone better for the job. She certainly knew her stuff, not necessarily about clothing design but after she looked at my work she had all these idea about who would look good wearing them, how the runway could be linked to be completely cohesive with other designs from the DB team, pulling together the whole look of clothes, hair and make-up and all these other brainwaves that would make a runway show capable of blowing every other designer away. If Harry had created an opportunity for her because he had a thing for her, then great, because at least she would make an amazing job of it. She had been doing long hours in the office too so we had gotten chatting loads over the last few weeks, though I have to say this week had been difficult because I was dying to let loose on everything that had happened between Dale and I and literally had to use every ounce of will power I had not to not open up. Instead I listened intently to her talk about her excitement about the show, her birthday and of course Harry. She was certainly hung up on him and knowing exactly how she was feeling I felt like the perfect agony aunt, pretending I was recalling past experiences, hiding the fact that I was caught up in the same situation, going between fighting my conscience over what is right and feeling my heart break at the thought of knowing that the right answer would be to forget the conversation Dale and I had, and block out my feelings. On Tuesday night last week, she brought some of her work down to the work room and chatted away.

"So you think he likes me, like seriously likes me, really likes me, like the same way I like him?" She was getting slightly excited about everything and because I said I was convinced Harry had a thing for her this was the fourth time she had asked me the exact same question. In so many ways Sasha seemed the same age as me, but hearing her talk about Harry was like listening to a school girl with a crush, not in a bad way, it was sweet but funny coming from someone who only seconds before was giving me a run down of how the work for the show was coming along, adding in the intricate details, the well thought out plans and the carefully connected elements that I didn't even realise went into a fashion show, and now suddenly, she sounded like a 15-year-old. It cracked me up and I knew, given the chance I would probably be doing the exact same, asking over and over if she thought he would come back and want to be with me. I wasn't ready to open up to anyone about all of this yet. I wasn't sure if when I knew what was happening next week if I would speak to her about it all, but I am more than aware of how easily things can slip out even if you don't mean them too. I had to wait until Monday anyway regardless of anything else, but by allowing myself to focus on Sasha at least allowed for some much needed distraction.

"Yes, yes, yes, yes, yes, yes, yes," I grinned, and

continued, "and for good measure, Yes. I was actually shocked when I first started here and discovered that you weren't a couple already because he certainly looked at you like you were his. He gives you little glances and stares at you for longer at the end of conversations than people usually do. Honestly Sasha, he likes you, and given by those looks, a lot." And I meant it. Harry was definitely into her, whether he would ever admit it was another thing. But I had an open mind after everything that had happened with Dale, so I was going to be crossing my fingers for her too. At least if they got together there were no kids to worry about so it would possibly be an easier situation to manage. That was my main concern with Dale, a wife is one factor, but kids, that is a whole different ball game to try and sort out.

"I am so happy you said. People have made comments before about him and I but I just thought they were hoping for some gossip but with you only starting and noticing it, well that definitely gives me hope. I've just never felt this way about anyone before in my life; he is just the most amazing person ever." She looked so happy talking about him and from the look on her face I could tell she felt the exact same way about Harry as I did about Dale.

"Honestly, I believe 100% that he has some kind of feelings for you and in no way do I mean just as a friend. And this isn't something I'm just saying because I know that's what you want to hear. There is no doubt in my mind that if Harry wasn't married he would have asked you out already."

Sasha looked so happy and danced around the work room in a daze that looked familiar of my own from last week. I wish I could've just told her everything and made her see how easy it can happen for someone who you think is completely unattainable to suddenly turn round and tell you everything you want to hear but no, I was keeping this to myself, at least until after I spoke to Dale again.

Watching Sasha dance around on Tuesday night made me wonder if I looked like that when Dale was around or if I was doing a good enough job at hiding my true feelings for him. Anyway, I was determined not to think about that and being in a health spa shovelling sushi into my mouth was helping. I was so glad Sasha had invited me along. She really was becoming a close friend, something that over the last few months I had lost a lot of, so she had definitely shown up at a great time. I was getting lost in my thoughts again and would've quite happily daydreamed to myself all day but Victoria started to speak and I didn't want to be rude and zone out on her.

"So are we all done with our treatments? I'm going to have a quick swim and then I'm booked in for a cut and colour, you are too Susie, am I right?" Susie just nodded, herself wrapped up in the sushi and smoothies. She was quite quiet compared to the rest of the girls but with such big personalities all round it would be easy to get lost in the crowd, I was almost feeling that way myself, not that I minded.

"Ok, so Susie and I will meet you all back at the Waldorf and we can get ourselves set for our big night out." Victoria started to pack up and as her and Susie walked towards the Salon, obviously forgetting her swim, she looked over her shoulder and added, "Can't wait girlies, get your Kinky Boots on and let's get ready to make sure New York really is the city that never sleeps."

We all got ourselves organised and little over an hour later we were all in the Penthouse Suite of the Waldorf. I don't even think words could describe how perfect it was, right down to the last detail. Lisa and Heather were having a lie down before getting ready and I had just started to curl my hair when Sasha came in and sat next to me.

"Thanks for coming today Kier. I know I haven't known you for very long but I can already tell we're going to be great friends. I feel so comfortable telling you anything, I haven't even confided in Heather or Susie about my feelings for Harry. To be honest, I don't think they would understand, whereas you, well you just take it in your stride and you seem to know the right thing to say, every single time. I appreciate you listening to me go on and on about Harry. It's just, when I start talking about him, I can't stop. He is amazing, wonderful, fantastic..." I was listening to Sasha but it was so hard not to drift away to thoughts of Dale because that's what I thought of him, that he was amazing, wonderful and fantastic. "....and he just gets me." Sasha was smiling into a dreamy space and all I could think was "ditto", that word that made me smile. That was our word. And all of a sudden Monday, yet again, seemed so far away.

The night was turning into an amazing success. The dinner in Nobu had been great. Again it was just the six of us and when we finished we headed to Bed. It was a little before eleven when we arrived, so it would just be starting to pick up. Sasha had booked a private "bedroom" and there were fifteen others meeting us there, including a few from the office, of course, including Harry. Louise would be there too and was coming with Paula (the girl who apparently had an affair with Dale and who Sasha said still has a massive thing for him) as well as the accounts manager Jacqueline and the International Relations Manager Calvin who completely loved Sasha in a platonic way. He was hitting fifty and I think saw her as the daughter he never had. They were joined with a few of Sasha's friends from outside work, so it was set to be a wicked night.

An hour later, the cocktails were flowing, the wine was going down by the bottle and we were all having the night of our lives, in fact, I think everyone felt like it was their 21st all over again. Sasha was filled with complete delight the whole night and when she eyed up Harry, who was looking, and even I'll admit this, very handsome in dress trousers and a very clean cut black shirt, I thought she was going to die. She proceeded to spend most of the night glued to his side, while I worked the rounds to distract people away from this. I was quite happy doing it and again, it was a welcome distraction from obsessing over Dale. Everyone seemed nice enough, well everyone except Paula who gave me the distinct impression that she didn't want to speak to me. Sasha had, however, warned me about this. She said Paula got jealous very easily if anyone became close to Dale in anyway. Apparently that is why people thought they were having, or had had an affair at some point. They use to go for lunch together and she would be first on the invite list for any award ceremonies or fashion dinners etc, and now I had shown up and almost taken the "spotlight" away from her. Not that Dale had invited me to anything but obviously he paid me a lot of attention and according to Sash, this would be driving Paula insane. Wonder how she would feel if she knew he had told me he was crazy about me, told me I was constantly on his mind, if she knew he had kissed me in a way that couldn't be faked because it was filled with such passion, such emotion I knew straight away he meant every word he had said to me. I didn't let Paula bother me, this was Sasha's night and I wasn't going to let someone's petty jealousy ruin it. Although I had to admit, I don't think she would have noticed anything that was going on apart from between her and Harry. Their eyes were fixated on each other and I had to admit they looked great standing together and watching them standing there I had to say brought a smile to my face. Don't think for minute I advocate cheating, although I know I could say that because of my situation, but I don't, not at all. Watching those two stand together though, I could see the spark, I could see that there was a connection between them, something that was obviously making them both happy and knowing she was happy made me happy. I'm sure this was a night she was going to remember for a long time, even if nothing happened between her and Harry, having had him there would be enough.

We stayed in Bed, the nightclub that is, until around 4am. Sasha was fairly drunk and openly hugging Harry, which raised a view eyebrows but nothing that was going to cause any hassle. He didn't object at all and I think this was maybe the cause of the raised eyebrows, not that either of them noticed which I was more than glad about. I hadn't had too much to drink and had made myself responsible for making sure Sasha got back to the hotel in one piece and free from Harry. As much as I believed they would be great together I wasn't going to allow it to happen through a drunken night out, Sasha would regret it if that's how it happened. So using a vice... I'm kidding...I wrenched her free from Harry's grip and lead her outside and into a cab. I was thankful she didn't object and I think Harry knew my reasoning behind taking her home and he looked grateful in return. Sasha was almost falling asleep on me in the cab but still managed to chat away in the drunken slurs that were becoming easier to understand as I became accustomed to them.

"I love Harry. I know you'll think I'm crazy but I do. I love him A LOT. Uh Huh, I do. I really really do. Really do…" Her words started to fade as she passed out against me and in my mind, once again, all I could think was, "DITTO."

Sasha's birthday was a roaring success and I loved how much of a distraction it had been away from Dale. I had also told Aiden I wasn't feeling too great over the weekend and that's why I couldn't see him. I felt awful lying but I knew I also couldn't deal with the added worry of having to force myself to be normal with him. By the time Sunday night came I was about set to ship myself off to Australia just to get away from everything. OK, slight exaggeration but I couldn't help being dramatic. I couldn't have been happier that it was almost Monday but at the same time I was beginning to worry about what would be the outcome of tomorrow. I had torn apart every last detail of the conversation we had, of the text message he sent and pretty much anything else that had ever happened between Dale and I in the last two months, just trying to get some ounce of sense out of what was going to happen when I saw him. I had over analysed everything so much that I no longer had any idea what was going to happen. It had taken me this long to realise that I hadn't even contemplated what would happen after tomorrow; on one hand he may come back and tell me he still feels the same and then I have to deal with if I'm ready to give up Aiden for the sake of an affair. Or, he decides he doesn't want to go any further forward and we just have to repress how we feel about one another and I have to deal with getting over him and putting every morsel of my being into loving Aiden, which of course I should've been doing all along. Whatever was going to happen, in twelve hours I would be back in the office and so would Dale.

CHAPTER TEN
09.00am

I was nervous. I had been sitting in the workroom since 7am, and since sleep wasn't happening I thought I would just finish off the second jacket I had been working on and pray that Dale would come in early too but no such luck. He still wasn't in; I hadn't had any text message saying when he wanted to talk, if he wanted to talk, nothing. I had asked Sasha to call me through when he arrived making the excuse that I needed him to look at the rest of the clothing I had designed for Keep Me Cupid and wanted to catch him before everyone else did.

By 09.32 she called.

"Hey sweetie. Dale has just come in but he's going straight back out again. He asked if you were in but said he would catch up later regarding some fabric samples."

I quickly said thanks and hung up. Later? He'd catch up later? I had just gone through nine days of waiting for "later" and now he is finally back and he is still stalling? I wanted to speak to him now, get whatever he had to tell me out the way so I could get some sense of order back into my life. So now it was the same again, yet another waiting game, another God knows how many hours of fretting, worrying and panicking about what was going on. Chill out Kier, he'll speak to you. He has to speak to you. I had to admit, I was glad I was in the workroom myself because I wasn't sure if I was speaking out loud or just in my brain. This whole fixation on what was going to happen was turning me into a schizophrenic. The men in white coats would be coming to take me away if anyone had a look in here and saw me wandering around having a conversation with myself. I couldn't help it. I had waited nine days. NINE DAYS. I couldn't wait any longer. And to make matters worse I had to go out and pick up some more fabric so I wasn't even going to be around all day to catch him as soon as he got back. I wanted to text him and ask when we were going to catch up but I thought that was probably a bad idea. The ball was in his court and I couldn't be the clingy needy person; that was one role I definitely wasn't comfortable playing. So a waiting game it is. Maybe being out of the office was better, I wouldn't be watching the clock or phoning round to Sasha trying to suss out if he was in or not. Being out was definitely a better option and maybe I could stretch it out a little and take some time away, see if maybe not being in the office would actually allow me to get my head in order and to breathe again. I had just worked a 70-hour week; a little R&R was deserved of me.

I decided to stay in the workroom until a little past 11am. As I left the office I let Sasha know I had to pick out some new fabrics and I would be gone for a few hours. I was lying; I had chosen the fabric weeks ago, I literally just had to pick it but I decided to go to the park and sit by the lake for a while. I liked the lake. It was the one of the few places in New York that no matter what was happening, how loud the world was, it still always seemed serene and peaceful. Plus the bonus was I could grab lunch at the Boathouse restaurant too so I could unwind before deciding whether I should drop Dale a text message or not.

To my surprise the park was quiet, which I was more than glad of. It was starting to get cold outside given it was late October and I was wrapped up tight with my black loose fit baggy trousers on, an oversized cream jumper all teamed together with a black hat, scarf and glove combo. I was tempted to make a big effort for seeing him today but decided that really wasn't me. I wasn't the fancy trouser suit wearing girl around the office and I wasn't about to start just for the sake of maybe swaying his decision towards me more. If Dale wanted me, it was me he was getting. Skater-Girl Kier, who was a little accident prone and who more than often forgot to brush her hair before pulling a baseball cap over it. That was who he would have to want, not the Kier that had been dressed up at the meeting on the 17th of October. I know I was over scrutinising everything now, which, let's be honest wasn't going to help matters, make time go faster or make Dale try and get in touch with me any sooner. I'm just very aware of people liking me one way and not the other. Aiden can be guilty of that. When I'm around his friends I have to be the perfect little girlfriend and almost hide my own personality and replace it with someone that Aiden is proud of. Maybe that's the reason I had fallen for Dale because he didn't do that to me. He liked that I danced around the office and sang up and down the corridors and my Skater Style never seemed to bother him so I'm not sure where my little outburst there came from. I was just starting to panic again I guess. Dale had been on my mind everyday for two months now and it's a bit daunting to think I may need to try and forget about him. This would all be a lot easier if I knew what the hell was going on.

And as though by magic my phone was ringing and to my surprise Dale's name was flashing on my screen.

"Hi there." I wanted to sound calm and as relaxed as possible. I didn't want him to think I was high maintenance and had secretly been stressing out over having not heard from him already.

"How you doing gorgeous?" I tried not to get excited and think that this was good start. "Are you planning on staying in the office all day today?" Straight to the point. Wasn't sure if that was a good thing or a bad.

"I'm doing ok." Stay calm Kier. "I'm actually just out picking up some fabric and looking for new material while I'm here. Not sure when I'll be done here or if I'll have time to come back." I looked at my watch, it was 12.56pm. I was hoping to stall for longer. Wasn't sure if I could face being in the office if I knew he was going to be around, not at least until we had spoken, which of course couldn't happen with so many people around.

"Well, how about you don't go back to the office. Let me come and meet you somewhere, wherever is easiest for you."

I was stunned. He wanted to come and see me. I was still trying to keep myself together and refused to get ahead of myself. This doesn't mean anything, Kier, relax. Yet again with the pep talks, what else could I do, well aside from go completely insane.

"Well I'm at the Upper East Side of Central Park. I was planning on getting myself some lunch but I can wait if you want to come and meet me. Are you coming from the office?" I wanted to know how long I would have to prepare myself for seeing him.

"Actually no and funnily enough I'm only about ten minutes from you. Do you want to hang around the entrance near Park and I'll come get you? We could go to the Boathouse for lunch if you like?"

Ten minutes! I had ten minutes to calm my nerves and prepare myself for what could be the most important lunch date of my life. "Yeah that's not a problem Dale. I'll be the one messing about on my skateboard, so I'll be hard to miss." I wanted to be as much like the real Kier as I could and the mention of me and my skateboard is enough to put anyone off.

"Great. Looking forward to seeing you." And that was it. He said good bye and I patiently waited on him to show up. Looking forward to seeing you. I really do pull everything apart. At least he didn't react badly to me being on my skateboard which was a big positive. I had a look down at my outfit and checked everything still looked ok. This was probably one of my more "dressed up" skater outfits and to be honest I felt good in it. Fingers crossed Dale would think the same.

I had Evanescence blaring in my ear and didn't notice Dale come up behind me and put his hands on my hips.

"Looking good beautiful. You hungry?" Dale looked incredible. He was tanned, looked relaxed and was dressed to stun in a white shirt and grey slacks that were honestly making me go weak and with his long black overcoat on to finish off his outfit, he looked amazing.

I instantly smiled looking at him. "I am starving." My grin was huge and as I picked up my skateboard I felt Dale brush his hand down my arm. And as I turned towards him he added,

"You're certainly a sight for sore eyes. Can't believe how good you look." And again he showed off that amazing smile that made me fall for him all over again.

"Ditto." We both laughed before I realised I just wanted to hear what he was thinking, I really couldn't wait any longer. "So lunch it is then?"

"Yeah, let's go." As we walked towards the Boathouse, Dale continued to talk away, "It's been a hectic morning but things are coming together for the Walkerton Show. Sasha has been doing well; she has an undeniable eye for styling. I've been very impressed all morning hearing everything that has happened over the last week." I loved listening to Dale speak about work, he was so passionate about his company and he loved knowing all the people working for him were as passionate as he was. It was yet another reason why he was so easy to fall for, he constantly thought of other people over himself.

"...I really think this is going to be the best show we've done. Everything is coming together and all the designs are looking amazing. And of course each of you girls will be showing something too, a little earlier than expected, but I think it's time to show something. Have you decided what you are going to put down the runway?" Dale had been talking all the way to the Boathouse and this was the first mention of me and work. Was this his way of bringing up us? Was this his way of telling me that's what we are; colleagues?

"Em...the show? Yeah, I had Sasha down during the week and of course she knows everything else that is in the show, so her recommendations were the basketball skate jacket, the satin type boarder pants and the red and black vest top. I know it's just one outfit we have each and I think this is something that will make an impact. Or I hope at least." I rambled on and on without taking a breath. I was trying to get Dale to talk about more than just work. I wanted to talk about him and I. I wanted to straighten out what had happened ten days ago. I wanted an answer.

"Sounds good. And good call by Sasha. That girl is going places; I'm going to make sure of it." He led me up the steps into the restaurant and just as I was about to ask if he got a lot of thinking done or something to that effect, the head waiter came over and ushered us to a table.

"So work has been ok this week? I have to admit I had a look into the workshop before I left the office and I can't believe how much you have done in the last week. Your work is just getting better and better. I'm totally blown away by you Kier." Me or my work? "I was really looking forward to seeing you today." And with that he reached over and took my hand. "I missed you this week."

And I smiled, relaxed and for the first time in over a week I could breathe again.

"I spent the last week just replaying our conversation over and over again. I would be walking down the beach and I'd be thinking about you. Everything there reminded me of you. In fact one night, I just lay awake the whole night thinking of what I was going to say when I got back here and even now I still don't know what to say except taking your hand again feels amazing, and this is going to feel better." He stood me up, looked straight into my eyes and as he twirled the front strands of my hair, he kissed me. I let my whole self fall into his lips and let go of everything around me, and although we were in the middle of a restaurant I wasn't even worried about anyone seeing us, all I cared about at that moment was that he was kissing me. And as he pulled away, his whole face was beaming and WOW did he look good. "That is the best I have felt since the last time I saw you." And as he said this, he lightly kissed my nose.

"You have no idea. I have been thinking about you constantly since I last left you too. I couldn't get you out of my head and after that kiss, now I remember why. That was incredible. In fact, I hope I don't sound really full on but well, you're incredible." I felt a little, well coy saying that. I wasn't use to being this forward with anyone, but Dale just seemed to draw something from me that I would tend to keep reserved from others.

"Well I think you're pretty incredible too Kier." We sat back down, but he continued to hold my hand and stare straight at me. "This has been a tough week for me. I was on vacation with my family and as much as I had an amazing time with my boys it was so difficult being with them and knowing I couldn't stop thinking about you. My wife is a fantastic person and she is very attractive but she has something missing that you seem to have but honestly, I don't know what that is yet. All I know is the last ten days have been arduous for me, knowing I have a family, who I should have been focussed on but I wanted so badly to see you. I can't help but feel like I'm a horrible person." He looked down and for the first time ever, he looked lost.

"Hey, please don't think that of yourself. You're an

amazing person, it's not like you walked into work one day and thought, you know what I quite fancy being attracted to a skater chick. Things happen Dale, things out with our control."

He smiled again and almost laughed a little. "You know, you make a lot of sense when you're not really trying to. And for the record, you were definitely one person I had no way of stopping being completely attracted to. I noticed you straight away."

"On the first day, really? You noticed me? You sure that wasn't just down to the baggy jeans and baseball cap?" I honestly wasn't trying to make a joke here, I was being deadly serious but Dale continued to laugh anyway.

"The first day yes, you looked amazing but I mean that day at Bachoa, remember you were showing some of the dresses you had designed?"

That was the first time I had ever seen Dale, the day when I acted like a complete idiot, when I made the jokes and just kind of died on my feet.

"You liked me from then? Are you being serious?" I was shocked. How was this even possible that he liked me from the same day I fell for him?

"Deadly serious. You were so different from everyone else and you showed up in the clothes you always wear and you done your speech about having won Young Designer of the Year and I was instantly drawn to you. You had this amazing smile that seemed to have the whole room captured under a spell."

I couldn't take this in. He thought I had people under a spell? Did he even realise it had been him who had me under his spell. It was him who I couldn't stop thinking about from that very first day.

"I can't quite believe this. I can't believe you are saying these words. Wow I suppose seems an apt word to use. This is when I should say I noticed you that day too and I'm not lying. You really got under my skin, in a good way, and then when I heard I had the job and I walked in and you were just there in front of me, looking amazing, well what can I say, I was hooked."

And for a few seconds we said nothing. We both seemed to take in everything the other had said, realising we both had this instantaneous attraction to one another, this same rush of feelings towards each other that we couldn't explain. Finally Dale broke the silence.

"Well, Miss Scott, I think we have gathered the two of us have a pretty big thing for one another, in fact I can put my hand up and swear to God himself I have never fancied anyone as much as I do you." He had the most boyish grin on his face and once again he was driving me crazy. "So now we just decide where to proceed from here. Any ideas?"

I had been thinking about this question all week, going over every scenario a million times. I had come to the conclusion that he would always have a family and that him and I would always just be a fling and to be honest, to be in his arms, close to him for even a few hours, I was willing to accept that. I was honestly nuts about this man and I felt like if I didn't do something, even the smallest thing with him I would live to regret it. So I just said what I felt.

"Well, Dale, a little fun never hurt anyone and what people don't know won't hurt them, so why don't we just see how we go, have our fun and just enjoy each other's company for a while." I couldn't believe how calm I was saying this. I had re-played it in my head so many times and had it word perfect for the occasion. And it must've worked because Dale leaned across the table, kissed me gently on the mouth and said, "You are amazing. How could I not have wanted something to happen with you?"

We had spent little over an hour in the Boathouse before we reached our conclusion and once we did, we spent another three hours talking, laughing and just getting to know each other even better. This was the longest I had ever spent with him and he was becoming more and more fantastic. He had this way of speaking and wording things that drove me crazy and I had never had anyone make me smile or laugh so much. Regardless of where this went from here, I had officially just had the most amazing, well "First Date" ever. Dale Brenton was one incredible person and I couldn't wait to spend more time with him, however long it lasted.

CHAPTER ELEVEN

A little over five weeks had passed since Dale got back from his vacation and our "affair" was in full swing. We had spent most of our time together in the office, staying late when everyone else had left to go home. He would come down to the workroom or I would head up to his office and we would talk for hours, kiss each other (which is still unbelievable) and just spend as much time getting to know each other as we could. It was a strange situation to be involved in because, to me, I always considered an affair to be something sleazy, where you would go to a hotel room, screw each other's brains out for a few hours and then leave, making a very dirty and sneaky situation. I mean yes, Dale and I were sneaking behind peoples' backs, including my boyfriend's, who I was still very much in a relationship with, his wife's and of course the entire workforce at DB Designs but we hadn't slept together. We hadn't even come close. To us sex hadn't become an issue at all. We were so content just sitting in each other's company, talking. I would tell him about my basketball games and how I was involved in dance as well as the other sports I took part in, and he told me all about how he was so close to becoming a pro footballer but gave it up to pursue a career in design, little realising he would become a worldwide recognised name. His football career had left him still with a love of everything to do with sport but given he ran a very successful company and had a family to look after now he didn't have much time to do any training. He mentioned how both his sons were sporty, though I have to admit he was a little reserved about mentioning them at first; possibly worrying I would freak out at the very mention of children and run a mile. But to me that wasn't something that put me off him, in fact, to be honest, it had the opposite effect. I loved how much he bragged about his boys, how much he was evidently completely crazy about them and wanted them to have the best possible life he could give them. Up until he mentioned them I didn't think it was possible to fall for him anymore but looking at his eyes light up when he mentioned his boys was something special. It amazed me the way he would say one thing about one of them and that would lead him onto boasting, in a good way, about how wonderful they are or how much he loved them. I had never seen someone be so involved in their kids' lives and just want to show that off. It was incredible. This man was someone who from the outside should've been a boring self-involved boss type, and yet behind the scenes he was caring, loving and to him DB Designs was just something that could help him give his kids the future he believed they deserved. In the last five weeks we had talked for hours and hours and he had never once mentioned how great he was or came across as being arrogant about his work in anyway. He was self-assured about his work but again in a good way. What I mean is, he wasn't ashamed to say how good he was at his job and being the competitive person he is, he would compare figures between himself and other designers or he would see any negativity towards the company as a fight that he had to win, which he usually did. He just amazed me and where in the past I had always been conscious of hiding my competitiveness he thrived on hearing me go on about winning this and that and being the best at anything I took part in. He said he drummed that into his boys, not to be afraid to show what you're good at and illustrate your talents whenever they could. His youngest son, Kaih, like me, was into basketball. He was tipped to be something special in the future and had already placed top 5 in the country for his age category, which lead to a few holiday programme scholarships and training opportunities. Dale said he loved how great Kaih was but worried because he got really nervous before a game and would go into his shell, which for a 10-year-old wasn't something that made Dale happy to see. I think he was more worried Kaih felt he had to play basketball because his dad loved him being an athlete, not because he wanted to. I told Dale with how close a relationship they had I was sure his son would tell him if he genuinely hated playing, which he said he appreciated. His oldest son, Regan, was fifteen and had a passion, like Dale, for football. He was already 6'3" and was making massive moves towards setting himself up a career with the Giants. He played with their youth team and although not as naturally gifted at sport as Kaih, he certainly gave it his all. Dale said he worried sometimes about jealousy arising between the boys because Kaih was such a natural sports person but Regan had to work so hard to be at the same level. I could tell he tried to give them both attention, encourage them both equally which was great but deep down I think it was obvious he and Kaih had a special bond. He had been telling me all about Kaih's last basketball game as we sat in his office one Wednesday night.

"Honestly Kier, it was incredible. He just ran like the devil was chasing him. Nothing could've caught up with him, not a chance. And well, bam, straight to the net. I couldn't believe it. He is the most amazing kid ever, when he gets that ball he instantly knows what to do, where everyone is. He can read any game situation like a book, he just knows. Do you know what I mean, I mean he just knows." Dale got like this when he spoke about the boys. Rushed excitement when he spoke as if he was really trying to emphasise how great Kaih was. "If he can push through those nerves of his he could play for any team. Maybe become a Knick one day?" Dale winked at me, knowing my obvious love of the Knicks.

"You never know." I smiled. "I love hearing you talk about your kids, in fact I think it's one of my favourite things about you." Dale smiled at me, leaned over and kissed me, first on the lips and then the forehead. As I smiled again, I bite my lip a little and asked "What was that for?"

"Well, most girls, in this situation, would be too self-involved to want to hear about me or more, me and my kids. It would freak them out or make them feel uncomfortable because it emphasises that I have a life away from them or in some cases they would get jealous of the boys, as stupid as that sounds. But you, I don't know, you're not like most girls. You don't have that jealous gene; you genuinely seem interested when I speak about Kaih or Regan. How did you get to be so incredible?" As he asked this he looked almost confused but confused in a way that made it seem like he couldn't believe someone could be like this.

"Well, I live in the real world and I know you have this life outside our little bubble. A life, which for all intents and purposes, especially when it come to your boys, makes you very happy, so why would I not want to hear about that. Why would I not want to hear you brag about something that gives you a smile like that across your face? Why would I not want to have even a smidgen of involvement in that life of yours? It's a very attractive quality you have there. Most men, involved in this situation..." I couldn't say affair, not in front of him, "...would be thinking solely about themselves. They wouldn't want to talk about anything, they wouldn't want to share experiences or to talk about their life, and it's those things that make you who you are and I like knowing them." Without realising it my smile had grown throughout that whole talk and Dale had taken my hand and moved closer to me. As he kissed me again, this time slowly and filled with feeling, he pulled away and stared at me for a few seconds before talking again,

"You are incredible Kier Scott. How did you manage to become so wonderful and well just so...you? Where on earth did you come from?" This was obviously a rhetorical question but I couldn't help myself from saying,

"Cumbernauld." With a cheeky grin.

Dale laughed, wrapped his arms around me and kissed me again.

"You really are incredible. I've said it about six times in the last half hour, but it's true. You make me laugh so easily Kier. No one, well aside from my sister, can make me laugh this easily."

Dale had spoken about his sister a few times. He described her as this fun-loving girl who still seemed like a 19-year-old even though she was in her late 30s. They had a very close bond and Dale had said many girls from his past found this hard to deal with, but again I just found it as something to admire. I had three older brothers, Christian and Cameron, who were twins and are twenty-eight in a few weeks' time and then Jayden, who was thirty-one and my favourite person in the whole world. I was closer to Jayden than to the twins, I think because the twins were always together so Jayden and I formed a bond, which by the sounds of it was similar to how Dale and his

Sister, Riley, were. Jayden himself had three boys, who were 4-year-old triplets, Lucas, Tristan and Logan, who I adored, so I knew what a father and son bond was like. Maybe this is why Dale and I connected so well. We had so many things in common and could understand each other's situations through experiences of our own. I loved every second I spent with him but at the same time, I was still feeling awful because in the background Aiden was still very much there. Dale must've sensed me thinking about him because at that moment said,

"So your other half? I'm a bit wary about this one, in case he suspects anything or comes by the office. I know I sound paranoid but this could get a bit messy if it got out."

This is when I worried. When he worried I panicked and wanted to walk away but at the same time I knew I never could. Dale had been at a dinner two weeks ago and someone had made comment about how close he and I were and my knee jerk reaction had been to walk out of his life and cut ties but after seeing him I couldn't do it. I was crazy about him and he was right, Aiden wasn't the type to just find out I had been seeing someone else and let it go. He would do everything he could to find out who it was and search them out.

"I have been thinking about him and well all of this. Aiden and I, well, we've obviously been together for a while, but there really is no spark. Nothing at all. We have nothing in common, he hates my taste in music, he hates that I'm competitive; he hates me bragging about, well, anything. So I was planning on ending things and not just because I met you." I wasn't lying, well not completely. Aiden and I had lost a lot of what brought us together and my relationship with Dale had just confirmed that. With Dale it was easy, it was all so easy. We gelled and we could waste hours just talking, nothing else. On the other hand, some nights Aiden and I barely said two words to each other. I knew what I had to do, and as hard as it would be it was the right choice.

"I'm seeing Aiden tonight so I think it's time to call it a day there. Regardless of you and I, there is no point staying with someone who I don't really have anything in common with."

Dale just looked at me and smiled, before adding what he always felt the need to add.

"You know I could never promise you anything Kier. As much fun as we have and as connected to one another as we are, I still have a family and my boys mean everything to me. And I love my wife too."

I paused slightly; I didn't know if he was saying he loved his wife too, like he loves his boys, or if he loves his wife too, like he loves me? He had never said that to me, in fact quite the opposite. When I spoke to him on Monday, his last words to me before saying goodbye were, "Now let's not go falling for each other." Little did he know I already had. I was, without a doubt, in love with him. At the very mention of his name by anyone my heart melted and my knees turned to jelly. He was the only person who I had ever had such a strong connection too, who made me feel like me. Of course, I couldn't tell him any of that, so I simply turned and said,

"I know, don't worry about it. This is just something I have to do for me. Anyway, it's getting late and I was supposed to meet Aiden fifteen minutes ago. I'll send you a text later; let you know what's happening." Dale had gotten a second number that only I used, so it was safe to text at any time and he would get it when he could.

"Ok beautiful." I loved when he called me that. "Hope everything goes ok, and don't forget, no matter what, you are a very special, very amazing woman."

I kissed him again, walked towards the door and said goodbye. As I walked onto 22nd street my heart was pounding. I was about to end a relationship I had spent two years in, all because I had spent five weeks with someone. Was I crazy? And all I could think was, yes, you are crazy. Crazy about Dale Benton.

CHAPTER TWELVE

Sitting in Aiden's apartment felt uncomfortable. I knew exactly why I was there, but of course he was completely unaware of what the next few hours were going to bring. I had walked all the way here from work, and I went back and forth between ending it and staying with him. Being with Aiden since I'd met Dale didn't add up anymore, it didn't feel right sitting next to him, didn't feel right kissing him, pretending to want to be there. I didn't love him anymore, in fact I don't know if I'd ever really loved him. I don't know if I'd ever really loved anyone anymore. What I feel for Dale is like an adrenaline rush of emotions that makes me smile when I'm near him, miss him when he says goodbye and no matter how long we spend together, it's never enough. I've never had that with anyone else. I've always been comfortable spending time on my own, always wanted my own space, time for just me, but now, whenever I'm on my own, all I think is I should be spending time with Dale. My head and my heart were fighting against each other at every turn; my head saying, don't be so stupid, he's a married man who will never be yours but my heart keeps saying this is real. This is true love, movie love, the fairy tale, that special something that doesn't happen every day and if you hold on in there it will become a reality for you. It's just time that I have to fight against now. I've never had such a big fight with myself. The sensible option, the option which most people would see as being right, would be to forget about Dale, move on and just remember the times when Aiden meant everything to me, when I thought in my head, he really is the one. But then, when I say that statement, the only person I see as "the one" is Dale. Even after such a short time I have this bond to him that I can't describe. I feel like when I'm with him I'm complete, I'm finally the real Kier. How is that possible after little over a month? How could I feel more for him in that short space of time than I had ever felt towards Aiden? In actual fact more than I even felt for Damien who I was engaged to. The rational side of me was trying to take over my thoughts, but the irrational side, the side that wanted to be in Dale Brenton's arms forever was winning any battle. I knew what I have to do, and I couldn't allow my head to try and win this. I have to do what my heart wanted. For one it's not fair to pretend to be in love with Aiden when I'm not and for another, I was going to drive myself insane trying to put on an act that I was happy with him.

"So how was work? That place is running you ragged." Aiden had heard every excuse I could think of over the last five weeks. Everything from late night meetings, to going over financials, to having to go to the emergency room after getting hit on the head by falling materials. I couldn't lie anymore, I had to choose to stop seeing Dale altogether, or give up Aiden, and unfortunately for Aiden, he didn't make the cut.

"Yeah, but it's my dream job, and I love it. I have to do everything I can to prove I am the best." I was being so off with him I was surprised he didn't already realise what I was thinking.

"Not everything is a competition, Kier. You don't have to come out on top at everything." Aiden never got this side of me. He would complain about me boasting about my success, or how my competitiveness was a very unattractive quality. This is where he and Dale are polar opposites. Dale encourages me to strive to be number one, whereas Aiden would be happier if I sat in the back of a sweat shop sewing other people's designs. I decided this was it. The perfect time to say what had to be done. No going back.

"Why do you not get me? Why do you not realise that is who I am? I am the person who wants to win. I want to be the best, I want to be the one standing front and centre with everyone seeing that I am number one. You're always bringing me down, making me feel like I'm not good enough. Well I am Aiden, I am the best damn fashion designer on that team, and I will continue to work my ass off until I'm the best in the company." I was going red and tears were in my eyes. I wasn't sure if I was angry or if the guilt was beginning to creep up because of why I was kicking off into an argument.

"Hold on Kier. I never said that. I just meant you need a

life away from DB Designs. You spend every waking minute in that place." Aiden was trying to reason, and any other time I would've just apologised and moved on but not this time. I had to push through.

"I don't need a life away, DB Designs is my life. It is the opportunity I have been working my ass off to get to for the last seven years and you are not going to take that away from me, or make me feel guilty for wanting to prove I'm worthy of being there." The tears were streaming down my face and I felt awful. Yes I hated that he made a big deal out of me being in the company, but I also knew deep down that I wasn't staying late to work. I was a horrible person, but I couldn't let guilt stop me.

"Aiden, me and you, we're different. We have different interests, beliefs and outlooks on life. You want the 9-5 Monday to Friday 2.4 family life. Me, I want the dream. I want my designs to be viewed at New York Fashion week. I want people to know my name. I can't promise to be home every night by 6pm. I can't promise to see you every night. I can't promise I'll ever want to get married or have kids, because to me, that's not in my plan. But I know it's in yours. It's part of you. Maybe it's time to give up the ghost, realise we aren't right for one another. You want a life. I want a career."

Aiden looked shocked. I felt shocked. The words had actually come out of my mouth and instead of feeling gutted, for the first time in months I just felt relief. As Aiden stepped forward to try and hug me I took a step back.

"What are you doing Kier? Why are you saying this? We're perfect together, you can't deny that."

Aiden had tears in his eyes, but I couldn't let his emotions get to me.

"No Aiden, we're not. We use to be, because I made sure I was the type of girl who was perfect for you. I never stepped out the box. I never acted like the real me. I never tried to be anyone other than "Aiden's girlfriend" and I can't do it anymore."

Aiden looked broken. I couldn't believe I was doing this, but I just couldn't live a lie anymore. I couldn't pretend to be someone I'm not anymore. For the last two years I had pretended to be this quiet perfect little girlfriend and Dale had shown me I don't have to be her. I can be proud of wanting to be the best, I can view my competitiveness as a positive instead of hiding it away and being scared to show that is who I am. Aiden would never get that because to him life should be simple. People should go to work, start at the same time everyday and finish at the same time every night. He wanted a big white wedding, he wanted babies; he wanted the whole package. But me, I just want to be a fashion designer. No, I want to be the Best Fashion Designer. I want the dream; I don't want to just settle.

"I can't believe this Kier. We can work through it. We can make it work. You know we're supposed to be together. Everyone always comments on how great we are together. Please, let's just try."

Aiden looked frustrated. His fists were clenched, his eyes were red, and his cheeks were tear-stained. He was gritting his teeth and trying to grab hold of me. I was struggling to look into his eyes, so I just focussed on the floor.

"I'm sorry Aiden. This is not what I want anymore." I didn't know what else to say. "I'm going to go. Please believe me, this is for the best. We would've made each other miserable."

Aiden was quiet for a long time, aside from the sound of him sobbing as quiet as he could manage. But eventually he spoke.

"Fine. Go. I hope you realise what you're letting go of. Goodbye Kier."

He turned away, and as much as I wanted to just walk away, I felt I had more to say.

"I am sorry..." was all I could say before Aiden erupted.

"JUST GO!!!"

I didn't wait around. I grabbed my bag, and walked out of the door. And as I got in the lift I couldn't help crying. I didn't know if I was crying because I was going to miss him, or if it was all the tension of the last few months finally being released, but the tears didn't want to stop falling down my face. In fact, as I left Aiden's building and walked towards Central Park I was still crying. I replayed so many memories him and I had shared, played back all the times we spent together that had ever actually meant anything. And the more I did, the more I cried, but this time I knew it wasn't because I had made a mistake, but because all I could think of was three events. Three times that I had loved being with Aiden. Out of our two years relationship I had three good memories. So this just made me realise that I had been with Dale for five weeks and every memory was not just good, but amazing and we didn't even do anything aside from sit and talk. My heart knew what the tears were for even if my head wasn't willing to accept it. They were for him, for Dale and for the relationship I feared we would never get to experience together. They were for the life I wanted but in my heart I didn't know if I would ever get the chance to be a part of.

CHAPTER THIRTEEN

I didn't get home until well after 2am. That's the good
thing about New York; even in the middle of the night
there is plenty to do to keep you amused when you don't
want to face reality. And tonight, I didn't. I wanted to walk
around and try to not think about Dale, a hard task when
every single thing reminds me of him. I had my iPod
attached to my ear as I strolled from one Starbucks to
another, and found myself constantly replaying Hallelujah
by Jeff Buckley, over and over again. Since the moment I
first heard this song it had become my favourite and even
after what must be thousands of times listened to, I still
wasn't bored of it. But as I strolled down Broadway I
suddenly understood the lyrics. I got what it was Leonard
Cohen had written about. He was talking about the
difficulty of love. The endless struggle to do what feels like
the wrong thing at the right time, and to overcome your
fears and go forward or at least that's what it sounded like
to me now as I thought about the situation Dale and I were
in. I'm not saying he loves me, or will love me, but in my
heart I know I love him, as ludicrous as that sounds after
only five weeks, especially when I know whatever is going
to happen is going to be hard, but even now, for him, I'm
willing to fight any battle and win that war. For him, I feel
like I can do anything. Even I can't believe this is what is
going on in my head. I'm rational, sensible, and sane. I'm
not the type of girl to take a risk; I'm not the type of girl
who is labelled as a home wreaker. That's not me at all.
But with Dale, I don't know, it seems like a bigger fight to
stop seeing him than keep seeing him. Every second I
spend with him I just can't stop smiling. I can't stop feeling
like finally I have something to be happy about, even
though, in all honesty, I know he shouldn't be the one who
makes me happy, because he already has a family to do
that for. So why, if I know all that I still feel like I can't let
him go?

I tossed and turned the whole night and by 6am I couldn't
stay in bed any longer, so I got up and made my way to the

office. If I wasn't sleeping I may as well get on with some work. The Walkerton Show had gone by without a hitch, and my designs got raving reviews. I couldn't believe I had shown pieces at an actual fashion show. Suranne was less than impressed. Over the last three months her dislike for me had turned into hatred and going into the office knowing she was there was becoming an endless battle. I swear if it hadn't been for Sasha and Dale I don't know how I would cope. They both told me that Suranne had a habit of this, picking on young people, maybe through jealousy but more because she had some sort of self-esteem issue and didn't like to see people do better than she had. Her skills as a designer were questionable, or more she hadn't evolved as well with time as other designers, and this caused a major problem when it came to picking items to be showcased and 9 times out of 10 Suranne's no longer made the cut. Dale had made her up to management status a few years back when he took on a lot of interns and needed someone to "babysit" them, and from there she just stayed in that position but she had always made her role in the company out to be more than it was. I found out before the five of us came along she hadn't really been doing too well at DB Designs and by mentoring the five of us it was Dale's last ditch attempt to get something out of her. Yes it was harsh, and yes it was horrible to think people knew she was very near the chopping block when she had no idea, but to be honest, I had seen a different side to Suranne. Where before I looked up to her as exactly what she was, a mentor, I now only saw someone who made me uncomfortable, frightened and who made me question my work when others were complimenting it. I know my obvious "friendship" with Dale had shook her up even more so, but she obviously didn't realise the extent of it because she continued to mock my work, try to put me down and single me out a lot of the time, thinking that Dale, or anyone else in Senior Management, would never find out. Obviously I was completely straight with Dale, but I had also told Calvin a few details too. He was such a great guy and I had a great amount of respect towards him, so it felt right to open up to him about a few of the things that Suranne had directed my way. I wasn't being bitchy, just honest. Calvin had noticed me looking a bit down in the workroom one day after another onslaught of Suranne's negativity, and commented that I didn't have my usual "sunshine" surrounding me. So he gave me a hug, made me smile again and I told him just the basics. He told me to ignore her jealousy and just kept doing what I was doing because I was a great addition to the team. And since then that's exactly what I've done. Rome Fashion week would kick off in a little over two months, and yet again, three of my designs were making their way down the runway, only this time not as part of the sportswear collection. Dale had seen a few other sketches I had been working on, including a dress worthy of the Emmy's, a trouser suit, that I thought about making for myself and a beaded jacket that still had my skater edge to it but also looked stunning when I finally made it up, so he decided he wanted these for Rome, which also meant I was getting to go to Rome. He had told me to choose one of the other girls to go with me, but in the end I managed to convince him to let me bring Sasha along. I made him see that if she wanted a career in runway show design this would be a great experience for her, and I meant it. She had already proven her obvious talent with the work she put in at Walkerton and needless to say she almost laid an egg with excitement when I told her about Rome, and she was even more excited by the fact that Harry was going to be there too. I was hoping there would be some way for me to be able to sit next to Dale and for Harry and Sasha to end up together too on the plane. I had to admit a nine hour flight to Rome sitting next to Dale seemed like a dream come true, I just wasn't sure how it would work. I wasn't sure what other members of staff would be attending but I was hoping there would be a chance to spend some alone time with Dale once we got there. I couldn't imagine going to the most romantic city in the world, with the man I was falling madly in love with and not be alone with him. I'm sure Sasha had the same idea in mind. She had asked another thousand times whether or not I thought Harry still liked her. I didn't know how many more times I could say yes to try and convince her, and since her birthday night out I had noticed how more full on their "friendship" had gotten, in fact, I wasn't the only one. Arlene and Louise had been trying to do a bit of bitching about it, commenting on how he was disgusting for taking advantage of a young girl, and she was a tramp for going after a married man. I tried to make them see they were just friends, though I had also heard from Sasha they weren't too nice about me behind my back, making comments regarding Dale and myself. No one ever said anything had happened, but there were a few rumours going around that we were heading in that direction. We just had to be careful, people would run a mock if they ever thought something had happened between us, and obviously the number one priority was keeping this away from Dale's family; his two boys were the most important factor to consider in all of this. That's why I had to be careful with Rome. Feathers were already ruffling because none of the other girls' designs had been chosen. Ashleigh was trying to pretend she was fine with the whole thing, but it was obvious she was annoyed. She had been making comments regarding the structure of my designs and adding in how she had been designing some amazing creations with an "Italian feel" to it, but she didn't realise that we were allowed to stray off of our current job, which is complete nonsense. Suranne made it clear we could design what we liked, as long as our other work got done. She had been trying to pull it out of me how exactly Dale had seen my other designs, and in turn I came up with an elaborate story saying I had left some drawings lying on my work bench one day when I went to buy fabric and Dale had come down to the work room to see if any of us were around and he had a look at them. Really he just asked me straight out if I had anything else that I was working on during one of our late nights together. He was genuinely impressed, and I knew he was too professional a person to just be saying that to make me feel good about myself because he would never send anything down the Runway that wasn't up to the standards of DB Designs. As much as I worried that people would think, "Oh, there is something going on with them, that's why she's going to Rome," I knew the truth, I knew that I had wowed Dale and to me that felt amazing. I was proving myself more and more every day, and it wasn't just Dale who noticed. Two of the other head designers, Nigel and Taylor had also commented on how my designs were taking the company in a new direction and that they were so happy to have me on the team. In fact, although Dale had already decided I was going to Rome to show the three pieces, it was Nigel he took the sketches too and it was him who said I should be there, so it took the heat off of Dale and made it seem like it was all coming from other factors. My career was definitely heading in the right direction, and it made me feel better that it wasn't just because Dale was a driving force behind that.

As I walked towards the workroom, I noticed the light was on and was shocked anyone else was there so early, but then my face lit up as I saw Dale standing looking through the piles of fabric I had been working with.

"Hey you." I couldn't help but smile. "Why are you in so early?"

He walked over, slipped his hands round my waist and gave me a kiss that just made the world stop turning.

"To see you of course." Before I could answer he kissed me again before pulling me close and hugging me tight. "I was worried because I didn't hear back from you last night. And I just kind of lay awake and decided to come in here and have a look round. I felt like just having some kind of sense of you around me. It makes me feel close to you when I'm in the presence of your designs."

I smiled again, and looked straight into his eyes and kissed him. "Well, no need to worry; I just didn't want to say in a text what I would prefer to say to you face to face."

He stepped back slightly and looked a little panicked, "Is this bad news?"

I laughed, "Not at all. I ended it with Aiden. I walked all the way to his apartment last night, and I went back and forth between my options, and as much as I know Aiden is the sensible choice, I couldn't stay with him when I feel the way I do about you." Dale tried to jump in but I continued to talk, knowing exactly what he was about to say, "and I know you can never promise me anything, I know you can't say that this time next week you and I won't have anything going on between us, but I didn't think it was fair to stay with someone else, when I know I have strong feelings for you, regardless of what happens."

Dale stared at me for a few seconds before talking.

"You are amazing. You always know exactly what I'm going to say, exactly how I feel. And I know how hard last night must have been for you, but I'm glad you done it. I have to admit, I was worried, a lot. I had this feeling that you wouldn't go through with it and you would come in here today and tell me that you and I had to stop seeing each other, and I know that is so unfair of me, because I can't promise you anything, but I also hate the thought of you with anyone else too. It drives me crazy thinking about someone else touching you or kissing you. You are just this amazing beam of light that has come into my life and allowed me to be completely myself, and I've never had that with anyone else. And even though I have never met your boyfriend, or ex-boyfriend now I suppose, I couldn't stand the thought that he had you because I would love that to be me. I would love to have you as mine. Even after only 5/6 weeks I just want to be near you all the time, I want to be sat next to you, talking to you, holding your hand, stroking you. Just be with you. And it drives me insane that I can't. I have two boys who are everything to me, and the thought of not being there for them, I just can't process that at the moment. I've tried to image it, tried to picture it, but the thought of something happening to Kaih and I'm not there, I just can't process that. But at the same time, I've never felt as happy in my life as I do when I'm with you. I hate thinking that I may have to one day let you go, and know that I have to let go of the best thing that has ever happened to me. Kier, I know that we have only been involved with each other for little over a month but, well, the truth is, I love you. I honestly, love you. In fact, I'm falling more and more in love with you every second I spend with you."

I couldn't believe the words that had just escaped his mouth. Did he honestly just say that? Was I hearing things? I realised I hadn't spoken in about thirty seconds, and Dale, again, looked panicked.

"Do you mean that? I mean, you're not just saying it?"

"Kier, I don't open up to my feelings, ever but with you I want to tell you everything, let out every emotion, I want you to know exactly how I feel about you, and I love you, so much."

I grinned and I collapsed into his arms, "I love you too. In fact, to be honest, as crazy as this sounds, I've loved you from the first moment I laid eyes on you."

"Ditto" as we both laughed. Dale kissed me again, "You are so beautiful Kier." He kissed the outside of both of my eyes, and the corners of my lips, before saying, "that's just mine, round the world with you."

As the rest of the world blurred, I got lost in Dale's arms and fell more in love the man who I now knew loved me too. Any thoughts of this going wrong, for the moment, were a distant memory, and all I wanted was to focus on me and Dale, how perfect time is when were together and how complete I felt being in his arms.

CHAPTER FOURTEEN

Little over a month had passed since I heard those amazing words fall from his lips, and in twelve hours we would be jetting off to Rome for five days. Sasha and I had gone crazy buying new outfits, picking out shoes and getting ourselves excited about the whole trip. We discovered we all had our own hotel rooms, which was a welcome surprise as I assumed I would be sharing with Sasha, but relieved that it meant I would have more of a chance to be spending some alone time with Dale. Things were working out better than expected; there were six of us altogether, Dale and myself of course, Harry and Sasha, as well as Calvin and the Business Manager, Steven. I couldn't believe how good we'd lucked out, because Calvin and Steven worked closely together and had told Dale they hope he didn't mind if they sat together on the flight because it would allow for them to discuss work and some new ideas coming up and of course, Sasha and Harry were more than happy to be together, which left Dale and I. I couldn't believe how easy it was. Sasha didn't think anything of me being completely fine with sitting with Dale, she just thought I was being a great friend and "taking a bullet" by sitting next to him. Now though, I had a bigger reason to want to be with him as much as possible, but that can be explained later.

Dale had been in constant contact over the last month. We had gone from seeing each other every day or so, to spending as much time as possible together. We must have visited at least twelve different Starbucks, and had a great day together; an actual whole day spent just the two of us. His wife had been away for the weekend, and on the Sunday the boys were doing their own thing, Regan was away playing with the Giants and Kaih was on a day out with the basketball team he played with, so Dale set aside a whole day for us to be together. He couldn't believe that I had never been up the Empire State Building, even though I had stayed in New York for so long, so that was the first point of contact. We met at 10am on the Sunday morning at the lake in Central Park and that's when Dale told me his plans.

"All this time in New York and you haven't even seen the best view? You're having a laugh, surely?" Dale actually looked shocked. He couldn't believe that someone could stay here and not have done all the sights. To be honest I hadn't seen much. My days revolved around sport and fashion, nothing else really slipped in, and to be honest, I didn't have much spare time to sight see.

"Honestly Dale, never been. I spend most of my days sketching or playing basketball, so that leaves no time for anything else. Anyway, it can't be that great, it's just a building. My Dad worked in Trump Tower and well, I've been on the roof there a few times."

Dale put his arm around me, quickly kissed me and added, "Kier, Kier, Kier. You really have been living a sheltered life. It's time for me to open your eyes." He kissed me again. "Let's go."

As he grabbed my hand we walked out of the park and towards the Empire State Building. Although we were still in New York, we strolled along holding hands like a regular couple, laughing and joking, and just loving every moment that we spent together. Our plan, if anyone saw us was to simply say we were discussing final plans for Rome. Dale had told Steven and Calvin that he was going to try and catch up with every one individually before we left including me and Sasha so we all knew exactly what we were doing once we got there. It wasn't completely true, but at least if anyone saw us and mentioned anything, the two men had our back. I wasn't exactly sure what Dale had planned for the rest of the day, but in all honesty, we could've done nothing, spent the day sitting drinking coffee in the most rundown little coffee shop and I would still be happy just to be spending time with him. Over the last few months we had gotten so much closer; in fact I was closer to him that I had been to anyone else in my life. I could finally just act like me with someone and he loved it. He didn't get put off by me breaking into a dance in the middle of a busy street, or me challenging him to a competition over everything, including climbing the stairs in the office. He loved my competitiveness, he loved how much I loved sport and for the first time in my life I fully believed that someone loved me. As difficult as this situation was, and knowing he still went home every night to his wife and his boys, I didn't care. I loved him. Full Stop. This wasn't just an affair, it was so much more. Although we had fooled around, a lot, and had some fun, aside from a few "fumbles", we still hadn't slept together. We had never had the opportunity to be alone together in a bedroom, my place was right in the middle of Greenwich Village, so Dale worried about bumping into people he knew, so really the workroom was the only room we ever had private alone time in, and I didn't want that for our first time together, I wanted it to be special, and so did Dale. He wanted us to wait until one of the nights we would be in Rome. We had been booked into the Weston Excelsior and it was stunning from the pictures I had seen, so I knew that it would be perfect. Over the last few months he had become even more perfect in my eyes. Everything in my life seemed so much better since meeting him. I was already aware of how unbelievably handsome he was, but into the bargain he really was a completely fantastic person, who to me, just brightened every aspect of my life. He wasn't just there to have fun either, when I needed him because things were difficult or I was upset, he was there too. Of course Aiden and I had split but that didn't stop him coming to my office and trying to see me, or going round to my parents' house and trying to get them to convince me to give him another chance, and Dale was there making sure I was ok every single time. It was difficult seeing Aiden because there were aspects of him I missed, just the closeness of having someone of my own, but to be honest, what I had with Dale was worth 10...100...1000 of what I had with Aiden. I could say it a million times over but I had truthfully never felt this way about anyone. I had never been so connected to another human being, not my best friends, boyfriends, no one. Dale and I could sit in Starbucks for hours just talking and not realise time had passed. In fact, three weeks ago I met him near my apartment and we drove towards a bar called Envy, but we didn't make it out of the car. We sat and spoke for four hours, in a car; just a car, parked on the street. It was unbelievable. I thought love like this only happened in movies but here I was living it. And no it wasn't perfect and yes I could get hurt at any turn, or things could become a complete nightmare very quickly, but to me none of that mattered. When I was with Dale I was in this different world. A place where no one else could come, a bubble that belonged to the two of us and nothing could pop it. And here we were, walking hand in hand about to step onto the elevator of the Empire State Building, a place, that Dale promised, would take my breath away as soon as I viewed New York in a completely different light. "You're going to love this Kier, I promise. I'm so happy it's me that's taking you up here for the first time. This is a memory I want to save forever with you."

I smiled and gazed deeply into his eyes, "I'm glad it's you too. And just in case I forget to say later, today was perfect."

Dale wrapped his arms tightly around my waist and kissed me on the nose before adding, "Just like you. I love you Kier."

"Ditto." And with that we arrived at the top.

I had to admit, the view was phenomenal. The outline of the park, the Brooklyn Bridge, the Statue of Liberty, everything just looked perfect. New York looked like a puzzle map, a maze, another planet. As my eyes dotted around the sights I had walked past a million times I got lost in the moment and was only brought back by Dale's hand slotting into mine and I realised then, this moment was flawless. This really was something special, and regardless of the negative side, in Dale I had found something unbelievable that nothing would replace. At that moment it sunk in...he really is the love of my life. My true love. My soul mate. I turned to look at him, and without saying a word I felt he knew what I was thinking. He gazed into my eyes in a way no one ever has, he looked at me in a way that I knew meant he wanted me to be his. I was his. I was in his heart right now, tomorrow and the next day. Whether we made it past the finish line or not, we were experiencing something that I don't think anyone else in the world could have, or to me that's how it felt. I couldn't imagine two people being so close, being so perfect, and being able to fit together in the most amazing way.

"Can't believe how great it feels seeing this with you. I've been up here so many times and not once have I ever seen it like this. You really are the perfect girl for me. Honestly, if I could create my perfect partner it would be you. This may sound too full on, but with you I don't want to hide anything I'm thinking, I want to be completely honest with you. With you, regardless of the outside world, I'm me. I'm the real Dale, I don't have to put on some kind of pretence of being super serious and acting like fun is a word that should never be used alongside my name. Kier, if I'm honest, you feel like my soul mate, you feel like the person I was supposed to be with on this earth and it kills me knowing I met you too late." Dale looked down at his feet. It was my turn to put my hand under his chin, look into his eyes and smile,

"No matter what, we still have all this. We have these memories, we have this time together. And just so you know I was thinking the same thing, you feel like my soul mate too. I couldn't imagine finding anyone else in this world that makes me feel like you do." I wrapped my arms around his neck and held him tight, and we stayed like that, hugging each other close, loving each other like nothing could break us. "I love you." I whispered it gently but every inch of my soul meant it, I meant it like I had never before, felt it like I had never before.

We stayed at the top of the Empire State Building for two and a half hours. More than enough time for us just to enjoy the moment, to block out the rest of the world and be engrossed in this bubble that was just us: Dale and Kier.

When we left there we went to a quaint little Italian, grabbed a bite and then hit a Starbucks for dessert. The whole day had been like I said before it started, perfect, in every way. But it also made it ever more present in our minds that we would have to face reality and try to come to some conclusion on how this was all going to play out between us. We had just spent the most amazing day ever together, where we didn't really do anything special except be with one another, but we had to face the fact that we weren't with one another. Dale had a family that were his everything and me, I was just an addition to his life, and to be honest, it was tough knowing I was complicating things for him. As we climbed into his car we both turned to each other and spoke at the same time, and as we did, laughed.

"Ok, you first." I wanted to know if he had been thinking what I was.

"I love you Kier. Like nothing else, like no one else. You came into my life and changed things. You changed my view of life, how I viewed everything. I didn't think it was possible to feel this strongly about anyone, where no matter how long we spend together it never seems enough time. But at the end of the day, I have a family. I love my two boys so much; I just can't bare the thought of not being there when they need me. I wish I knew an easy way through this, but I don't. I have a wife, and I don't know anymore."

I stared at my fingers for a few seconds, wrapped around his, the same way they were on that first day all those months ago. And I asked the one question I swore I would never ask, but now I needed to know, so biting my lip I let it out, "Do you love her?" I couldn't believe I was asking, and I didn't know if I was ready for the answer.

"Honestly, I don't know. I don't know anything anymore. I don't know if I've ever loved her, at least not in the same way I love you. When I married her, for four years after it I thought I had made a mistake. I was sure I had married the wrong woman, but then we had Regan, and life revolved around him and then we had Kaih and well, I settled into thinking this was my life. This was it." Dale looked lost and at the same time relieved that he had said something he had obviously been bottling up for a long time.

"But why marry her if you weren't sure?" I had no right asking these questions, but I needed some clarity on everything.

"My mum, as crazy as that sounds. She told me I would never find anyone better, that Sarah and I should just go for it. So I did, and well, it's been fifteen or so years now and you just get use to that being your life. I never expected in a million years for anything like this to happen, to finally meet my soul mate when I'm forty. I don't know how to deal with this situation because I've never imagined myself in this situation." He was half smiling; obviously trying to tell me at the same time how much he cares about me without making me feel uncomfortable by the fact he was spilling his heart out about his wife.

"Same here. I mean obviously different situation, I wasn't married to Aiden, but when I met him I thought that was it. I thought he was the one for me. I really did, and then I met you and everything stopped being black and white. Suddenly it wasn't about pleasing someone else, I was allowed to venture into that grey area and stop hiding who I was. I started to see the world so differently. You became this person who allowed me to express myself in the way that I wanted to, it was like even before anything happened I could feel that connection between us, and nothing could stop me falling for you because you liked who I was." It was my turn to half smile, and at the same time I felt tears in my eyes. "Dale, you don't have to answer this next question but if you didn't have the boys, could you leave her?"

He didn't say anything. He held my hand tighter and just stared at me.

"I don't know Kier. When you spend that long with someone evidently there would be aspects of them you would miss. I'm sure you even felt that with Aiden, and I would feel that with Sarah, but you know what, I think I know in myself, if I'm honest with myself, I could leave because I couldn't pass up the chance to experience true happiness like I have with you."

His words were amazing, he was amazing. He made me so happy and listening to him sound so confused killed me. I was about to speak when he continued on,

"Believe me though, if I didn't have those two boys my decision would be easier. It would be difficult leaving my wife, and not because of the way I feel about her but more because I know I would hurt her. But there is no way I could ever stay there knowing you were on the other side. I have known you for a fraction of the time I've known her and the feelings don't compare in the slightest. With you I feel true love, real love. So just always know, it's not her that's holding me back, it's just my boys. I can't leave them." I couldn't believe it, but Dale was welling up. I pulled him close to me, and kissed his forehead. "I don't think I've cried in years. I just hate that I love you, I mean I love you so much and knowing I can't be with you hurts so badly. I would love a life with you."

I didn't add anything to what he said. Instead, I just held

him tight and felt him close to me as we embraced each other's emotions, allowing the tears to run down both our faces. Ten or so minutes passed before I finally spoke.

"Dale, you know I love you. I would do anything to make you happy, anything to make you feel as great as you have made me feel and it drives me crazy to know that I have complicated your life and that I have made you feel confused and mixed up and lost. I hate that I'm the cause of that. I want to be the smile on your face every day, the one who makes you feel complete."

Dale cut in before I could say anything more, "You do make me feel complete, but it just so happens that my boys need to be a part of my life to make me feel complete too. And just now they need me. Not so much Regan, he's growing up, but Kaih still needs me there. He still needs me to turn him into the young man that I know he can be. You don't complicate my life Kier, you make it real, make it better. You make me feel like it is ok for me to step out of the box and be myself with someone so never think you are anything negative to me. But, saying that, I think it's safe to say that we can't keep doing this. You deserve so much more than someone who can only give you his all part time, and for now that's all I can give. To be honest I've been thinking this through so many times, over and over in my head, and I can't leave the boys, I know I can't, well not just now. I need to make sure I'm there to help Kaih grow up, so for the next eight years I have to be with him. And I know that's a long time, and I would never ask you to wait for me, but that's what I need to do." He broke down before he really finished the sentence properly. I felt broken. I knew we loved one another, I could feel how much he loved me because of how upset this whole situation was making him, how much it was breaking him into pieces trying to think of his boys' happiness before his own.

"Please don't cry Dale. I understand everything you are saying. I understand this whole situation, and I understand why you have to say all of this. I love that you are honest with me. You never make false promises; you never lead me on or made me believe that you and I are going to be together when we both know that may be something that can never be. And as hard as this is, we know we have to walk away from each other at some point, and I suppose put it into God's hands to allow us to be together again one day, when it is right. You have to know though, if I have to wait eight years for you, I would. I would wait until the end of forever for you. You make me feel brand new every time you smile at me; you make me feel like nothing could ever go wrong every time I'm with you. But I don't want to hurt you, and I know leaving your boys just now would do that." I tried to smile, to fight through the tears that were once again stinging my eyes, and as Dale looked up, he kissed me so passionately, so filled with feeling that I could smile.

"You do know that leaving you will hurt just as much, but my boys have to come first, I have to put them before me." He paused before continuing. "I think, after Rome, we have to let go. We have to find a way to not be together. Some way to try and bring some normality back to our lives. I have to be there for Regan and Kaih. Please tell me you understand why I have to do this?" He was again fighting through tears to speak. I wasn't doing much better, but I knew I had to respond.

"Of course I understand. It's that very reason why I love you so much, because you would do anything for those boys, including hurting yourself. You amaze me more and more every day, and I understand every reason you have. So let's just make Rome our farewell, but hopefully not a goodbye. I would love to believe that one day, we can come together again and this time it will be forever." I cried and smiled at the same time, praying hard inside to God that this would come true. Dale embraced me once again.

"I would love to end my life with you. I would love to wake up next to you, fall asleep next to you. I would just love to know I had my soul mate by my side everyday, and as crazy as this sounds, in eight years it will be easier. This next statement is going to sound a bit, well crazy, but let's set the date. Friday the 17th of October, 2016, at the top of the Empire State Building. My boys will be turning into men, starting to lead their own lives and they won't need me anymore, and I can finally be with you, if you still want me that is?"

Again I smiled, "I will always want you, no matter how long passes. I love you now, for always, forever. And in eight years I'll gladly be there and be ready to begin my life with you."

"Ditto."

We held each other again, and kissed, again with such passion, knowing we would have to give up something amazing, to hopefully get something better. Every hug, every word for the next few weeks would be cherished and stored until the day came that we could do it every day and not have to let go.

We stayed in the car for another hour, talking, laughing and trying to suck up every second we had left together, every moment we would make a memory of that could be called upon to keep our love alive.

Kissing Dale goodnight that Sunday was hard. I cried myself to sleep and tried to get my head around not doing that anymore. Not feeling his love seep into my pores every time he touched me, not looking into his eyes and feeling like that's where I belong, knowing that now, in little over a week everything he said that night would have to come true. I was going to have to face up to saying goodbye to the love of my life. I know every reason behind us ending, I know it's nothing to do with him not wanting to be with me, he just needs to be with his boys more. I have to keep my fingers crossed and hope that one day it's all part of God's plan for us to be together again. That sounds crazy. We are doing something so wrong, I'm making Dale commit adultery, but at the same time praying that God will see we love each other like nothing else and that he has made us meet for some reason to be together. Can that even be possible? I didn't know how I was going to forget about him after Rome. We were so perfect for each other, and losing him, even after only this short time was going to break my heart.

CHAPTER FIFTEEN

E ven though it was the 3rd of January the weather was great. The sun was shining and felt warm against my skin, and in return made me feel relaxed, calm and happy. No, a heat wave hadn't suddenly taken over the -10 degree weather in New York; I had just stepped off the plane in Rome and felt the heat instantly take hold of me. I had heard some people in the airport say that it was quite cold, but when you come from New York, if it's over 0 degrees in January it's classed as warm. Sat on the plane for the last nine hours had been amazing. Dale and I had sneakily been holding holds, staring at each other and even stole a few kisses on the flight. We were seated in first class, Steven and Calvin were sitting right at the front, Harry and Sasha were just across from them and Dale and I right at the back. We had planned it almost perfectly to be seated together, but we couldn't have planned it any better being seated where we were. Of course we were happy to be going to Rome together and to have spent the last nine hours talking and just basically being with one another, but of course, deep down we still had to keep in mind that after the next few days this was it, we were done. We had tried to be together as much as possible before today; in fact since our day out we had spent time together every single day. Dale hadn't tried to hide how scared he was of letting me go and how much it terrified him of thinking about saying goodbye to me and knowing that I would end up with someone else. He said that was tough to handle. It was too much for him to imagine me giving the love I had shown him to someone else. But to be honest, I didn't think that was possible. I had been trying to get my own head around being with someone else but I couldn't. How was I expected to move on from who I thought of as my soul-mate, who I knew was my soul-mate? It's such a contradiction, and I had to continually tell myself that I did in fact have to just settle for second best, I had to make myself move onto someone who I could already tell I would never really love. Just now, I hated even thinking about it.

I hated the thought of having anyone's arms wrapped around me, of looking into someone else's eyes and loving the fact that I was doing it. I couldn't begin to imagine what it would feel like kissing someone else and feeling that kiss be as mind-blowing as it felt when I kissed Dale. I guess it would never be easy moving on from him, moving on from something so faultless. How could anything else ever compare? I just had to tell myself it would eventually be worth it. I had to believe he would eventually be mine.

After a day in Rome it was already turning out to be everything I ever wanted. Although we were busy with the fashion shows, Dale and I were still spending as much time together as possible without arousing suspicion. Luckily, Harry and Sasha were in a world of their own, with Harry claiming to be 'training' Sasha on his job and Calvin and Steven were constantly in and out of meetings so no one realised we were actually together most of the day.

On the third afternoon we went outside Rome, away from everyone and for the first time we could act like a normal couple. We held hands, we laughed and joked in public and acted like the two people in love that we were. Although the time together was amazing, it was still locked in my head that in a little less than three days we wouldn't be able to do this anymore. There would be no more hand holding, no more kissing his lips softly and leading them into long lingering kisses filled with passion and love. My everything would soon become nothing and I would have to let go of the only person who had ever truly made me feel alive. When I was with him I was complete, I was me and now, knowing that it would all be gone was becoming too difficult to understand, in all honesty it felt like my head was simply unable to process that as factual information. How was it possible to be so in love and yet we had to end something that brought the two of us so much happiness? Most couples break up because they don't want to be together, but Dale and I, we were breaking up because we do. This was a scenario I never expected, my heart yearning so much for someone, them yearning for me, and yet it has to end but even knowing that wasn't making me end it any sooner. I was happy knowing I at least had him for the next few days; I just had to deal with the dull ache I got every so often when I imagined him no longer there. When I thought about him not being mine it felt like my heart was being ripped from my chest and all that was going to be left was a hole that no one else could ever fill. I couldn't imagine any other man making me feel the way he does, found it impossible to comprehend another man kissing me and making the rest of the world disappear into the background. Dale was someone who had come into my world without warning and now my world didn't make sense without him. Before Dale of course I had been in relationships, I had even thought I had found my special someone, but nothing could've prepared me for meeting him. With Aiden I thought it was love, I even called him "the one" but nothing I felt for Aiden was anything like what I feel for Dale. There was this unbelievable connection between him and I that seemed unbreakable, so having to break it didn't seem right. Why break something that works? But of course I couldn't be selfish. I had to keep in mind that he had something else more important than me to consider, and for Dale his boys would always come first, they were his world. And that didn't bother me. I didn't feel jealous of his kids for having him; I didn't even feel jealous of his wife. I just felt more in love with him because he was so unwilling to be selfish that he would put his own happiness last in line.

Walking through the streets of Rome that day felt like nothing else. I could feel the elation of my emotions shining from me. I'd never had such a feeling of contentment. Every now and again Dale would lean across and kiss me slightly, or he would wrap his arm around my shoulder or around my waist and hug me from behind...all the things a couple in love should be doing, and to look at us people would believe we were so happy that nothing could break us. If only they knew the truth, if only they knew that we had to end the most fantastic relationship because we were never supposed to have fallen in love. I often wonder how people would view us; me, the dirty mistress, Dale the older man taking advantage of a young girl. Or would people see it as it is that we are in love and we can't help how we feel. Human nature is to judge, but humans also adjust just as quickly. Maybe if people knew about us they would make comment to start with and then they would see that we were so amazing together that they knew it was real. But let's not get caught up in the fantasy and let it take over reality. My brain was living in a pipedream thinking that this is going to happen. It wasn't about whether other people could accept us as a couple, they weren't the problem. Dale assured me he would be with me if it wasn't for the fact of him wanting to be involved in his boys growing up. And I believed him, but always, locked in there was the thought of his wife, the thought of what he felt towards her. I tried not to ask about his wife, and he had told me he loved her before, but I wasn't sure if he still felt that way. I didn't even know whether if he knew the boys would be fine it would make a difference to him leaving.

"This is none of my business, and if you don't want to answer then please don't. I know I asked about your feelings for your wife before but if it wasn't for the boys, if you knew they would be ok, and there would be no issue with them, could you leave your wife?" I just blurted it out. No pause, no thought, just out with it.

Dale took my hands and stared at me.

"I'm not going to lie, Kier, as I've said before it would be strange leaving her, and I would probably miss certain things about being with her, purely because we have been together for so long, but don't let that upset you because what I feel for her is nothing compared to you. I have never had such a bond to someone, felt so close to another person. I've already told you, my wife is very attractive, and a fantastic person, but we have nothing in common. She likes to garden, I don't. I love sport, she doesn't. We go drives in the car, she falls asleep. We can't chat for hours like you and I do. I don't kiss her every day, I don't tell her I love her every day, I don't even know if I do love her. I know I love you, I know that more than anything that I love you. Sarah is the mother of my children, so I don't know if my love for her extends to that. I know for sure I am not in love with her, I don't know if I have ever been in love with her. But after fourteen years with someone, they become a part of you, whether that is in a good way or not. Maybe I shouldn't be speaking like this. I know how hard this is for you Kier, and I hate that I'm hurting you."

I had to jump in. "Dale, you are not hurting me. This situation maybe, but you, you could never do anything to hurt me. The last three months of my life have been fantastic. I've felt more alive, more like me than I ever felt before. You have never made me any false promises. You have never said that you would be with me, or that we would run away together...you only ever told me the truth. How could that hurt me?"

Dale leaned over and kissed me softly, "Why are you so amazing?"

There was only one answer to that, "Because you make me amazing."

We kissed again and let it linger. Every kiss with him now was being locked tightly into my head and into my heart. I couldn't believe he thought he was hurting me. How would that even be possible? It was hard knowing that he was no longer going to be mine, but I knew it wasn't because he didn't want to be with me. The reason he was walking away was so that maybe one day he could be with me. This situation was a complete mess, but my faith was going to God that there was a reason for it all happening, and one day I would know what that reason was. I just hoped deep inside my heart that reason would be for us to be together and be able to start living the amazing life we knew we could have with one another. We would just have to wait until the time was right for this to happen.

That afternoon passed quickly, just like every other time we spent together. Too quick. I wanted minutes to feel like hours, not the other way around. As we walked back to the hotel, just before we headed in separately, Dale stopped me and looked into my eyes,

"This scares me, Kier. All of it I mean. I've never felt such an intense feeling of wanting someone and now thinking about letting you go terrifies me. For the last three months, you have been at the forefront of my life. You have been my reason to want to wake up every day. You have been everything to me. And now, I have to let you go, which is the most frightening thing I've ever had to deal with. I hate the thought of allowing you to walk away, knowing you will probably find someone else, and they will get to experience how amazing your love is. Someone else will get to kiss your perfect lips, hold your perfect hands and run their hand across your cheek." As Dale said this he cupped his hand around my cheek and I could see tears filling in his eyes. "This feels like nothing else. This feeling of being completely connected to you, and I have to let it go, I have to be the one who walks away from the love of my life, walks away from the one person who has made me happier than anyone else in the world." And with that he let go. The tears fell from his eyes, as he let go of everything he had been trying so hard to hold onto. "I don't want to let you go Kier. I don't want anyone else to have what I feel is always going to be mine. But I also can't let my boys down. I can't walk away from them. They need me to help them grow into men. I can't be selfish and think of myself. It's not fair. It's not fair I met you and I can't have you. Or I can have but can't be with you. I don't get into these situations. I'm usually the one who can solve any problem with the right outcome. But for me to have the outcome I want, for me to be with you, I have to hurt everyone else. I have to upset my sister, my parents and more than anyone: my sons. I don't know how they would react if I did leave. This is so difficult for me. I am more in love with you than I ever imagined being with someone. It's driving me crazy knowing I won't be with you, or I won't be able to just touch you, or when we get back I have to look at you and pretend I don't want you, that I don't want to just hold you in my arms forever. Kier this is driving me crazy. I wish I could just think of myself, but I can't."

I could feel the pain running through Dale, and it was transferring from him to me like electricity. I loved him. I loved him like nothing else in the world, and feeling his pain had only confirmed to me how real this feeling was. I wanted to make him feel better, I wanted to make him realise that everything would be ok, and if we were meant to be together it would happen, and it would happen at a time that was right for both of us. But I couldn't find the words. My whole body felt frozen, my jaw felt glued shut, and I was scared to talk. I stared into Dale's eyes and I could tell he knew what I was thinking. Him and I didn't need words to make things right. Every word I could ever say was said with that simple look. Again he cupped his hand round my face and through his tears he smiled and simply said, "I know."

Dale walked away from me before we said anything else. I was going to follow on into the hotel, but I felt the need to just be by myself. I about turned, took my iPod out my bag and just started to walk. As Hallelujah blared through my ears, I struggled to see through my tears. I had a firm belief in everything happening for a reason, but at that moment my heart and my head were in complete disagreement with one another, neither could believe what they felt. Half the time I felt like God was punishing me for having made a man commit adultery. I believed God was making my heart break because I deserved it for allowing our affair to turn into love. But then at other times, I thought maybe this is a test. Maybe God is testing my love for him. He wants to see if I'm willing to wait, wants to know that I am willing to put up with the heartache because in the end I will get him and it'll make it all the more worth it. The Gospel of St Peter does say: Love forgives a multitude of Sins. Would that count for our love? If God was making me wait to prove what I felt, Dale and I will appreciate our love that much more because we have had to wait for it. I didn't know. I wanted to put my every faith in God; I wanted to believe that whatever his will was going to be it would be the right decision in my life. The thought of ending up without him though was almost too much to take. I couldn't imagine going through my life, and experiencing a multitude of different things and not having Dale there beside me. I couldn't imagine having to wake up every single day for the rest of my life and not ever wake up next to him. If I didn't end up with him, I really hoped it would become clear why he had walked into my life.

CHAPTER SIXTEEN

I walked around for about two hours just trying to make sense of everything that was happening in my life. I was struggling to reach any conclusions, but I was just hoping my head would take over soon and stop my heart from pining. When I got back to the room I had three missed calls from Dale and a few texts as well. I quickly text'd back saying I was fine, just needed to clear my head but not to worry. I was about to call him, but Sasha appeared at the door, red faced and looking like she really had to speak to me.

"Are you ok?" I almost laughed. She looked like she had just run a marathon.

"Ok...em...I have to tell you something...Oh, my God...Yeah."

I laughed again. Sasha was a bumbling wreck. She didn't look upset and I didn't expect anything bad had happened, she looked more 'flustered' if that's the right word to use.

"Sash, are you ok? Has something happened?" I was still laughing, and Sasha had a wide eyed look with an almost smile starting to form across her face.

"Ok, yes. I mean. What? Ok, I have to calm down." Sasha was a complete mess. But suddenly, she took a deep breath and made a noise, that I guessed was supposed to be words. "Harry kissed me." And literally before she got the words out she screamed and the noise was possibly only audible to dogs. She was going crazy. Her whole body was moving as she jumped up and down and continued to scream her heart out. I was going to try and interrupt, get some actual information, and find out if what I thought she said was what she actually said. I was almost positive she had said that she kissed Harry. I didn't have to wait long, because she eventually collapsed on the bed with a massive smile on her face and spilled all.

"Kier, can you believe it? I mean, Harry kissed me. He kissed me. I can't believe it. I'm waiting to wake up and feel completely gutted that it's been a dream. I mean it's Harry. HARRY!!"

So my ears hadn't deceived me, she had actually kissed Harry. I was in shock.

"Are you being serious? How, when, where? Did he initiate it, what happened?" Now I was a bumbling wreck.

"Oh, Kier, it was amazing. It was...amazing." Sasha was really working hard to elaborate.

"What happened? Details, Sasha, I need details." I was practically shouting. I couldn't believe this was happening.

"Ok, well we were over at the venue, and I was checking how cohesive the line looked with the new designs that Dale had ordered in." Even the mention of his name gave me goosebumps; I had to work hard not to smile when Sasha said it. "And then we messed about with the lighting and the music a little, rearranged the orders and other bits and pieces. Anyway, when we were done, we were walking back and Harry said he wanted to show me something. So we walked about fifteen minutes out of town and he took me to this garden and Kier, believe me when I say it was beyond stunning. There were white and red roses growing all over it and it was so green everywhere. Anyway, with Harry there it just looked even better." She gave a girly little grin as she said this, "So we were wandering around and he was asking if I was having fun and just having general chit chat, and then he said the whole trip was just made so much better because I had come along. Anyway I started to blush and he kind of touched my cheek and said he wasn't kidding, and then he leaned in and kissed me. And it wasn't just a little kiss it was a full on, earth-shattering kiss and I swear fireworks went off. And it wasn't just the once, we walked for a bit and he would just stop and kiss me, and kept telling me I was beautiful and he was just being so sweet and it felt amazing. Anyway when we got back here, he asked me into his room, and I was barely in the door before I was on the bed and well, one thing led to another." She has a sly grin on her face, and mine in response was a wide eyed, open mouth expression.

"You slept with him?" I was in shock. I couldn't believe what I was hearing. Dale and I hadn't quite got there yet, and we had been together for three months.

"Yes," she said coyly, "it was total spur-of-the-moment, unplanned and well, amazing. It felt so right, Kier. And I know, before you say it, I'm a horrible person for sleeping with a married man but I am so crazy about him. He is like everything I have ever wanted, ever could want." I didn't have any right to judge anything. I was patiently waiting for the moment when Dale and I and would be able to do that, to be honest I thought it would've happened by now, we'd been here for two nights now, tonight would be the third, but Dale hadn't mentioned anything about it. I didn't want to say for him to come to my room, or for me to go to his, but I hoped he would say something. The previous two nights we didn't really have the opportunity to sneak about. The first night here we all went for dinner, Sasha ended up a bit drunk and I had the privilege of holding her hair while she was sick and last night was really our first day here and there was a welcome meal for all the designers and their staff. After the meal Steven caught up with Dale regarding some new information he had heard regarding Dale's biggest manufacturer and I didn't want to raise any suspicions with me hanging around, so I just went to bed. Dale did text me when he had left but I was fast asleep and didn't get it until the morning. Tonight Calvin and Steven had a Business Managers' meeting that Dale doesn't have to attend, and after the news about Sasha I was guessing she wouldn't be hanging around for me so I was hoping tonight would be it. All of that was beside the point though; I couldn't believe Sasha had slept with Harry.

"Of course I don't judge you. I know how mental you are about Harry. But I just, I can't believe it. I actually can't believe you two had sex. I mean, OMG." I could hear the shock in my voice, and I hoped it wasn't coming across at all as disappointment given my current situation.

Sasha was completely beaming. She looked so happy, so content and well to be honest she had a glint in her eye that I could tell meant what she was feeling for Harry was close to what I felt for Dale.

"Kier, I don't do things like that. I mean I don't just randomly sleep with people, but with Harry, Oh, my God, with Harry it felt so right. It felt so amazing. The closeness of it was just beyond comparison. It was indescribable Kier, and now all I can think is when it's going to happen again."

Sasha looked in a daze. This was a girl who was completely infatuated.

"Where is Harry now, I mean how did you leave it? Was anything more said?" I was hinting to find out what they were planning for tonight. I wanted to know if I would have a window of time to spend with Dale.

"Well, he had to meet Dale, so we had to stop what we were doing, but he said he wanted to see me later and if there would be anyway for that to happen. I know Calvin and Steven have that dinner meeting but I think Dale had hoped we would all be going for dinner together. And I don't want to be selfish and I don't want to make you do something you don't want to do but could you maybe make up a reason to have to talk to Dale on your own. I know he's a bit boring and I know that I'm being totally unfair asking this, but I just, I just can't help it." Sasha was almost pleading with me, and I felt so bad because I was going to have to lay it on thick at how 'unhappy' I was to be having to spend the night with Dale, when really this was hopefully going to work to my advantage.

"Em, ok. I'll ask Dale if we can have a chat about some ideas I have for next season but you owe me big time, I mean a night alone with the boss. If you come back and I'm no longer alive, it's because I've died of boredom. I mean Dale is a lovely person but not my idea of a great night out. What if he doesn't go for it though and needs to speak to Harry?" I wanted to cover all bases and make sure that Dale and I wouldn't be caught out.

"Don't worry about that. Harry is going to tell him that he has arranged to meet some old friends tonight and if Dale asks where I am, I'm in my room with a migraine, or something similar, whatever you think works best. As long as it's ok for you to lie?" Sasha looked genuinely worried.

"Of course it's ok. I'm sure Dale will believe whatever I say, why would I lie?" I didn't plan on lying. Dale meant too much to me for me to hide secrets from him, so I planned on telling him exactly what had happened. "What time are you meeting at?"

Just then, as if by magic, Sasha's phoned beeped. I knew by her reaction and the smile across her face that it was Harry.

"It's Harry." As if I didn't know. "He wants me to meet him at his room at 6pm. Oh, my God that's in an hour. I need a shower, I need to get ready and make myself look great for him." Sasha was panicking just a little.

"Sasha, you had sex with the guy an hour ago. He has seen you looking exactly the same way you look now so don't get yourself panicked. You could show up with a towel on and he'll think you're just as amazing as you are now...in fact, thinking about it, maybe he'll like that even more." I was trying to make jokes to calm Sasha down because suddenly she looked ill.

"Ok, I just, I like him Kier. I really like him. I think he's amazing. And I know he has a wife. And I know I shouldn't even be considering doing anything with him, but I can't resist. I physically cannot resist."

A tiny part of me wanted to open up about Dale and I. I wanted to tell her everything and I wanted her to hear that I knew exactly what she was going through but I just couldn't, not yet. Not until I completely trusted her 100%.

"Don't worry, Sasha. Do what you think, or feel is right. You're in Rome, you're with someone you have feelings for, just go with it." I think I was trying to convince myself more than Sasha. "I'm going to go down to Dale's room to speak to him about tonight. Say something about my designs or something like that."

Sasha launched herself towards me and hugged me until I could barely breathe.

"Thank you, thank you, thank you, thank you. I actually love you, so much. You are the best. Honestly...the best. Anyway, better go, and thank you. I hope your night isn't too bad with Dale. I definitely owe you, big time for this." Little did she know I was thinking the same thing.

CHAPTER SEVENTEEN

After Sasha left I went for a shower, dried my hair and made sure it was super straight before pulling on my cream shorts, a light brown short sleeved top and a pair of cream stilettos. Before coming to Rome, I decided to splurge on some "girly" outfits, given we would be attending various meals and events. I hadn't planned on going straight to Dale's room, I was going to call first, but Sasha knew I was going anyway, so no one could say anything if they saw me.

I was beyond nervous walking towards his room. I'm not really sure why. This is the same man I had been involved with for three months. A man who made me feel amazing, a man who I was falling desperately in love with, more and more every second. I hesitated a little before I knocked and when Dale opened the door I was met by a massive grin.

"Well isn't this a pleasant surprise? You look stunning." Dale looked phenomenal. He was obviously just out the shower, his hair was a little wet and all he had on were cargo shorts and I got a look at his amazing physique. It was very obvious he had been a sportsman; he was toned and looked unbelievable.

"Wow, you look...wow." I didn't know what else to say.

"Come on in, I'm leaving you standing there like an idiot." Dale had a look around, obviously checking that no-one saw me go in. "So what do I owe for this visit?"

I smiled again. I loved the way he put things, but I was struggling to put words together.

"Well, you see. Wow, you look so good right now. Kier focus." I must've looked insane. "Yeah, turns out Harry and Sasha; they have a little, how you say, *tete a tete* going on with one another. I think Rome is having an effect on people. So I am here to occupy your attention so you won't ask them to meet tonight. Sasha practically begged me to make some excuse up so they could spend the night together, and thinks I'm doing her the biggest favour ever." I smiled.

"You're kidding. Harry? I just had a meeting with him; he

said he couldn't make dinner tonight because he was meeting some old friends." Dale pretended to be angry but then laughed. "Oh, well, I had my suspicions that something was going on with those two."

"Well, Sasha thinks I'm talking to you about work-related issues and that I'm hating the very thought of it." I was struggling to put words together. Dale's physique was captivating every bit of my concentration.

"So work-related issues? And what issues would they be, Miss Scott?" Dale stepped towards me, placed his hands round my hips and pulled me close to him. "Does this cover any of your ideas?" As he kissed me softly on the mouth.

I was breathless. Actually breathless. I knew I had to speak, but staring into his deep brown eyes and feeling his warm smooth body next to mine was something else. There were mini explosions going off over my whole body and I was struggling to control myself. Taking a deep breath I managed to whisper.

"Maybe just a little." I swallowed hard. "I do have a few ideas that need to be explored in more detail." I stared at Dale with what I could only hope was my most seductive glance, I bit my lip and ran my hands up and over his chest until they were wrapped round his neck, and then running my fingers through his hair, I pulled him close and kissed him again, softly at first but without realising it, the passion I felt for him took over and I could barely control myself. Dale's movements mirrored my own, and before I knew it, he grabbed me closer and kissed me hard, and yet it still felt gentle. He ran his hands up and round my back, before bringing them round and taking them slowly down my breasts, along my stomach line and then travelling back up, this time taking my top with them and slowly letting it slide up over my head and dropping it on the floor. Without warning, he left my lips, and travelled down and round my neck line with his tongue and continued around my bra line, before easing down over my abs. When he reached the line of my shorts, with no hesitation he slowly opened the button, and allowed the shorts to drop to the floor. Before he continued any further he took a step back and stared up and down my semi-naked body. I had put on one of the many new underwear sets I had brought to

Rome with me. Cream lace French knickers, complimented with a matching bra that made my breasts look perfect. And with my stiletto heels still in place, my legs looked long, lean and extremely toned. From the look on Dale's face, he obviously agreed.

"You are stunning. Look how amazing you look, your legs, your abs, your arms, and your ass. Kier, you look phenomenal." Dale was actually ogling me, and I liked it. I should've got embarrassed by him saying this, but it just made me feel sexy. I stepped towards him and without wavering, Dale again ran his hand all over by body, covering every inch of flesh that he could, before unclipping my bra and letting it drop to the floor with the rest of my clothes. He slowly ran his tongue around my nipples, and round the curve of my breasts. His left hand started to venture alone towards the line of my underwear, and this time it didn't stop. Dale ran his hand down and the excitement took over as he touched me in a way I had never felt before, ecstasy didn't come close. My whole body completely surrendered to him. The explosion I felt was shortly enjoyed as Dale dropped to his knees and slowly slid my French knickers down, and as if in perfect co-ordination, slid his tongue down to meet when his fingers had just been. He lifted one of my legs and placed it on his knee, before caressing me again with his tongue. Although this time it took a little longer, the end result was even more of a rush. My whole body was screaming in exaltation. I was about to push myself forward to return the favour when Dale lifted me up, and laid me across the bed, and again, he ran his tongue over every part of my body, working from the top of my head, making sure to give me a long and lingering kiss before continuing down, and then finishing by running his tongue all over my legs. I felt so unbelievably amazing, my whole body was drawn more to him now more than ever, and I couldn't hold back, I had to feel him closer to me. As he moved up towards my lips, I allowed him to kiss me again before I placed my hands on his shoulder and let him lay where I had been. I followed on from where he left off, running my tongue over his perfect body. And this time when I reached his shorts, I took them off and continued on. Dale moaned with pleasure, but before anything happened further, he climbed on top of me, and without another word, our worlds met for the first time, and I couldn't believe how right it felt being with him. It was like no other experience I had had before. Of course I wasn't a virgin, but being there with him was like my first time all over again. Only this time it just felt like I was meeting with my soul-mate.

The whole sessions seemed to last for minutes, but I was surprised when we stopped and I looked out at the moonlit sky, which meant that it must have passed 9pm. I had arrived at his room at 5:30pm. Dale was lying snoring softly, and I couldn't help but fall more in love with him. The soft white cotton cover of the bed was draped lightly over his body, but still allowed for me to see his muscled back. I traced the outline of his muscles with my finger tips and he stirred, opened his eyes and smiled at me.

"Hey you." His voice was quiet, almost a whisper, but along with it was a smile that melted my heart. "You were amazing." As he said this he reached over and pulled me close, gently kissing me, before pulling me on top of him. I gently stroked his face, running my fingers along his eyebrows, and staring straight into his eyes. "I've never experienced a feeling like that before, Kier. It felt so, so right. I've never felt a connection like this to anyone before. Never felt like I wanted to give so much of myself to another person, not even my wife." I tried not to react at the mention of his wife, but he obviously sensed my tension. "Sorry I shouldn't be mentioning her. I wish I had a better resolve for this. If it was just me and her, then no problem, I'd be with you, but my boys, Kier. Those two, next to you, are my whole world," I smiled as he said this, "and I just can't imagine not being there for them. I can't imagine not seeing them grow up into amazing young men. It just kills me to have to give you up to do it. It's so difficult, but we both know I can't be selfish. I can't just think about what I want. When I had children they became the number one priority in my life and I have to continue making them my number one priority." His eyes were again filling with tears, and I was about to talk when he continued, "I love you Kier, I love you with every ounce of my existence, in a way I've never loved anyone. You make me feel like me, in fact with you I can be totally me, I don't have to pretend to be something I'm not, to be someone I'm not. I don't have to be Dale Brenton Designer, I can just be Dale, who loves Starbucks and loves joking around with the girl he loves. To my wife, the fact that I have a successful career and no financial problems are a major bonus. She loves the attention she receives when she attends events with me. She loves that people know who I am. To her, sometimes I feel like I am just a name. Don't get me wrong she has a great job herself. She is a psychiatrist dealing with high-end clients, but it seems more important that I have the great job, that she can tell people who her husband is. I just feel like it's all very superficial. I don't doubt she loves me, and I don't doubt that we have a relationship that has obviously worked given how long we've been together, but we have no interests in common. Like I said, to her sport is just a word, she doesn't get my love of sitting drinking coffee, watching the world pass by. We don't have these amazing moments together where we just chat for hours on end and think it's only been a few minutes that have passed and having no knowledge of what we just spoke about. But we have these two wonderful sons and that's what keeps me with her. Like I told you, I always thought I had made a mistake when I married her, always sensed I was with the wrong person, but I got comfortable. I had two babies with her and then that was my life. I'm not saying I've been an angel Kier, I told you I've strayed a few times, but nothing would've made me leave, but suddenly, you came into my life, and I felt complete. I felt whole. And tonight has just confirmed that for me even more so. I've never had an experience like that before, a feeling of belonging with someone, to someone."

My eyes didn't leave his the whole time he was talking, and I barely blinked, but each time I did, I was aware of the tears falling on to his chest. This was difficult to hear, and not because I was upset I couldn't have him, but because of how upset he was. I felt his pain like it was my own. I felt everything he felt, in the same way and I hated how much hurt I was causing him.

"Kier please don't get upset. You have been the best thing that ever happened to me and I would never change any of it, the only thing I worry about is how you will deal with all this. I don't want to hurt you."

He barely finished the sentence before, again, I butt in, "You could never hurt me. Dale you have never lied to me, you have never lead me to believe that something will happen here that isn't going to. You have been perfect in every way. I mean I'm not going to lie, this situation could maybe hurt me, but you couldn't. I love you Dale, with all my heart. I love everything about you, and I love the way that you love me. Being with you has made me feel like me, made me feel like I'm worth something, so even for that I owe you so much. Being here with you tonight feels amazing and I know it maybe wasn't the best idea doing what we just done, but to feel that way, even if it is just once, well that's a memory I will never be able to erase from my mind, one that I wouldn't want to erase. And as hard as the next few days, weeks, months, whatever are going to be, I know how good the last few months have been, and a thousand hours without you are worth the few I have had with you." The tears were now streaming down my face as the realisation of letting him go was getting closer to me. I had just spent three or so hours in heaven, and in two days we were done. Reality isn't so good when it hits you after you've been blocking it out.

Dale obviously sensed what I was feeling and grabbed hold of me close and kissed me gently on the lips, "I hate that this has to be over too. I hate that I'm going to have to walk into the office or into the work room and know you're no longer mine. I hate that I have to let you go and you will meet someone else and I'll have to imagine them with you, see you with them. But we just have to pray for some kind of answer, some kind of outcome. If we are meant to be together it will happen. We will come together at a time that is right, at a time where it will cause as little damage to others' lives as possible." Dale stopped talking and buried his head in my shoulder. I could feel him sobbing from below me, could feel his tears on my skin, and as much as I wanted to comfort him, I couldn't do anything but breakdown along with him. This was killing the two of us to let each other go, but there was nothing we could do, or say that would make it any easier. We were just going to have to deal with it being hard, or feeling like we were lost. I didn't know what else to do, so I simply kissed Dale on the nose, on the lips and then on the forehead.

"At least we have tonight and tomorrow. Can we just at least enjoy that together?" I stared at him and smiled.

"That to me sounds perfect." As he smiled back

We lay in each other's arms for a while, talking and laughing before we realised it was almost 10:30pm and we hadn't eaten since lunch.

"I'll order some food and have it brought here. Now you're in my room I am not willing to let you go." He had a cheeky boyish grin on his face and I fell even more in love with him, "What do you fancy?" He threw the menu towards me, but I threw it back and simply said, "Surprise me."

"No wonder I love you so much Kier. It's little things like that that make me fall in love with you all over again. You're the only girl in the world who would just happily eat anything that someone gives them."

I looked at Dale with a confused look, "That's why you love me?" I was slightly puzzled.

He laughed and then kissed me lightly on the tip of my nose, "I think they call it low maintenance."

Now it was my turn to laugh, "Oh, and I just thought it meant I was a complete grubber who would eat anything put down to them." I had a huge smile across my face as I leaned over his naked chest and nuzzled into him. I gazed up at him, took a deep breath and then just zoned out for a minute or so, looking around the room. "You ok?" Dale seemed a little concerned.

"Me? Couldn't be better. Why?"

"Just the deep breath and the long stare into space, just checking you were ok."

I smiled and softened my gaze. "One thing you never need to ask when I am with you is if I'm ok. As long as you're with me, I'm always ok. I'm just, you know, making a memory of now. I don't want to forget a single detail of this moment, not the smell of you, the colour of the room, the way the moonlight is hitting through the window. Oh, God, I sound insane." I got a little embarrassed and could feel my cheeks burning up and I could tell straight away they were red.

"Wow." Was as much as Dale got out before the tears started in his eyes again. He took a few breaths and started to talk again, "It makes me feel so happy that you want to remember this moment. That you want to keep a memory of this moment." He just stared into my eyes for a moment. "No matter what, never forget that I love you. And that's forever."

We spent the rest of the night talking, laughing, joking, and again lying in each other arms, pretending that this week wasn't going to ever end. I fell asleep in his arms, he fell asleep in mine, and we continued to just enjoy each other at various points throughout the night. It may have been the worst idea we had allowing ourselves to give into temptation, but at that moment, sense wasn't something that we were going to listen to. It was about Dale and I and nothing else mattered.

CHAPTER EIGHTEEN

The rest of the time in Rome was a complete blur. The fashions shows went by in a flash and DB Designs were hailed as champions of the show. Although I was only supposed to have a few pieces shown, I ended up with more than expected, along with some of my Sports Wear. My designs had caused a flurry of excitement and I have to admit, I was getting thrilled by it all. Three of my dresses were being considered as the styles to wear to the Oscars, and the Sportswear was being hotly tipped as the fashion of the season, not just for sport, but everyday wear. Having already been snapped up by Keep Me Cupid, every fan of theirs had been calling DB Designs ever since, hoping to get a hold of the designs, which weren't due to hit the stores until March, with the rest of the spring collection, but knowing the demand was high had me living on Cloud 9, unable to believe these were my designs.

On the last day in Rome, I was overjoyed when Steven and Calvin came over and said Dale wanted to speak to me in private. The success of my designs meant Dale and I had been able to do some more sneaking around than we had hoped, as he used this as an excuse to have to speak to me. I walked towards the small meeting room at the back of the event site, smiling already before I even got to see Dale's face, and when I actually saw him, my smile grew further as he looked at me in a way that made me melt as always.

"Hey handsome, how are you? Today has been amazing." I babbled already, and Dale laughed.

"You are the most overexcited person I have ever met in my life. Why has everyone not completely fallen in love with you?" Dale stared at me, and I could almost feel how much he loved me.

"Because, you're the only one who has Kier goggles on and doesn't find me annoying." I grinned, and giggled at the same time.

Dale laughed again, "Their loss." He looked around, stole a kiss and continuing the conversation. "Anyway, I do actually have you here for a reason, and not just to kiss you, unfortunately." Dale took a step away and directed me towards the couch on the other side of the room. As we sat down, he held my hand, again keeping himself aware of anyone looking towards us. "Ok, as you know, your active wear range has been going down a storm, getting major amounts of attention. There have been a few sports persons attending the shows, as well as people linked to them, PR, HR, agents, you know the script with these people. Anyway, Rory White and his entourage were at Wednesday night's show...the one that had some of your skate gear in it, so Rory and his team had decided to have a look. Anyway Rory fell in love with your designs and wondered if any of them could be altered into snowboarding attire. Now I know you have snowboarded, and I know how well you design, with a variety of fabrics, so I didn't hesitate before saying yes, but then realised it is a big task for you, on your own, especially with how well things are going with the dresses and evening wear, and Keep Me Cupid, but this is a massive opportunity for you Kier, and well, if you want to take on the job, you don't have to include it under the header of DB Designs, it can be all you." Dale looked serious for once, and I realised I was squeezing his hand really tightly.

"*The* Rory White. As in the world champion snowboarder? He wants me to design for him? Me? Are you serious?" I had said the sentence in about a second, with every question running into the next. "Well, I'm glad you said yes." Smiling doesn't cover what was on my face. I was beaming from every area of my body. "OMG, Dale, this is huge. First, Keep Me Cupid, then three actresses and now Rory White. Pinch me. No way is this true." I was screaming. My body was so overly excited I actually couldn't believe this was true.

"So you're happy?" Dale said this a little sarcastically, but not in a nasty way.

"Happy, I'm ecstatic. This is unbelievable. This is phenomenal. This is, this is WOW!" And suddenly I couldn't hold back any longer, I let go of his hand, wrapped my arms around his neck and hugged him. At that moment I didn't care who saw me, elation had overtaken me and I wanted to scream to the world. "Thank you so much Dale. None of this would've been possible without you. I can't believe this. I actually can't believe this." I let go, and sat back. I breathed as I finally allowed the information to absorb into my brain. I was being recognised as a designer, me, Kier Scott. "This is unbelievable Dale. I mean, this is unbelievable." I stopped for a second, took his hand again, and allowed myself to be serious, "And before we go on, I want it under DB Designs. That's who I design for; you are who I design for. If it wasn't for you, I wouldn't be here. I wouldn't have any of these opportunities, so I don't want to fly solo. You are my inspiration to do well, and I know that after this week we will have to be nothing more than colleagues again, but you are still my inspiration to do well. You are my inspiration to succeed, so I want to be under your name." I babbled, but I wanted him to know, it was him who had made me into the designer I now was.

Dale was silent for a bit. He inched closer and again took my hand, imitating that day in the restaurant on Park Avenue. "You don't have to do that Kier. It's you they want, not DB Designs." Dale seemed almost taken a back, in shock. "Do you want time to think about it?"

I didn't hesitate to answer, "I don't need time Dale. It's your company they saw my designs under. I want it to be a part of you. I still want to be a part of you, in any way possible." I grimaced, "That sounded incredibly cheesy didn't it." I screwed up my face, and then a smile spread across when I looked at Dale smile back.

"Yes it is cheesy, but it also makes me feel great. I don't mind you doing this on your own Kier; I'd do anything to help you out that I could. If you want it to be Kier Scott Designs, go for it." Dale looked at me again with a serious glance.

"Honestly Dale, I want to be under your name for now. I'm only twenty-five; I don't need that type of responsibility just yet. I like knowing I have your backing, and even though now it will just be as my employer, I still know you're there. But thanks all the same. I know there will be a lot of cash in this contract and thanks for thinking of allowing me to be sole benefactor of this, but these designs will be as much yours as mine. Like I said, you will always be my driving force." I kissed him lightly, forgetting to look around, relieved that no one could see us. Dale allowed it to last longer than it should have, and as I pulled away I stared at him, "What was that for?"

"Because you," he tapped me on the nose lightly, "are the most incredible human being ever. How unselfish are you. Any of those other girls in that team would've jumped at the chance to design under their own name with a definite sale at the end, but you, you're amazing. No other word for it."

I blushed, and kissed him on the nose, "Thanks. And by the way, just because I can say this, I love you." There was no reasoning behind me saying it; I just wanted to tell him.

"Ditto." Dale smiled

I couldn't resist the urge to laugh. Instead of kissing him again, I just laced his fingers and smiled, before letting go and walking towards the door. Just before I left he shouted after me,

"Can we spend the night together again? I know we're supposed to have the big round up meal, but I can get us out of it. I want to feel one last time what it's like being with you, feeling like your mine." Dale walked towards me.

"Sounds perfect. Just let me know the arrangements. But I would love that." I smiled, although this time I was the one with sadness in my eyes.

"Also, can we not say goodbye tonight? I'd like to meet somewhere back home, and have time ourselves to say goodbye, if you don't mind?" Dale took a deep breath and I could see his eyes glaze over, and as he shook his head I realised he was going to break down at any moment.

"Of course. I better go Dale. Text me and let me know where and when tonight."

"Ok you. Oh and Kier, I love you too." The sadness lifted for a moment from his eyes, and I felt the words deep inside my chest.

"Ditto." I smiled as I about turned and headed towards Sasha.

She was messing about with Harry, and even if I didn't know the truth I would've guessed it quite easily. They were like a pair of love sick teenagers, with glances of affection towards one another and gentle touches towards each other every now and again. If they were trying to fool anyone, it wasn't working. Since Tuesday, the two of them had been inseparable. Sasha couldn't thank me enough for covering for her, all the time being unaware that I was thanking her situation just as much. It meant Dale and I had gotten our first night together, and we had spent last night together too. Harry and Sasha had stayed in her room last night, with the cover story of him going through the events process procedure for certain shows. Of course no one knew they spent the night, except Dale and I, and Steven and Calvin were too involved in everything to realise any of us were even there, and that included Dale.

"Hey you two, what's happening?" Sasha glanced over with a love struck grin on her face.

"Harry is being an idiot and causing oodles of problems for me." I laughed at the term oodles. Sasha was acting overly polite and could barely take her eyes off Harry, even as she spoke to me.

"I am not. I simply said that Sasha maybe wants to not pack things like they are heading for a rubbish tip." He squeezed her hips and they continued to laugh. I couldn't believe how obvious they were being, unless Sasha told him I knew. That must be it; they didn't feel they had anything to hide in front of me.

Sasha laughed, "Yeah right. I had packed everything perfect, and Mr Smarty pants here," Sasha poked Harry in the ribs, "decided he wanted everything packed in order that the colours went back in the office. Obsessive compulsive much." She was trying to sound mean, but the undertones of her voice proved she was mocking him in a caring way.

"I was just trying to lighten your work load at the other end. Though, I suppose I've just doubled it by making you do it here." Now Harry erupted into laughter, with Sasha following and I found it difficult to believe he was thirty-one, he was acting like a 16-year-old.

"Ok." I was feeling like a third wheel, so I decided to spill my news out so I could leave them to it. "Did Dale mention anything to you Harry?" They both shot me a worrying glance.

"About what?" He sounded nervous, obviously expecting

me to mention something about the two of them.

"Rory White?" I questioned.

"Rory White? The snowboarder?" Harry looked puzzled.

"Yeah, well it's actually pretty amazing. He loved my skateboard designs, from the show on Wednesday night, and he approached Dale to see if I would be willing to change them about to suit snowboarding. Isn't that phenomenal?" I grinned, and could barely say anything more before Sasha launched herself towards me.

"Kier, that is amazing. He wants you to design for him? He asked for you. That's outstanding; you must be over the moon?" I wasn't sure if this was genuine elation at my good news, or more elation that it wasn't something to do with her and Harry. Harry also looked happy for me, though I sensed the relief in his face that his boss wasn't about to attack his affair with a colleague, though he couldn't have passed judgement anyway.

"Yeah I can't believe it. I mean after the show on Tuesday with my three dresses being enquired about and now this. I can't believe it. Rome is certainly being an eye opening experience for me." I smiled, hiding what was the real eye opening experience for me. "I'm still trying to process it all to be honest."

"Well done, Kier. That's some opportunity being thrown your way. Dale must be thinking he struck gold finding you." Harry seemed genuinely pleased for me, though I still sensed his slight liberation of not being involved in what Dale had said. If he only he knew Dale knew everything. I smiled, thinking, yes Dale had struck gold, in more ways than anyone would ever know. "Where is Dale? I actually have to speak to him quickly regarding tonight." I stared at him, and panicked, was he going to ask him for a meeting, would my night be ruined, but before I said anymore, Harry, completely unaware of my panic, continued to speak, "I know we are all supposed to go for that round up dinner, but I could really be doing with missing it. I wanted to finish packing everything up, and Sasha offered to help. I just don't want anyone messing anything up. Think he'll mind?" Harry quizzed me, not in a way that made me think he was suspicious, but more in a way I could tell he was hoping he would get to spend the night with Sasha.

"I don't see why not. To be honest, I think he was hoping to ditch it too. I overheard him mention to Calvin that he had a few calls to sort out and would most likely spend the night in his room and try and catch up. So he'll probably be relieved." I tried to remain composed, acting like I was just passing on information and not lying in anyway.

"Great, that works out well. Actually, I'm sure Steven is meeting with that business manager from Sightgate International tonight, I heard them talking earlier and it was easier to catch up here than arrange a meeting in England or back in New York. Wouldn't Calvin be going to that too? He is the manager for business in that area?" I could feel Harry reassuring himself that tonight he wouldn't have to cover his tracks too much.

"Yeah possibly. I was planning a quiet one tonight, so that would be good if the dinner wasn't going ahead. Dying to get stuck into some design ideas and get them ready for back in New York on Monday." I was even convincing myself that I believed this.

"Cool, be back in five. I'm just going to confirm with Dale what the plan is." Harry left and I saw Calvin head into the room Dale was in too. I knew he wouldn't make any other plans for tonight, but I still panicked that he would maybe worry about arousing suspicious if Calvin asked for a meeting and he yet again had other plans. I knew he didn't want to have anyone asking questions, I just hoped Harry was right, and Calvin would go along with Steven, maybe that was what he was going in for.

I was staring in to space when Sasha patted me on the shoulder, "Hey space cadet, you ok?"

"Yeah, sorry, I'm completely dreaming. There is just so much going on I hardly know where to start." Yes I do, I start by having an amazing night tonight with Dale, and then try to go on living without him in my life. "I hope the dinner doesn't go ahead, would let me get at least something started." Again I sounded convincing, with the right level of panic, which I may add wasn't directed towards work, it was all going into hoping that tonight I would be with Dale.

"Yeah I hope it doesn't go ahead either. Harry and I were planning on spending our last night together. Nothing

137

excited, well we were just going to stay in his room." Sasha smiled a cheeky grin.

"I wouldn't worry. Dale sounded stressed when I was speaking to him, so hopefully it will all be off. By the way, when we get back, what's going to happen with you and Harry?" I was genuinely interested if this was heat of the moment, we're in Rome, let's have sex kind of fun, or if they did genuinely feel something for one another.

Sasha grinned again, "He wants to keep seeing me. I know it's a bad idea, and I know he has a wife, but I just love spending time with him, the sex is beyond amazing and we just have the best time together." I loved how the whole idea of sex came into play. This almost made me believe that for them, that's all it was. I think the fact they slept with each other on the first night was a massive indication of the way their relationship would go. I had been with Dale for three months before anything happened. We had declared our love for one another before we even contemplated being with each other in that way. To be honest he had doubted if it would ever go that far. Dale had made a comment before we had slept together saying he knew it would be that good being intimate with me that nothing else would ever compare, so letting me go would be twice as hard. To be honest I had to admit, it was amazing. I had never felt so attracted to someone, never wanted to feel someone's hands on me so much. But at the same time, if someone told me I couldn't have that, if all I got was his company, it was enough. I felt so content when I was with Dale, speaking about everything and anything all at once, losing hours and wishing time would stand still so I didn't have to leave him. Being in Rome, feeling what it was like to not say goodbye just felt right. I loved the two nights I had fallen asleep next to him and woken up next to him. I loved seeing his face first thing, feeling his skin on mine, everything. I loved him so much; sex wasn't even an issue between us. I just hoped that Harry wasn't using Sasha for a bit of fun. His wife wasn't the "fun" type, and Sasha offering him it on a plate wasn't exactly playing it cool. I didn't want to say anything to her, the damage had been done, and I couldn't judge. Maybe there were genuine feelings there and I had no right to make comment until I knew one way or the other. Maybe I was just feeling a little deflated hearing when we were back home, they would still be having fun together and I'd be doing everything in my power to repair my broken heart. Jealousy wasn't something I ever felt, but maybe I was just slightly envious towards them, though I shouldn't be. Did they really have the same feeling towards each other that Dale and I did, were they lucky enough to feel the same passion, the same connection, the same everything that him and I had between us? I had to just be happy I had that and if what Sasha and Harry had was the same I just had to be happy for them too.

"Kier you're spacing away again. What is with you?" Sasha knocked me lightly on the head. "You ok?"

"Yeah I'm so sorry. I'm just thinking about work." I wasn't lying, Dale was related to work. "Look there's Harry coming. Oh, by the way, did you tell him I know?"

Sasha widened her gaze, "No, he doesn't know a thing." Then she stopped, "Why?"

I couldn't help laughing, and was glad Harry was speaking to Calvin as it gave me time to talk, "Well he's not exactly hiding the fact he likes you. He was all over you when I showed up earlier." I barely got the words out before Sasha was beaming.

"Oh, my God, I'm so happy. Wow. Thanks, Kier." Sasha danced around a little, and again I laughed.

"You're nuts. And I didn't do anything so don't thank me, and anyway…" I couldn't say anymore, because Harry was right next to her by this time.

"What ya saying, Kier?" Harry, oblivious to the conversation, was obviously just being nosey.

"Nothing much, just saying I hope dinner wasn't going ahead because I've got so much to do tonight." I hated lying, but what else could I do; even I didn't believe all of this was happening.

"Well you're in luck. Steven and Calvin are going to sort out some business, and Dale said he has too much work to catch up on, so he's not to be disturbed no matter what. So that's us all off the hook. You still up for helping me Sash?" Harry must've thought I was an idiot and hadn't caught the cheeky wink he directed towards Sasha. Yeah helping you out; out of your clothes is my guess.

"Of course. Anything I can do is all experience." I burst out laughing without thinking, and Sasha shot me a look that could kill, while Harry just looked confused.

I tried to cover it up, "Sorry that wasn't directed at you was just thinking about something in my head. Sorry, again." I looked at Sasha with an apologetic glance.

Sasha laughed nervously, "Kier you are crazy. Anyway, Harry, we should get organised. Do you want to grab some food first before we start? Kier you can join us?" I could see from the way Sasha looked at me she was saying, you dare say yes and I will kill you, so I smiled and simply replied.

"No, it's ok. I'm going to get some room service and do some work. Have fun you two. Don't make too much of a mess." I realised how much of a double-edged comment that was, but this time resisted the urge to laugh, so instead I just hugged Sasha, and said goodbye.

As I walked towards my room, I got in the lift, removed my phone from my pocket and looked down, before I could do anything else, the door re-opened and Dale walked in.

"Hi beautiful." And waiting for the door closing, he wrapped his hands round my waist and kissed me as though it was the last time he ever would. His hands were frantically trying to touch every part of me, and as he closed off his kiss, I caught my breath.

"What was that for?" I continued to catch my breath and smiled at him.

"Because you have been walking around all day looking completely stunning and all I've wanted is to grab you, kiss you and feel you as close to me as possible. Do you even realise how much of a beautiful princess you are?" I was completely taken a back. Dale was always complimenting me, but I felt like he just wanted me then and there. "I have been getting big time withdrawals from you the whole day. Just been dying to get a hold of you all day and I couldn't wait until tonight to just have you to myself again. How quick can you be ready?" Dale was still holding me tight and kissing me between almost every word.

"Quick shower, and pull on some new clothes, then I'm good to go. Say half an hour?" I kissed him this time.

"How about, you grab clothes and come to mine for a

shower?" Dale flashed his cheeky grin at me and I couldn't help but melt.

"It's a deal. Well, as long as you are a part of that shower." I stared seductively at him, as I slowly traced his lips with my tongue.

"Wouldn't have it any other way." He was about to say more, but the lift came to a halt and the door opened, as Dale moved away from me. My room was on the 5th floor and his on the 7th, "Just grab your stuff and come up, have a check around before you come in." He kissed me quickly before I left, and as the doors closed I ran towards my room.

CHAPTER NINETEEN

I didn't want to waste a minute without him. Running into my room, I was glad I had left clothes sitting for tonight, a tight fit cotton dress, and another pair of cream heels. I grabbed the clothes, picked up my hair dryer and straightening iron and put them into my bag. I also lifted my small make up compact, locked the door and rushed towards the elevator. The whole process had taken less than five minutes, but when I arrived at Dale's door, he pulled me inside, "What took you so long?" I didn't get a chance to answer, as his lips were already pressed to mine, his hand undoing my shirt and the button of my shorts, as he pulled me towards the bathroom. He had a suite in the hotel, and his shower was huge. As we both stripped each other, we went into the shower and continued to allow our passion for one another to overtake us. Sex in the shower had never appealed to me, but being there with Dale was something else, it was yet another amazing memory that I could log in my thoughts. We stayed in the shower for around half an hour, before taking advantage of every surface of his room. I was shocked again, when I realised the sun had yet again set, and Dale and I had lost another few hours wrapped up in our own time bubble.

"I can't believe it's night time again. Minutes really do turn to hours with you." Dale was smiling, but I sensed something else was going on behind his eyes.

"Are you ok? You seem a bit distant." I was slightly worried. I had been panicked a bit more than usual with Dale since we had slept together, aware that this may make reality all the more clear to him, and I worried that he would be feeling more guilty with me than usual.

Dale, obviously realising I was feeling a little stressed, pulled me close to him, and gently brushed my hair off my face, as he looked intently into my eyes. "Sorry. It's nothing to do with you; well it is but nothing bad. I just can't help but think that we spend this time together, and just feeling you with me, feeling your skin touching mine is all so perfect, and I want time to stop so I can spend more time with you. And now, here we are, having spent another three hours together, and I can't help but think we only have twelve hours left together. None of this makes sense to me. Nothing about this situation makes any sense at all. You are my perfect woman; everything about you matches exactly what I want from a woman.

I stared intensely into Dale's eyes. I processed everything into my brain. He was right. None of this did make sense, but at the same time, we couldn't continue on as we were. Dale was married. Simple. He was married.

"Dale, have you ever read any work by Bernard Shaw?"

Dale looked completely confused, but he went along with me anyway, knowing I was probably going somewhere with it, "Can't say I have, why?"

"Well, he once wrote, there are two tragedies in life, one is to lose your great love, and the other is to find it. I think he meant that finding it leads to you being more aware of what you have to lose, but to be honest; I don't think he was right. Finding you could never be described as a tragedy, and the pain that I feel from losing you or the fear I will feel of hoping I get you back will only indicate that I had something worth losing, I had something worth making me feel this way, and therefore how could that be a tragedy? Emotions that we feel allow us to know we are alive, allow us to know that we have lived. So even if I lose you, I've still gained because I had you. I found my great love, and how many people can honestly say that? But I understand you have a life to lead and so do I. You have kids to bring up, to mould into something great, and I have to realise that you still have a wife, whether you want to admit to me your true feelings for her or not, I know there will still be some sort of love there." I bit my lip, and took my eye gaze away from him, and looked to the floor. I didn't want to cry but I couldn't help tears falling from my eyes.

Dale put both his hands on my shoulders and slightly crouched down so he could look at me.

"Kier I wish I wasn't doing this to you. I wish I could just take you in my arms and hold you there forever. Believe me, if it wasn't for my boys I would be with you. I may have a certain degree of love for my wife, but it is nothing compared to what I feel for you. When I think about leaving you it hurts me. If I was with you I'd never want to spend a night apart. I'd want to fall asleep next to you every night, wake up next to you everyday. I'd want to share every experience of my life with you there. God, Kier, you're the love of my life, it's completely unfair that I have to let you go." I could feel the hurt running through Dale's veins, the anger that he was feeling mimicked what I was feeling. We were like one person; we shared a bond to one another that made us feel exactly what the other was feeling.

"Dale, let's not dwell on this anymore. We both know what is going to happen when we step off that plane at JFK tomorrow. We could go round in circles a hundred times describing the love we feel for each other, going through how unfair this is, how much hurt we both feel and how much heartache we are going to feel, but that's just making it worse, and cutting into the time we do have left together. I just want to block out the fact that we don't have much longer left together, and I want to pretend for the next twenty-four hours that you really are my guy and I'm your girl. Can we do that?" I swallowed hard, and faked a smile.

Dale looked warmly into my eyes; his deep brown eyes making me melt as always, "Anything for you." He wrapped his arms around me, and then again stared into my eyes, "and just so you know, in my eyes, you will always be my girl." And he kissed me.

That night with Dale was an experience I can't even describe. I honestly felt like we were one person, moving in synch together, being able to assume where the other was going, what the other was doing, how each other was feeling. As I drifted off to sleep I listened to his heart, I watched him breathe, I took in the smell of his skin, every sound he made, and thought about how much I would miss this, even though it was only the third time I had experienced lying next to him. As I stared at him, I stroked his skin as lightly as possible so as not to wake him and realised that I was here with him, I was breathing him in, feeling him next to me, and I missed him. I missed him. I knew I had him here, but my heart was aching knowing I was going to have to let him go and I had no choice. I couldn't change that he was already married, I couldn't change that he had a life that didn't involve me. Dale and

I had our own world, and it was so hard beginning to process that was it, our own world. I had to be strong, I had to get myself through this and try to smile and learn how not to be with him. As he stirred under my hand, he turned to look at me, pulling me in and kissed me lightly.

"You look stunning in the moonlight." Dale smiled at me, as he gently brushed my hair away from my face. "Are you ok?"

I couldn't lie, "Not really but I'm dealing with it. It's just taking my heart a little longer to catch up with my head. Feeling you lying here, breathing you in and experiencing what it's like being with you, I'm going to miss it. I'm going to miss everything. I'm going to miss you. This is going to sound so cheesy, but over the last few months you have become my best friend. You have become the person who makes me smile when I'm upset, who lifts my mood when I'm feeling down, and now you're not going to be there. I'm just going to miss it." I was determined not to cry again.

Dale didn't speak for a bit. He just played with my hair and smiled at me, looking at me the way he always did, in that way that made me know he loved me like I did him.

"Well maybe we don't have to stop all contact. Maybe we can still text, or talk on the phone. In fact we can still catch up once a week, grab a coffee outside work. Obviously we have to be careful, but I don't want to miss you anymore than I have to. I've never felt so close to anyone as I do to you. The thought of losing that closeness all together, I don't know if I want to imagine that."

I suddenly smiled, and this time it wasn't false, or forced.

"That would be amazing. Honestly, Dale. That was what hurt more, the thought of not speaking, not catching up with you, not knowing how you were doing. Are you sure that will be ok?" I was getting excited at the thought of still going for coffee and getting to gaze into his amazing eyes, even if that's all it was. Even if I couldn't kiss him, or touch him, at least he would still be in my life; we could stay a part of one another lives. "I can handle that. As long as it's ok for you?"

"Kier, having you as part of my life, at the moment, is all that matters. I can't be with you in the way I want, but I still want to be with you in some way. Just know, I would always prefer the first option, every single time." Dale leaned over kissed me again, and then hugged me in close. And I felt myself smiling as we both drifted off to sleep, entwined in each other's arms, his skin on mine.

CHAPTER TWENTY

Being back from Rome was tough. Dale kindly offered to drop Sasha, Harry and myself off after we arrived at JFK, obviously covering up that he was going to say goodbye to me, or at least a goodbye to us being something more than friends. Harry and Sasha were subtle, she asked me earlier if her and Harry could both be dropped at her house. Her parents were away for a few days and Harry had told his wife he had to stay in Rome for a few more days. It made me wish Dale and I had thought about that, though, truthfully, if we had spent forever together I still wouldn't think it was long enough. Dale and I said our final goodbye near the lake in Central Park. It seemed the perfect location given that's where all this started, and now here we were saying goodbye to what I saw as perfection. We kissed, we hugged, we cried, and we said goodbye. Dale wanted to drive me home but I wasn't quite ready to go back to reality. I wasn't ready to face people or speak to anyone. I didn't want to cry in front of people, didn't want questions being asked. I needed to cut people out for the moment. I was getting good at this, avoiding people, being myself, and trying to suss out a way to live without half my heart. That's how it felt. Dale had made me complete, he was that other half that God had created that I was always meant to meet, but for some reason it just wasn't meant to happen, at least not just now. On the last night in Rome, Dale handed me a gift and when I opened it, I discovered a black sports watch. He said although he and I could no longer be together he hoped this would help to make it seem as though we were still tied as one, in some way, forever. Looking down at it now, I pulled some strength from it, and almost felt the love Dale had for me trickling from the dainty black watch and into my heart. Even without the watch, Dale would always be present with me. A thousand memories would make that possible. I walked to our favourite Starbucks, located on 34th Street. You have to love New York, purely because everywhere is always opened. It reminded me of when I went home (to Scotland) and I was visiting relatives, and at 1am, I got an urge for Starbucks, and was destroyed to learn most places are closed by 9, even the airport one closes between 1 and 5. That didn't make any sense to me, but living in New York you get use to 24-hour everything.

I sat in Starbucks for two hours. I wrote in my diary, I cried into my coffee mug, I listened to some music, and I tried to make my heart comprehend what my brain had always known. I knew Dale wasn't going to all of a sudden be mine. He had a life he had to sort before him and I would even become a factor. It was just difficult being this in love with another person and having to become aware that as much as we want to be together, as much as we feel like we are made for one another, we can't be. I almost felt like I deserved to be feeling like this. I felt like I had disappointed God and made him angry, so therefore I was being punished by feeling my heart break. And I knew God could heal that broken heart, but he needed all the pieces to do this and maybe he was keeping a piece back as a constant reminder of what I had done. I had to keep faith that if that's what God was doing, if he was punishing me, then I deserved it. I had made a man commit adultery, I had lied to my family, to my friends, and I had committed sins that I wasn't sure if God could really forgive. I know he loves love, but does he still love illicit love? I was no longer sure of myself as a "good" person, and felt I had gone against my religion, my faith for my own selfish need to be with Dale. I had to believe that God would see the good in us, that he would see this was genuine love. It wasn't about sex, it wasn't about just lust or passion. We fell in love, simple as that sounds, that's what happened. I didn't choose to fall in love with a married man. I didn't wake up one day and think, you know what I fancy having an affair with a married man, I really want to see what it feels like to end up completely in love with someone that I can't have, to end up feeling like my heart has been ripped from my chest, and my whole world turned upside down. That's exactly what I decided. HA! Hardly. If I could've resisted him, if I could've stopped myself falling for him, stopped myself craving the need to be near him, I would've. But at the same time, would I have? Would I have really given up the last three months? Would I have given up feeling so close to another human being? Would I have given up being with my soul mate, even if it was only for the short time I was with him? I loved him, I loved being with him. It just hurt knowing it was over now and I wasn't with him, that I couldn't be with him. Every ounce of my soul was fighting for survival. I felt like I was going to drown in the tears falling from my eyes, felt like I was unable to catch my breath and my lungs would eventually stop working. This was the worst pain I had ever felt – I had thought my heart had been broken before, but I didn't even feel like me now. How was that possible? I had been with Dale for three months, but it could've been a lifetime with the way I was feeling. It was like I had lost a leg...an arm...my heart. I didn't know how to function knowing he wasn't going to be in my life anymore. I knew we would still speak everyday, I knew I would still meet up with him, still be able to look into his amazing eyes, but would that be enough? Would I miss leaning across and feeling his lips on mine? Would I miss linking fingers with him and knowing that I was linked in with my other half? Or would I be able to get used to knowing that's all we were now? That I couldn't take it any further, and it was good enough we were still meeting up as friends? My stomach was in knots and I felt ill. How could I just be his friend? How could I pretend I wasn't completely in love him, that he wasn't the only person who I could ever imagine spending the rest of my life with. Why was life so unfair? Why do some people meet their soul-mate, feel that amazing rush of love and still not get them? Is this just a cruel twist of fate; is it a punishment for being swayed by a married man? Was meeting Dale some kind of test from God to judge my character and show me that even though I believe I am this great person who is completely unselfish, really I'm just a dirty mistress, swayed by an amazing smile, good looks and witty banter. Or, is this all part of the plan, part of God's Will? Are Dale and I destined to be separated, so that, in years to come, we can come together again and having spent so much time apart we'll appreciate it all the more that we finally get to be with each other? I honestly have no answer to this, and I feel like I'm constantly asking the same questions without any resolve because at the moment there isn't one. The only thing I know as a definite is that I need to put more faith in God than I ever have before, and I need to pray for some sort of strength to get through all of this. I had written Dale a text message, basically just saying I loved him more than words, and I would always be here if he wanted me. Very cheesy, I know. And he replied, with the most amazing text ever, that simply said, "( )...2 halves of the one whole." Those two little brackets were amazing. They were like our own little symbol and I seemed to draw strength from knowing that's how he felt about me, I was his other half.

As the weeks past, things got harder instead of easier. I saw Dale every day in the office. He would send me text messages with the brackets in it, and even if that's all it was, it really did make me feel better. We still met up at least twice a week, and we resisted the urge to not just fall into each other's arms and forget about the fact we're not allowed to be together. Dale said he couldn't resist every urge, and when I drove around with him he still insisted on holding my hand. I didn't know if this was worse or better, still feeling that electrical spark I did when my skin touched his. I had to use every ounce of will power I had to resist the urge to just make him kiss me. Every time I left him I tried to convince myself it was ridiculous putting myself through this, I wrote out so many text messages saying it was over, or that we should just cut all ties, but every single time I stopped myself. I couldn't cut him from my life. I couldn't force myself to give him up. Holding his hand, staring into his eyes and still loving him, it all had to be enough.

One Saturday afternoon we had decided to meet at Starbucks, and sitting across from him, staring into his eyes and realising this is where I want to be, tears stung my face.

"Kier, please don't cry. I can't stand that I'm making you unhappy. I can't handle the thought of making you feel upset." Dale ran his hand down my face, and cupped round my cheek, "Do you feel that." He looked at me and smiled, "That is how I know everything will be ok, Kier.

When I touch your face, when I connect with your skin it's like magic happening, it's like no other feeling I have ever had. We're connected Kier, whether we make it in the end, we are still connected together, and that's forever. I promise." Dale let his hand loose from my cheek, and went back to his coffee.

I stared into his eyes. He was fidgeting with his muffin, taking tiny bites, and looking nervous. I panicked. Was he worried about what he said, did he realise he shouldn't be saying anything like that to me, or was he panicked at the thought of us not being together ever again? I tried to analyse his expression, his actions, but everything pointed to him being nervous as he continued to take tiny bites of the muffin and avoid eye contact with me. I couldn't take it anymore,

"Are you ok? Don't worry about what you said. It's ok, I'm just being stupid getting upset. Ignore me, don't stress yourself out." He continued to look down and eat his muffin, as I got more and more stressed out over having upset him, "Dale please, speak to me." Now I was starting to get upset again. I was about to speak again, when Dale looked at me and without warning his cheeks exploded as a spray of muffin covered my whole face and hair. I stopped every movement and for about five seconds Dale and I just stared at each other, he was searching face for a reaction and I was searching his, unsure of what had just happened, but I couldn't hold it in anymore. As a smile crept across my face, I couldn't hold in a massive laugh, and as I erupted, so did Dale.

"OMG, what was that." I struggled to speak through my laughter. Tears were again streaming down my face but this time it was through happiness. Looking at Dale made me laugh even more, he was almost doubled over in two, and his face had gone a funny shade of red. "That was hilarious." I was still laughing so hard that it took me about ten seconds to get the sentence out.

Dale struggled to speak through his own laughter, "Kier, no other girl in the world would react to that like you, no one would laugh at me spitting in their face. How amazing are you?" And as though completely forgetting himself, Dale cupped my face, pulled me close and kissed me, and just as quickly, realised what he done and pulled away.

"Kier, I am so sorry. That was uncalled for. I just got lost in the moment I guess and I just, I'm so sorry. I shouldn't have let my feelings take over..." Dale tried to continue, but I placed my finger over his mouth, and whispered,

"Do it again." I stared straight into his eyes, and willed him to kiss me.

"But Kier..." He tried to continue but again, I wouldn't allow it.

"Kiss me again." This time I demanded it as I flirted with his eyes, and bit my lip seductively towards him.

And without any more persuasion, Dale leaned in and kissed me. Softly at first, as though feeling to make sure it was ok, and then he let go and just allowed himself to sink into the kiss, and suddenly, for the first time in weeks, the world seemed right again. My broken heart was suddenly put back together, the hole in my chest that had felt empty without him was filled, and I was whole again. We kissed with the same passion, the same emotion, the same want that was always between us that made every kiss feel like the first one all over again. I allowed myself to be completely taken over by him and pushed the rest of the world aside. It was just Dale and I and nothing else mattered. As we slowly started to allow the kiss to come to a close, Dale slowly pulled away, stalling to press his nose to mine, and then kiss my forehead.

Dale stared at me and smiled, although not a grin, but an almost sad smile.

"Are you ok? That wasn't really the response I hoped for from kissing you." I bit my lip, and looked down in despair from his instant regret of what had just happened between us. But I didn't have to worry, as Dale quickly took my hands, and kissed me again.

"Sorry about the glum look, but that felt amazing. Actually amazing." Dale sighed and it was his turn to look down.

"Why does that make you sad? I mean, if it felt amazing, is that not a good thing?" I quizzed his response and could tell I was squinting my face. Dale broke his sad smile, and laughed a little.

"Yeah Kier, it felt amazing, it felt like finally everything was right again. It felt like the last few weeks hadn't happened and yet again I was me, but that's not fair. How can it feel so amazing but be so wrong at the same time. I'm married. I go home to my wife every night and pretend I am Mr Family Man. I put on this pretence that I'm happy being there. Damn it, Kier I don't even kiss my wife everyday because I just don't have that type of bond with her. And here you are, and I'm doing everything in my power to stop me wanting to kiss you because I love you so much, and stopping myself needing to be with you because that's not what I'm supposed to want. I don't know how to do this Kier; I don't know how to stay away from you. I feel like I'm addicted to you and because I've had you I can't stop having you. I don't want this to end yet Kier. After Rome I thought my brain would switch into gear and I'd be happy enough to get used to being your friend, still chatting, occasionally holding your hand, but it's not enough Kier. I know I have no right to make a request or to even ask you to be with me knowing that I am married and have to stay there, but I love you Kier, please believe me, I love you with all my heart and being with you is like nothing else. And if it wasn't for the boys, I swear I'd be yours. I would. But like I said, I'm not in any place to make demands on your time, and I know you deserve more than the part time partner that I can be for you. I hate even saying this to you, because I want to be yours, full time, everyday I want to start and end with you, and its hurts, it actually hurts knowing I can't do that. I can only be with you when I can, and how unfair is that?" Dale was now fighting through tears to get the words out, his fists were clenched tight and I could feel the frustration in his voice. Everything he was saying was true, everything he was saying was unfair, but to be honest, I didn't care. I wanted Dale, even if it was only on his terms, and maybe I'm stupid for thinking that. Maybe I'm being completely crazy even willing to be "the other woman" to continue my role of what everyone else would see as me being The Dirty Mistress. I didn't want that as a title, but I also didn't want to let him go. The time spent away from him had been the worst time I had ever spent in my life. Every second was devoted to thinking about him, to picturing having him next to me, to imagining him being mine. And now having him offer me a way for that to happen, a way that, from the outside looking in was completely ridiculous, completely insane, but to me completely perfect, because regardless of the family, the kids, he would be mine for whatever time we spent together. I could be in his life, have him in mine and know we were together, even if it was just in our own little bubble. And that's what I wanted, him, in whatever capacity I could have him.

I turned to Dale, released his fists, and slid my fingers between his and felt that amazing electrical bond that I knew would tie us to each other no matter what. When I touched his skin, the butterflies took over inside my stomach and I was suddenly no longer in control of my own body, and without realising what I was doing, I leaned forward and kissed him again. I could taste his tears on my lips, before he released my hands from his, and wrapped them around my body, allowing himself to completely absorb me into himself. Although we were in the middle of Starbucks, it felt like the rest of the world didn't matter and all that existed was Dale and myself, exactly how I wanted it to be, exactly as I felt it should be. As I released myself from his grip, I ran my fingers down over his eyebrow, and down the side of his face.

"I love you Dale Brenton. I love you for who you make me, and for who I am when I'm with you. I don't care that I will only spend a few hours with you every week because those few hours are so worth it. I would rather spend one hour with you, than a lifetime with anyone else. Being with you, whether that is walking into a room with you on my arm, or having to pretend that you're just my boss, knowing that we are so much more, I honestly don't care. As long as I have even a small part of you then I'm happy. If this is going to be too much for you though, and if it's easier to walk away completely, cut all contact, whatever, then I can do that too. It won't be easy, in fact to be completely honest, it'll feel like I'm losing a part of me, but I will honestly do anything to make you happy." My face was focussed and serious, I wanted an answer, needed a resolve, and if that resolve was the hardest thing to hear, I still wanted to hear it, my head needed to hear it so I could attempt to move on.

Dale stared at me for what seemed a lifetime. He cupped his hand around my face again, lightly kissed my lips and then the tip of my nose before he spoke,

"You are what I want. Just you. And as much as I try to fight being with you, my heart knows what it wants. I just wish I could just be with you, but you know the story and I hate that I have to tell you that. I hate that I'm telling the love of my life that she has to be placed back seat, and that I can only give you snippets of my time, when really, what I want is to spend every minute with you, have you with me through everything. It just seems unfair me telling you that when I can't follow it through with a promise." Dale dropped his head to his hands, and then ran his fingers through his hair, grabbing it slightly. I placed my hands on his head, before slowly lifting his chin, and kissing him, the same way he had done me.

"Dale, I don't care about all that. What I care about is having you in my life. Having you by my side, and whether that is just in our little bubble, or whether I'm able to show you off to the world, it doesn't make a difference. Just now doesn't feel like the right time to let go. So let's just go back to how it was before Rome. I think we both have enough faith in God to know he will show us when we should let go. How does that sound?"

Dale grabbed me and kissed me hard on the mouth, pulled away, smiled and simply said, "I love you Kier." And that was it; I was given, at least for the moment, a resolve.

The rest of the night was amazing, we talked, we kissed, we spoke, we laughed, and because Dale decided he wasn't really up for saying goodbye that night, we checked into the Plaza for the evening. I don't really know what he told his wife, or where he said he was and really, it wasn't any of my business. Dale and I live in a world that wasn't part of the "normal world" and in my eyes nothing else really mattered outside our bubble. The night in the Plaza was unbelievable. From the minute we walked in the room, the electricity between us was indescribable, we were being pulled towards each other by a force that was greater than any of the two of us could resist. I was completely in love with him, felt him through every pore in my body and loved being entwined in his body again. Never had I felt more like me, more alive and more complete. Lying in his arms I smiled as I drifted off to sleep knowing this was exactly where I belonged.

CHAPTER TWENTY-ONE

The next few weeks were amazing. Dale and I tried to hide how crazy we were about each other in the office but when we were together outside the office, away from questioning eyes, we were the perfect couple. Every moment we spent together was a dream come true. We spent hours on end just talking and laughing. I had never felt so happy in my whole life, being with Dale was heaven; there was no other word I could use to describe it. He told me everyday how much he loved me. We spoke every morning on the phone before work and every night after. We would try to have even half an hour alone time together just so we could get a "fix" of each other. One night when I couldn't see him after work because I had made plans with Sasha, I received a text five minutes after I left the office that said, "Having withdrawals from you already." Sasha saw my face change when I received the text but I just said it was joke and somehow managed to get out of it. She was dying to fill me in on her and Harry, who were still having an affair of their own. We hadn't seen each other in a few weeks, so I was looking forward to the catch up, though it was gutting not seeing Dale. Sasha and I were walking towards The Copperton Café for a quick bite to eat, and she had already started to fill me in, telling me how in love she was and how she missed him every minute she was away from him. Half way towards our dinner location, she got a text from Harry saying he could get away for the night and as though I wasn't even a second thought she cancelled on me to go see him. She just turned round and said she was sorry but she had to take every moment she could while it lasted. I wasn't annoyed at her wanting to see him, of course I wasn't, but just annoyed because I had cancelled my own plans with Dale to see her. I didn't have to worry though because I quickly text him and said, "plan changed, much happening?" Yes the text was dry and not very entertaining, but when I text his work phone I like to keep it simple. The one he used for me he kept on silent so I worried he wouldn't see it, so whenever I text his normal number, I made sure it was as discreet as possible, especially when I didn't know where he was, or more importantly: who he was with. We also had a little arrangement where, if he wanted to talk to me, he would ring my phone and I would call him back. Our missions were very Secret Service. In fact I had a joke that Dale was my very own James Bond, my own Sean Connery...in fact that's what he was in my phone as, just in case anyone saw anything regarding him, they would see the name Sean and wouldn't be able to link it to him. After I text him, it took less than a minute for my phone to light up and flash Sean on my screen. So I rang back.

"Hey Handsome, how you doing?" I couldn't help but smile every time I dialled his number.

"Hello my beautiful," I smiled again, "I didn't expect to hear from you so soon." Dale sounded like he was smiling, which again just made me grin even more.

"Well, Sasha got a better offer from Harry and I got ditched. Wish she had told me sooner though, hate that I could've caught you for five minutes but didn't and obviously I couldn't act annoyed in anyway because given half a chance I would've ditched her for you." I laughed a little down the phone. "But at least I'm getting to speak to you."

"I can go one better than that, how about meeting at our Starbucks and you can see me too?" I could feel Dale's grin even through the phone line, and I loved how he called it our Starbucks.

"Seriously? I mean you don't have to get home? I know it's getting late now so I completely understand." I was getting excited. I loved nothing more than when I got to see Dale and when I wasn't expecting it, it made it even better.

"Of course I'm sure. I've been dying to get a hold of you all day. Anyway, my, em, she's away out for the evening and the boys are staying at friends." He never said wife anymore, not to me, and I appreciated it more than he could know. "So get your sexy behind to me now so I can show you how much I've missed you." Dale laughed, and I could picture him looking completely fantastic.

"Ok, I am literally five minutes from there. Can't wait to see you."

The Starbucks session went like every other one. Amazing and fun, filled with laughter and love like every other minute that we spent together. It was amazing how we had spent so many hours together and yet we still found so much to talk and laugh about. Dale would continue to spit muffin in my face, I would crinkle mine up and sprinkle it on his head. We would kiss, we would hug. Occasionally after these sessions we would go to a hotel or sneak into my apartment if no one was around, but to be honest, as amazing as the sex was, it wasn't really about that with us. It was more about just being together. Us, just being Kier and Dale, and forgetting everything else going on round about us.

As we continued through our coffee and muffins, Dale stopped speaking and just kind of stared at me, not in a bad way, just stared at me.

"What you looking at handsome?" I grinned at him with a cheeky glint in my eye.

Dale cupped his hand as always around my face and kissed me softly on the lips, "I'm looking at the most beautiful woman I have ever met. I love you so much Kier."

I bite my lip and smiled, and mimicking his actions, I kissed him back, "Well you are the most amazing man I've ever met, and into the bargain, you are ridiculously good looking." I giggled, and I swear I even frightened myself with how girly I sounded.

Dale flashed me the biggest grin I had ever seen and then laughed, "What a statement Miss Scott. Wow." And again he leaned over and kissed me. It was times like this it was hard to take in the fact we shouldn't be doing this, to realise that even though it felt like he was mine, he wasn't. My face must've changed because Dale changed his expression too.

"I know what you're thinking Kier. I feel the same. We're here, laughing and joking, loving being in each other's company, and from a distance, anyone looking in from the outside, would think we were the perfect match, the happiest two people in the world. Little did they know that when I leave you at night I have to keep missing you, and feeling like all I want to do is wrap my arms around you because then I can feel like me again. It's like there is this choice to be made, I can either make myself so unbelievably happy and be with you, or I can stay where I am and make sure my boys are happy. And I know Kier you would never make me choose, and if I was with you I could see my boys as much as I wanted, but I wouldn't be there everyday to see them smile, or to make sure Kaih was doing ok if he felt ill, or anything like that. I can't stand the thought of another man taking my place, playing dad with my boys. But at the same time, it kills me that if I'm not with you, you will be with someone else, and I'll have to imagine them touching you and kissing you and loving you in the way I want to. And I hate bringing this up because I love spending time with you, and I love every second I have with you. "

I just smiled at him; I didn't know what else to do apart from just smile at him.

"Dale please stop worrying. We can go round in circles 100 times, like we have 100 times before, but nothing is going to make this any easier. You don't have any choice to make. I understand where I stand with you, I know that you need to be with your boys and you need to do the right thing for you, I understand that more than you can imagine." I kissed him lightly on the nose before he spoke

"But Kier, what if what's right for me is you?" Dale, again, stared straight at me.

"Then I will be here for you forever and always, for the rest of my life." I couldn't have put it any simpler.

"Do you mean that? I mean, you're not going to come to your senses one day and realise what am I doing with him?" Dale sounded almost worried.

"Dale, I'm sorry to say this, but I love you, and no matter what the future holds for us, I am going to continue to love you, now, forever and for always. You are the love of my life, you are my soul mate. My true love. Can I make it anymore clear?"

And this time he didn't speak, he just embraced me in a kiss that allowed me to know he believed every word I was saying, that let me see that he loved me in a way I love him, he wanted me, needed me exactly the same way I needed him. And for that, as much as I didn't think it was possible, I loved him more.

"I love you." I whispered softly, still allowing my lips to touch his.

"D T O." He smiled

"D T O?" I questioned him, not really knowing what those three letters stood for.

"Well instead of saying Ditto, it's like our own little language if we simply shorten it to DTO." Dale laughed, and looked a little coy.

"I love it, almost as much as I love you. So that can be added to our little brackets." I made the sign with my hands.

"Yip, just for me and you. Those two brackets will forever represent the bond that is always going to be between us." Dale kissed me on the forehead and slowly ran his fingers through my hair.

"God I love you. I could say that a million times and never be able to say it enough for you to know how I feel about you. My heart will belong to you forever and a day." I realised how depressing we were getting, again, so I leaned over and gave him a massive smacker of a kiss, and then laughed. And while he laughed at me, I lifted a piece of muffin, and crumbled it over his head. And that did it, Dale erupted into laugher and I couldn't help but do the same.

"Kier, you're the most wonderful, fantastic, amazing princess I've ever met." Dale had the biggest grin on his face and had the expression of a kid in a sweet shop.

We continued to laugh like that for a few hours before Dale looked at his watch and realised it was 23:08pm. He screwed up his face, and then spoke,

"That's the problem with you Kier, there is never enough time. I should've been home by 10pm, but I just couldn't bear to say goodbye, again. I've got a proposition for you, how about, the weekend after Easter, you and I spend it together, the whole weekend? I'm sure I can make an excuse, or sort something out. And we'll go away, Vermont, Connecticut, anywhere outside the city, just me and you for two whole nights together." Dale moved closer to me as he asked this.

"Dale are you serious? I would love that? Honestly, I would love to spend time with you again. I mean Rome was amazing, but obviously we had to watch our backs a little, but this would be just you and me right?" Now I was getting excited. The prospect of a whole weekend with him was too much to take in. Up until a few weeks ago, we were supposed to be over, and now we're going away for a weekend together. This was insane, but to be honest, I wasn't sure when it would all be ending again, and I wanted to have every moment I could with him.

Dale was grinning, and looking at me with that same cheeky boyish glint in his eye. "Good. Then that is exactly what we will do. A weekend with you sounds like heaven. Knowing I don't have to say goodbye, knowing that I can just be with you, no distractions, no interruptions, just undisturbed Kier time." Dale's grin was one that I hadn't seen before. Although I believed him every time he told me he loved me, for the first time I really felt like he saw me as his everything, that to him, I meant everything. Without realising it was happening, my eyes were welling up and I had a tear dropping down my face. The grin on Dale's face turned to a look of worry, "Why are you crying Kier. Have I upset you, I just thought you would be as excited as me about spending one whole weekend together. I'm sorry if that's too much, if I'm pushing you for too much. I'm such an idiot sometimes." Dale dropped his head, but before he sunk deep, I grabbed both sides of his face, and smiled through the tears.

"I can't believe this is actually happening, but these are tears of joy; actual happiness brimming out of me. I have never felt like I'm, I don't know, special, or that I really mean that much to someone, but hearing you say those amazing words, seeing you say them with such conviction, I finally feel that I do. And it's just made me fall in love with you all the more." I had the biggest smile on my face as I said this. I could actually feel this massive beam of light shining from me and making me feel so unbelievably alive. I couldn't hold back, I wrapped my arms around his neck, pulled him close and kissed him with more sincerity than I had ever kissed anyone. Deep inside I knew I was where I was supposed to be, with the man I loved, the man I wanted to spend my life with and regardless of the current situation we were in, I was happy he was at least mine in some way.

CHAPTER TWENTY-TWO

The countdown was on. In three weeks we would be heading to Vermont for the weekend and I would have Dale all to myself. Work had been completely insane over the last few weeks. I was still staying as far away from Suranne as possible, and I had almost aliened myself from the other four girls. I still saw Ashleigh but I was so busy between my work for Rory White, Kiss me Cupid and the orders coming in for dresses that I literally went into the office at 7, and left at 10...granted between 7pm and 10pm, I was generally hauled up in Dale's office kissing him, chatting and basically just falling even more in love with him. I was in the work room one Tuesday afternoon and was shocked to see Sophie in too.

"So have you been kept busy?" I hated making idle chit chat with any of them, well aside from Ashleigh, but I felt I had to at least try.

"Well, not as busy as some, but doing ok." The tone of her voice was a little off and slightly unnerved me a little.

"That's good. You're designs great." Ok, I was lying and even I wouldn't have believed what I was saying. My voice went weird and I kind swallowed hard after the sentence.

"Thanks. I do work my ass off, and I've had so many orders." Now I knew she was lying. Dale told me that Sophie had been doing the worst out of us and had literally sold nothing of her own fashion range, and had only sold a minimum of her sportswear.

"Well that's good. Go you. I've been doing well too, Rome really worked in my favour." I was definitely forcing the conversation and wished to God I hadn't bothered asking her anything at all.

"Yeah would've been good actually going to Rome, could've picked up some more clients, networked a little, but we can't all be Dale's favourite can we." Sophie drew me a sarcastic glance and I tried to remain calm.

"I don't know what you mean. I was invited to Rome because of interest in my designs, nothing more. In fact I barely saw Dale in Rome, in fact I barely saw anyone, we were all so busy." My blood was boiling. I couldn't believe she was saying this.

"Ha." She said this with the most sarcastic undertone to her voice that I really don't know how I refrained from taking my hand across her face. Ok, I had a cheek, Dale and I were heavily involved in, as much as I hated to say it, an affair, but he never favoured me over anyone. I got to go to Rome because I worked my ass off and I was the best out of that group, the only one to actually be making a success of the sports label, as well as making designs for more areas of DB Designs. This annoyed me. I wasn't involved with Dale for success, I was involved with him because I was completely in love with him, Sophie was going by hearsay, stupid gossip and I couldn't handle it.

"I don't know what you're implying Sophie, but to be honest, I don't like it. I am not going to deny the fact that Dale and I are friends; in fact I'd go as far as to say good friends, but that's because I make the effort to speak to him. I speak to him about things that don't include work. We have a lot of interests the same, mainly due to the fact I play basketball and so does his youngest son." I was trying so hard to sound like I wasn't trying to defend myself, but more just try and tell the truth. Now it was my turn to laugh...the truth! If I told the truth I would look like some tramp who was after Dale for his money, or to get me a step ahead in my career, and I didn't want it to be viewed like that. Not at all. I love Dale because he's just Dale. I think by me putting the Rory White clothing under his company it more than proved that.

"Well whatever Kier. Everyone is talking about the closeness of you and Dale's relationship. So if you are trying to sleep with him to get a head of the game it's obviously working. Maybe I should try and work my magic with him." Sophie has a sly smile across her face that made me feel like slapping her, but I knew I had to remain calm. I couldn't give anything away that would indicate that anything was happening between Dale and I. So I took a deep breathe, disguised it as much as possible and simply said,

"Yeah maybe you should. You could ask him down here late on one night to check your designs and then screw him over your work desk." I said this with just the right amount of venom that allowed me to get my annoyance out, but still not seem like I cared about Dale in any way.

Sophie took the bait, looked disgusted and immediately launched the offensive,

"I wasn't implying I was going to do anything of the sort. Jesus, Kier, take a joke. Anyway, I was trying to give you a heads up. People are talking about how close you and Dale are, and that you got to go to Rome, and that it's your designs that are being chosen left, right and centre, so just be careful is all I'm saying. We wouldn't want anything stopping you being an amazing designer."

Up until the last sentence I was actually starting to believe that Sophie was being genuinely nice and was trying to help me out, but the last sentence sounded like a threat from someone whose own jealousy was getting the better of them. I decided to take the high road.

"Well you know what Sophie, I know my designs are good. And I know I could be great, and I definitely don't have to have some kind of affair with a married man to do that, so anything you think, or any jealous feelings you have bubbling below the surface, keep them there. I am a great designer, Rory White thinks so, Keep me Cupid thinks so, and you know what, Dale thinks so, so I don't need to "sleep" with him to get him to like what I'm doing." Ok, so I got the defensive up, but I was only saying the truth, minus the sleeping with Dale part of course. Sophie looked taken a back, obviously thinking she would strike some level of fear into me with her empty threat, and shocked when I retaliated with a level of assuredness in my own ability that would rival anything she could throw at me. She simply mumbled under her breath, picked up some sketches and left the work room. I felt proud of myself for standing up to her, for being strong enough to not back down. I knew people would talk, because human nature is to look from the outside, judge, make assumptions and well, bitch.

As I watched her leave, I took my iPod out, and put it in my ears. I didn't want to be rude when she was in, but music soothes me, and lets me push myself a little bit more. I must've got lost in my own thoughts, because I didn't realise Sophie and Suranne had come into the work room, or that Suranne was looking through all of my sketches while I had my back to her. Needless to say I almost had a heart attack when I turned round and she was standing.

"Whoh! God Suranne, you scared me. Everything ok?" I never had much to say to Suranne after the way she had treated me over the past few months. She had gone from someone who I looked up to, to being someone that to be honest, I had grown to loath. And she was another one who made a lot of judgements regarding Dale and I. Sasha has told me she overheard a conversation with her saying she thought it was disgusting the way we acted around each other and that she would make sure she put a stop to it sooner or later. I have to admit I was worried by this statement but she said it way before Rome and it was obviously just her ranting and relieving some steam. Anyway, she kind of looked me up and down with her usual smug expression and continued to look through my work.

"It does seem strange to me that you are the one designing the new collection for Rory White, when it is Sophie here who is our snow queen." She said this in her usual icy tone. "I struggle to understand how it suddenly came about that it was your designs that were chosen when, well, you don't design winter clothing." She sounded so cutting, as though she was accusing me of something.

I remained calm and composed.

"It wasn't actually winter wear he noticed. It was my skate gear he liked and enquired if it would be possible for something similar to be designed in snow clothing material. Simple as that." Ok I have to admit, I was being slightly sarcastic, but over the last few months I had lost all respect for Suranne. She was the most jealous woman I had ever met and that didn't compute in my mind. She was supposed to be my mentor, but seemed to do everything in her power to bring me down further and further. No way was I going to let her, I was stronger than that, stronger than she was, and just because she was failing in her career, I would not let her bring me down. She was still sifting through my designs, when I decided to add a bit more.

"Is there something wrong that I can help you with Suranne?" I didn't like her snooping around; I didn't trust her looking at what I was doing.

"No, nothing at all Kier. Just being nosey I suppose. What are these for?" She had picked up a few dress designs that I was working on following on from the success of the ones that had been snapped up for the Oscars. Two of the actresses had requested that I make them a few more dresses for any up and coming events that they would be attending, so I had gotten a head start. I explained this to Suranne, noticing her face go more red and more red with every word from my mouth.

"Mmm." She looked angry, "So you are designing for a band, you are designing for a snowboarder, you are designing for awards and what about the work you were actually brought here to do, managed any of that?" She looked at me again with the same self-righteous look she got when she thought she was going to catch me out. Little did Suranne know that I had completed both my spring collection and summer collection and was half way through my autumn and winter collection. The pieces had all been made, and approved, not by Dale, but by three of the Chief Designers, Julie, Trevor and Norm. I wanted to keep things as professional as possible, and had spoken to Julie regarding my "relationship" with Suranne, who gave me approval to go over her head at anytime I felt I had to, which I have to be honest, allowed me to breathe a sigh of relief. I took every part of my self-control not to brag and rub Suranne's face in it as I pulled the rails of clothes from my cupboard at the back of the room and sifted through them, pointing out details, adding in some comments and really strengthening how the design had a degree of cohesion through the various seasons.

"Quite the little worker aren't we?" Suranne was angry. I could see fire in her eyes and she was not impressed. "And how do you get time to design such a diverse range. I mean sportswear, casual wear, formal wear; it's a lot of work." I knew she wasn't being nice, and she wasn't trying to act like she was either. I looked at Sophie who looked at me, again with certain slyness in her eyes. I wondered how much she had said to Suranne regarding our previous conversation before she left the workroom. I wasn't going to tempt the beast out of Suranne, but instead play it down and let her ask the questions.

"What can I say Suranne, I love my job, and well, evidently I am very suited to what I do." I was calm. I had an image of Dale in my head and I focussed on that to keep myself in control. Even when he wasn't around he managed to soothe me.

"Playing much basketball or anything these days?" Suranne quizzed, and I knew a look of confusion was on my face. Why the sudden jump from my designs to my sport? It took about three seconds to click that she was trying to work out how I could design so much and play sport. I couldn't believe this. My guessing was Sophie had spread her little theories to Suranne and now she was allowing her mind to wander on overtime. No way was I going to lie down to this, Dale and I were having an affair, yes, but he had never once helped me with my designs, not in anyway. I worked 12-hour days; I pushed myself harder than any of the rest of them, so of course I was going to do better. And as it stood I still went to B-Ball training four times a week, granted on the Tuesday I went from 17:30 – 19:30 and generally caught up with Dale for a quick hour after, same with a Thursday, and a Saturday and Sunday I was still playing three hours each morning, and occasionally a Saturday afternoon game too. I wasn't about to back down, I just told the truth.

"Yeah I still train two nights during the week and a Saturday and Sunday too. Why?" If she wanted to nosey into my life I was certainly going to quiz her on it.

"Hmmm. four days training and you manage to design all of these too?" She said it in the most sarcastic tone yet, with an underlying implication that I was up to no good.

"Funnily enough Suranne, yes I do. I don't really have a social life, I design, I play basketball, I skate to and from work, and on the rare occasion I can, I go to the Broadway Dance Studio for a class. Do you want me to write you my weekly schedule?" I realised I was being off with her, but I was getting so angry. What a bitch.

"There is no need to be rude Kier. I was only asking as a

matter of interest." Suranne gave me a smile that would put the devil to shame. I tried to rise above her, I tried to not react but the way she was trying to imply that I was "cheating" at my job was too much.

"Yeah, a matter of interest Suranne, I'm sure. And have you been asking Sophie, or Ashleigh or any of the others these same questions? Maybe you struggle to keep up with us budding designers, but I don't. My talent and skill are what drives me forward and I'm not ashamed to admit that. What some people design in three hours I can do in one. I'm in this work room three days a week for twelve hours and two days for ten hours, so is it any wonder I manage to crank out a hell of a lot of work?" I realised my hackles were up and I needed to bring myself back down before it seemed like I was trying to defend myself. "Sorry if I sound a little off Suranne but to me it sounds like your being a little, I don't know, accusing towards me, when really you have nothing to accuse me of, except being the best designer on this team. And I know I sound extremely full of myself, but I know I am damn good at my job, and I'm proud of that. So, before you start throwing accusations my way, because I know that's what you're getting at, I work my ass off to achieve what I have, and the fact I still train four times a week just means I give up something else to allow me to do that. As you know I'm single at the moment, so I don't have to give any time up to see a boyfriend. I prioritise my life so I can do everything in my power to make myself always be at the top of my game, and if that means sacrificing a love life, and drunken nights out then I'll do it. Simple." Oh dear God Kier, you've just given an Oscar speech. I almost rolled my eyes at myself, but my eyes were fixated on Suranne's. I don't think she knew how to take what I had just said. I could tell her mind was working in overtime to process the vast amount of information I had just divulged to her. She kept going to speak, or at least she looked like she was and then she kind of stopped herself. This happened about four times, but she finally opened her mouth and allowed some words to come out.

"Well Kier it's good to see you're dedicated to what you do. But, I wouldn't big yourself up so much." Suranne got the same evil glint in her eye, "I think we're all aware of how close a friendship you have with Dale, and I don't think I'm the only one who thinks you may have an unfair advantage perhaps over some others in this office." Her voice remained calm, with that same tone that made me feel highly uncomfortable. I couldn't believe she was saying this, couldn't believe she was implying I got extra help, and what unsettled me more was that she said she wasn't the only one who thought this. Ok, she could be exaggerating, but I was panicking, though somehow, managing to remain calm and composed.

"Nice, Suranne." I was of course being completely sarcastic, "It's great to know my mentor has such faith in my abilities. Honestly, big thumbs up to your encouragement." Now I had gone beyond being rude, but I couldn't believe what I was listening to. Was she being serious? Dale hadn't even made any changes to my designs, they were 100% me. He had however given Ashleigh a load of help with her upcoming summer collection, and he had given the other three loads of advice. In fact he had meetings with the other four regarding their work and how he could help. This was ridiculous, and no way was I going to lie down and listen to it.

"I don't care if you dislike me Suranne, I don't care if you think my designs are the biggest load of nonsense you have ever seen, but don't ever, and I mean it, ever, make assumptions based on hearsay regarding my work effort. I have poured every ounce of my entire being into this job from the day I started and the fact I have a friendship with the owner of the company does not give you the right to assume he is pulling me through. As far as I know the other four have had more help from Dale than me, they have had meetings with him, design consults and what have I had aside from a few times he's popped down and gave me a thumbs up or simply approved something I have done. Like I said Suranne, I am damn good at my job, and I am not going to be made out to be a cheat or a fraud. I work my ass off for this company, I've secured some very lucrative deals, and all of which I could've produced through my own name, but didn't because I work for this company. So unless I'm getting some backhanded extra wage that I don't know about, I think you owe me an apology." I wasn't standing for this. Suranne could only push me so far, but I knew in my heart how hard I worked. Regardless of my relationship with Dale, this had nothing to do with my work load – and her implying that was making me slightly uneasy about Dale. I loved him with all my heart, and I was worried how this would affect him, how he would be feeling. I mean, would he panic? Would he run from me? Would this make him feel like we really couldn't go on anymore? I knew what we were doing was wrong, and I knew it could end at any moment, but would talk like this make it happen sooner? I couldn't let Suranne away with this; I had to take some kind of action. Suranne started speaking, but I wasn't really paying attention. She wasn't backing down, I could hear that much, so I decided to step in.

"Do you know what Suranne, if you are so sure I'm doing something so underhand, so wrong, then fine, let's go and speak to Dale and you can make these same accusations to him?" I smirked at her, and I could see straight away she started to squirm.

"Oh Kier, let's not be rash." Suranne was growing increasingly uncomfortable, and I could see that although she was quite happy to bully me, she hadn't quite expected me to come back and challenge her. "I mean, I'm just trying to make you aware of what has been said around the office. I don't want you feeling under pressure, or having to get caught up in a mess that is nothing to do with you." She was sweating now, I could feel her worrying, in fact I was pretty sure I could hear her heart pounding through her chest. I could've let it go there, could've been nice and said fine, leave it at that, but this person, this woman was trying to make me look to be an idiot, a fraud in the one field I know I excel in, so no way was I going to let it go now.

"Suranne, no disrespect to you, but you were the one throwing accusations at me a little over ten minutes ago, so in my eyes, that is you trying to put me under pressure. Regardless of your apologies, or your fake words of assurance that you are actually trying to help me, I don't really buy it. So, let's just go upstairs and speak to Dale regarding this, because I'm sure he would like these rumours put to bed too." I couldn't believe how strong I was being. I am well-known as the girl who, when faced with confrontation, tends to burst out crying and just agrees with whatever everyone is saying, but not with this. I felt like I had to stand up and protect Dale, I had to stand up and make sure everything would be ok with him.

I stared at Suranne. The colour had completely drained from her face, and I could see the terror in her eyes, the dread at her having to face her boss with these "accusations" and I knew at that moment she didn't really believe what she was saying, but I knew I had to keep going with it.

"So let's go Suranne, or would you rather I just speak to Dale on my own?" I remained calm, I remained composed and I knew Suranne believed 100% that I had nothing to hide. I stared at her waiting for an answer, but she just stared between myself, and Sophie, who herself was looking a little worried and obviously hoping she wasn't going to be drawn into this. "Ready?" I smiled towards Suranne, knowing how uncomfortable she was and wanting to seem as relaxed as possible, when, in reality, my heart was racing faster than it ever had and I was pretty sure I was about to have a heart attack.

"Kier, come on, let's not do anything we are going to regret later. It was a simple misunderstanding. There is no need to bother Dale, I'm sure he's very busy." I could hear her voice shaking, the tone was rushed and completely out with her control. I almost felt sorry for her, but I just stayed focussed on her accusing me of being a fraud. Me! My relationship with Dale may be a secret, but it wasn't a secret because I was getting some extra help or because I had the upper hand on people. Dale would never do anything to give me any sort of advantage, and he knows I would never expect one. I mean the only time he has ever done anything for me that wasn't for someone else, was with Rory White, and I think by me showing that I wasn't interested in working myself, it clearly showed that I'm not using his position to further my own gains. To me Dale was just Dale. He isn't some famous designer who can further my career. Not at all and that is exactly why I was going to make Suranne face him.

"This is not something I will regret later, not at all. I just want Dale to be aware of the type of staff he has. I'm sure you're all aware of his feelings on disloyalty. I'm going just now anyway, with or without you." I was feeling so strong. I wished I could've quickly sent Dale a text to warn him, but I didn't think I could without raising suspicion from Suranne, so it was a case of hoping he would pick up on that almost ESP that we seem to have and know to just go with me on whatever I was saying.

"Are you coming?" Secretly I hoped she wouldn't, that I could speak to Dale myself, but to my surprise, she just muttered under her breath, "Let's get this over with."

CHAPTER TWENTY-THREE

Dale's office is only a short walk from the workroom, but I swear I felt like I was running a marathon. I was terrified of slipping up, of Dale taking me saying something the wrong way and admitting everything. Although, I'm sure my heart wasn't going anywhere near as fast as Suranne's. She actually looked like she was going to be sick. Yet again, I almost felt sorry for her, but the dislike I felt for her over shadowed this, and to be honest I was struggling to care.

As we got to Dale's office I could see him through the window and noticed an intense look on his face. He had Paula and another manager Derek in with him. When he saw me, I could see him quickly rounding up the conversation, and leading the two of them out the door, but he looked shocked when he noticed Suranne coming behind me.

"Kier, Suranne, what a pleasant surprise. What can I do for you?" Dale about turned and walked behind his desk and sat down. I tried to catch his eye, and try and almost prompt him to what was coming, "My room has been like a revolving door today." He smiled, and even given the circumstances, I completely melted as always. My God was he gorgeous; I actually couldn't believe sometimes he wanted me!

"Ok, Dale. I'm not on here on the best of terms, unfortunately." I looked at him seriously, making sure I didn't stare too deeply into his eyes like I do when we are alone.

Dale squinted and dropped his eyebrows, "I'm sorry to hear that Kier, nothing serious I hope?" I could tell he was slightly panicking, so I just let it out.

"Well, it seems that some people in this office are misunderstanding our friendship as something more. In actual fact, there are people in this office who feel that I am being given a certain "advantage" over other people, perhaps getting some help with my designs or my work load?" I remained composed throughout the whole speech, making sure to sound as light-hearted about the situation as possible, "So, obviously, I'm a little annoyed that people are making their own assumptions from what can only be regarded as hearsay."

Dale stared at me, obviously searching for how best to react to the situation. And like a pro, he laughed and allowed a smile to spread across his face.

"You're actually kidding, right?" He said this in a joking way, obviously following on from my own light-hearted tone.

"I wish I was Dale. Obviously, some people have a problem with a male and a female being friends. Either that or they have a problem with someone excelling in their chosen profession, which I'm sure you won't mind me saying, I do." I was shaking, but I was determined to sound as self-assured in myself as I wanted everyone else to believe I was. I could feel Dale almost sending me some kind of comfort just from the look in his eyes that, in a strange way, almost felt like he was holding me.

Dale didn't say anything for a few seconds, before he just kind of grinned, "Well Kier, evidently I don't know my staff as well as I thought, or at least I thought I had employed staff who weren't so narrowed minded. It's a little disappointing to be honest. And I'm guessing Suranne is here to back up what people have been saying?"

Now it was my turn to laugh, "Actually Dale, and this is definitely a disappointing part, Suranne has been one of the ones making comment regarding your and my friendship. You see, Suranne seems to think I shouldn't be able to make my way through so many designs, have so much work on and still be able to keep training playing basketball. She made a reference earlier and this is why I thought it best to come to speak to you direct. To be honest, it wasn't just Suranne; Sophie was also making a few comments with regards to my workload. I did try to make them see that, without sounding cocky, that I excel in this field of work, and I also work close to 60-hour weeks so that I can get through the amount of work I do. I also sacrifice having too much of a social life so that I can design and do basketball, because to me these are what matters, not going out and getting wasted on a Saturday night." I smiled at Dale, proud of myself for keeping my cool, remaining calm, and at the same time, knowing I was protecting him from the vicious rumours that Suranne was trying to create.

Again Dale went quiet, and the smile on his face dropped, his eyebrows lowered and he had a look on his face I hadn't seen before. For the first time he looked angry, and I knew it wasn't with me. He stared straight at Suranne and I could see he was clenching his teeth and tensing his jaw.

"This is completely unacceptable, you do realise that Suranne?" She was about to answer, but Dale continued to speak. "You are a member of my senior staff, more than that you are a trusted employee, a mentor to these new girls, and you do this. What exactly is your thinking can I ask?" Dale had venom in his voice, a tone I wasn't used to hearing from him.

Suranne was squirming; she looked completely uncomfortable, completely uneasy.

"Dale, I think Kier may have got a little confused. I was merely trying to ask how she managed to fit everything in. She does in fact have a very busy schedule, and I was simply making a comment on that. I think she just got a little mixed up." Suranne sounded so smug, that I couldn't stop myself from butting in.

"So making comment about my busy schedule includes making comment about my "close friendship" with Dale." Now I was clenching my jaw. I saw Dale stare at me, and although his face didn't change I could sense he was thanking me for sticking up for the situation.

Suranne didn't say a word. She dropped her head and I think she sensed she was in trouble. Yes Dale and I were having an affair, but this wasn't what this was about. It was about the fact that she was making it out my work wasn't my own, and that I wasn't going to let go.

"Suranne I'm sure you know how big I am on loyalty." Dale's face was focussed on hers, although she herself still fixed her eyes at the ground. "And this is completely against everything I ask for from my employees. Kier has been one of the best designers I have found in years. Her natural ability to succeed and to design high-end creations is something that has completely impressed me. Add that into her love of sport of course we were going to have a friendship, we have a lot in common, as do you and Nigel, but no one makes reference to an apparent affair there. I have never given Kier any help with her designs, I have never set up any sales meeting, it has been all her. She works more hours than anyone because she wants this, and I think even you know that. So what is this, some kind of petty jealousy? Are you threatened by a fresh talent? If Kier and I were having an affair, that still wouldn't be anyone's business. We both have morals and I don't think either of us would use each other to gain any advantage. I'm sure Kier made you aware that Rory White wanted to wear designs by Kier Scott, not DB Designs, but Kier made it clear she designed for us. I was happy to let her go but she is a loyal employee and she wanted our backing. I am not about to stand by and allow you or anyone else in this office for that matter, accusing her of something that she hasn't done. Our friendship is completely separate from work, and I am not about to deny the fact that I have a great amount of time for Kier as a person, but that doesn't mean I give her any sort of advantage. She would never ask and I would never give. She doesn't need to. This girl is an amazing designer, in fact she is better than me at what she does and I am proud that we have got her as an employee, and as her mentor, you should've been proud of that too, not try to bring her down." I was staring straight at Dale and couldn't believe what he was saying. He wasn't trying to deny we were friends, and he was happily calling me amazing out loud. I thought he was done, but was shocked to hear what came next.

"As it stands, I was aware of people making comments, that is why Paula and Derek were in before, warning me to be careful with Kier, and they were told the same thing. I can be friends with who I like, and whether she is an employee, or the fact she is younger than myself, or female for that matter, doesn't make a difference. We have a bond of friendship, big whoop." I laughed a little at the "whoop". "I will not stand here and be accused of helping someone more than I help others. To be honest, I think I have given the rest of your team more help. Kier is the one person who I do not discuss work or have to give any extra help to. So why not pull the other four girls up and see what they have to say, see how much help I've given them, see how many designs they sell without my help. I'm sure you can tell from my tone Suranne I am not happy. In fact I am worse than not happy. You are trying to make comment on my integrity and that's something I can't stand for." Dale ran his fingers through his hair, and again clenched his teeth. He looked towards me, and un-tensed his glare, "Thanks Kier, I know how hard it can be standing up to a figure of authority, especially someone who is supposed to be your mentor. You can go back to the workroom, and please accept my apologies for having to listen to this nonsense. Suranne, I'd like you to stay for the time being." Dale ushered me out of the room, lightly touching my shoulder, and allowing me to feel that he was still there for me. "Keep up the good work." I smiled at him, and allowed my lips to move but only slightly so he could see me say "I love you" and in response he merely mouthed, "DTO". I walked away smiling inside, but tried to keep my face fixed on being angry. I couldn't believe Suranne had tried to make it out it was in my imagination, that I was making it up. As I walked into the work room, I grabbed my phone and sent Dale a quick text message,

"Thank you for that. You really are amazing and MTL for always ( )" The MTL simply meant my true love. I had never text that before, and was interested to see if he would work out what it was. I should've have, but sent it to his normal phone, knowing I was in it as a different name anyway, and was pleasantly surprised when he text back almost immediately saying, "DTO u r my true love too." I was on cloud nine and I don't think the smile was going to leave my face, even more so when he text again saying, "I want to see you later, BT." I assumed the BT meant Big Time and just replied "DTO".

CHAPTER TWENTY-FOUR

I worked around in the work room for another five hours, which passed without me realising it. My iPod, as always, was glued to my ears and I was shocked when I felt a tap on the shoulder and turned round to see Dale standing in front of me.

"God, Dale, you gave me a fright." I smiled, and brushed against him.

"You go into that little world of your own all the time don't you. Look at how much you've done today, yet again. You are amazing you know that, I wasn't lying when I said that to Suranne." Dale kissed me lightly on the lips and as he pulled away smiled, which was completely catching, as I found the same look on my own face.

"Thank you for that. I know that situation wasn't the best, but if I had lain down to Suranne I feared she would assume that you were helping me out, or giving me an unfair edge, or worse, clicked on to us." I was trying to almost explain myself in case Dale was annoyed at me for saying anything.

"Hey, stop that. I'm glad you done it. After my conversation with Paula and Derek I was slightly worried about how you would feel about everything. I was so angry at Suranne today. I can't believe she had the audacity to try and bully you, to actually try to suggest you don't do all your own work. It's ridiculous for her to imply that and no way is she getting away with it. I'm glad you came and spoke to me, and even more so that you brought her along. She is an idiot. She's has been spreading these rumours around the office now for weeks, since before Rome. Idiot." Dale's face was going red and I could tell he had anger surging through his veins. I placed my hand on his face and kindly traced his eyebrow with my finger, as I always did and I could feel him relax as a smile crept across his face.

"Thanks." He grinned. "I just can't believe out of jealousy or whatever it is, she does that. And Sophie better watch herself as well. That girl has been getting pulled through the job. Anyway, I'm going to be making a few changes and

Suranne is in hot water as far as I'm concerned." I wrapped my arms around Dale's neck and kissed him, actually for a moment forgetting we were still in work, but quickly pulling away again.

"God, I'm so sorry Dale. I got a bit carried aware there, forgot we were working." I laughed nervously.

"Kier, it's 8pm, everyone is long gone." He laughed and wrapped his arms around me and squeezed tight. "God I love you so much Kier. So much." He kissed me passionately on the lips and I felt a little shocked. As he pulled away, I stared at him.

"Where did that come from?" I smiled but with what I could tell was a shocked look on my face

"Because you're you, and I'm crazy about you." He kissed my nose and jumped himself up to sit on my work bench. He was like a kid, acting a little mischievous. "You make me feel alive I suppose. You're amazing."

I just kind of giggled, "And you, Mr Brenton, are crazy. But I guess I'm crazy about you too." I smiled, but then a wave of sadness gripped me, "Dale, if people are starting to talk now, what if someone finds out about us? I mean I know Paula and your wife are friendly, what if she mentions anything to her? What if she tries to take the boys away from you and stops you seeing them? I don't know if I could handle having caused that for you."

Dale's smile faded. The high he was on seemed to hit rock bottom in a matter of seconds.

"I know, Kier. I know how bad this could get if it got out, but that's a big if. I just don't know how to let you go. I mean I know I could risk losing my boys, but I don't know how to risk losing you. When we ended it after Rome, it was so hard. I missed you so much all the time, every minute of the day, and I don't know how to feel like that again." I could see the tears stinging Dale's eye, could see the sadness he was feeling, in fact I could feel it because it was exactly how I felt. Scared, lost and alone, that's the three words that match with a life without Dale.

"I don't want you to risk everything. I just want you to do what is right for you. Forget about everything else."

For over a minute he was silent, he stared at the ground and I didn't try to approach him either. I gave him his time, and eventually he spoke.

"Like I said, what if you are what's right for me?" Dale looked at me with the most serious face I'd ever seen.

I didn't respond straight away, not because I didn't want to, but because I wanted the words I said to be as perfect as the words he had just said.

"Then, like I said, I will be here for you forever. I will be there every morning, I will love you every day, and I will show you how lucky I am to have you every second." I kissed him lightly, but knew I had to say more, "But, you and I both know it's not really an option for you and I to be together just now. Those boys need you Dale, they really need you. I need you because I love you, but they need you to make them strong young men, to mould them into fantastic people like you are." I tried to hold back the tears, tried to say the words without allowing my voice to break.

Dale looked at me, slightly confused, "What does that mean then? We carry on as we are? We live a double life so we can be together?" Dale was panicking; I could hear his voice rush through the sentence in a state of worry.

I took a deep breath, knowing what I was about to say, but not really wanting to say it and I braced myself for the words to leave my mouth.

"I love you Dale, I do. I love you with such an unconditional love that I honestly didn't think it was possible. I didn't think I could love another human so completely that I would do anything for them, even something that would break me apart. But, I know you have a life without me, I know you had a life before I came along, and I have to take note of that. You have a wife who I know will love you, you have a family who need you more than I do, because I'm already moulded into me, and having been with you, even for this short time has moulded me so much more. I love you for that Dale, and I love you enough to let go. So after the weekend in Vermont I think that should be it. And this time we have to cut everything, no talking, no texting, nothing." I was now sobbing so hard that my whole body ached. Dale had wrapped his arms around me half way through the speech, in fact at one point he tried to make me stop but I knew I couldn't do this. People talking was bad enough, but what if it got out, then what? I couldn't do that to him.

"Kier you can't mean that. You can't mean no contact, we work together, we can't just miraculously ignore each other?" Dale was a mess. I could feel his heart breaking like it was my own. Could feel every single emotion that was surging through his body, because they were all the same as what I was feeling. I was now crying, harder than I think I ever had in my life.

"Dale, if there was any other option I would do it. I would do anything for you to be mine, just mine, but I can't be selfish, I can't take you away from your boys. You and I both know that's not what you want. I love you so much, honestly Dale, this isn't a way out. This isn't me thinking, oh, I'll just get rid of him, it's so not anywhere near that. I just can't do this anymore. I can't be afraid that something is going to happen that will mess up or complicate your life. I can't be the one responsible for messing things up for you." I was hurting so much just now. The tears felt like acid running down my face, and the pain in my chest was crushing me so much that I felt like I was going to collapse. I needed him to understand what I was saying. I pulled him towards me and kissed him with everything I had in me. I needed to show him I loved him and losing him was the same as someone taking away my heart. It felt raw, it felt painful and it felt wrong. I kissed him again, and this time I wrapped my whole being into him. I could feel him embrace me back, could feel his love for me pour into my body. And with that, suddenly both our tears stopped, and as we pulled away from each other, it seemed like that moment something clicked and we realised this was the right decision. The pain, the hurt, the heartache, everything, we just had to accept it all.

"You know this is right don't you." I was breathing deeply to allow me to talk, "This is no longer about you and I making ourselves happy, this about doing the right thing and making God step in, and if we are supposed to be together, it will happen." I sobbed again, but only lightly.

Dale stared at me for a bit, in fact for over a minute, then took a deep breath and smiled at me. He kissed me lightly on the nose, hugged me and then he spoke,

"I love you Kier, with every morsel of my being, but you're

right, we can't keep living this lie. For one, it's not fair on you. You are this amazing person, who deserves so much more than a part-time romance. But, I do want to be with you, when the time is right. I believe God has made us meet for some reason, and I believe it is so we can be together, just not right now. My boys are still so young and I need to be there every day for them. You understand that, I know you do. You've said so many times about your brother and his kids, so I'm sure you can imagine how hard it would be for me to just leave that whole atmosphere. To not hear Kaih every morning tell me something about basketball, or here Regan tell me how he destroyed some opponent at football, it would be too hard. Don't get me wrong, being with you would make all that easier, but that's completely selfish of me to want that." Dale laughed a little, "I'm rambling, aren't I. Anyway, what I'm trying to say is, I want you Kier, I would love you to be mine, I would love to walk into a room with you on my arm and be able to call you my wife." I smiled as Dale said this, and felt a wave of butterflies creep through my body; he wanted me to be his wife. Dale, again, kissed me lightly before continuing. "I know this is going to sound ridiculous, stupid, whatever, but obviously I need them to grow up into amazing men, I need to help them do that. In seven years those two will be men. They will be at College, living their own lives, and well, maybe then I can live mine. So, what I say is, let's meet, on the 17th of October, seven years from now, and then we can start our lives together, just like we said. I know it sounds extreme, and God I am asking a lot for you to hold off for seven years, but I can't see any other way. Once my boys are off living their own lives, I can just focus on mine and I want that to include you. I really want you to be there, experiencing everything with me." Dale looked serious and focussed. Me, I'm almost positive I had a look of confusion, excitement and heartbreak. I was excited about being with him one day but confused at the length of time and completely heartbroken at the thought of so long without him, but what else could we do? He was right and I was right, we couldn't continue on like this. Eventually people would get suspicious as to why I wasn't seeing anyone, or interested in seeing anyone. This really was the only way.

"I don't know what else to say Dale except, I would be there, no matter what. Yeah I'll probably have to move on, but if you ever came back, I would be yours, no questions asked. 100%. Forever." I was getting a little agitated because I knew this time when we stopped it would be it. I was playing with my hair and subconsciously biting my lip. Dale ran his fingers down the side of my face, and then cupped his hand round my cheek like he always done.

"I know this is hard Kier, it is not any easier for me, but I just know you are my destiny and this is the only way that we can be together. I wish it wasn't, I would love to just be able to sweep you off your feet, take you in my arms and love you forever, but at the moment that's not possible." His eyes were filled with tears, he was holding me so tight but it somehow felt comforting and I could tell this was wrecking his head. I wasn't about to be selfish, I wasn't about to make him choose me, and if I had to wait seven more years for him, then I'd wait the seven years.

"Ok. After the weekend away we end it. We go back to being just work colleagues, no texts, no calls, nothing. Giving up a few years to have you for life seems like a small sacrifice. I want you Dale. Just you. No other man has even made me feel like you do. No other man has even got me like you do. I'm not going to lie, I'm sure over the next seven years there will be other men, and I may find myself loving them in a way, but just be assured, none of them will compare to you. Even if you hear I'm ridiculously happy, or you see me and I seem happy, it will still always be you that I will want to be with. It will always be you that I want. You are the love of my life Dale Brenton, my true love, soul-mate, whatever way you put it, in my eyes you are number 1. I love you so much, and I know that will never change. Ever." I made it through the whole speech without allowing the tears to spill from my eyes. However, Dale hugged me, whispered "I love you" and of course I lost it, the strength I was clinging onto was gone and I allowed myself to be taken over by the heartbreak of having to face losing the love of my life yet again. There was no way of me saying anything else, getting anymore words out. This was hard. Harder than I thought it would be. So much for "just a bit of fun", I was the idiot who had to go and fall in love with him, especially when I knew the whole time he was married and he couldn't be mine. I guess this was just part of the package I was going to have to deal with.

We spoke some more and in typical fashion it was midnight before we left the office. Luckily Dale had called his wife and told her he wasn't going to be home until late on because he had a dinner meeting and he expected it to go on in to the early hours. I was glad, I felt like I needed as much time with him as I could get, especially if I was going to have to say goodbye in a little over three weeks.

He dropped me at my apartment and when I went in I went straight onto my laptop. The whole time I had spent with Dale over the last few hours I had a thought in the back of my mind about how hard it was going to be working in that office, having no contact with him, so it was time for me to do something about that. I had to find another place to work. I loved DB Designs, but I couldn't work there and still be in love with him. I knew my designs would suffer, and I would be a wreck all the time, I couldn't do that to myself, and I couldn't let him see me like that and make him feel like he had done that to me. To be honest I had been thinking about leaving for a while, thinking about trying to get into something else, go somewhere else. In actual fact only this morning I had emailed a family friend who works for a designer in Scotland. I know it's drastic, and moving 3000 miles away may be quite insane, but now it just seemed like a better option. I couldn't handle the thought of being near him if he wasn't mine, if we had no formal connection to each other. The last time was hard and at that time we were still speaking, meeting up, and still almost being us. And now what? Pretend I don't love him, pretend I don't care? I couldn't do that. I couldn't imagine doing that. The company in Scotland wasn't as big as DB Designs but I thought that I could at least get a fresh start, be away from Suranne, away from that "team" and just begin my life over. Little over six months ago everything in my life was perfect, I had a boyfriend I loved, started my dream job, and now it's all a mess. Suranne messing into Dale and I was just the start, I know it was. People would start to talk, they already were and I wasn't prepared to cause anymore upset in Dale's life than I needed too.

As I opened my emails, I was almost shocked to see I had a reply from David Masters, the CEO himself from the company in Scotland. Clicking to open it my heart stopped as I read on,

"Dear Kier,

Thank you for your interest in my company. I am very aware of the work you have been doing for DB Designs, and even more aware of the designs you have done for Rory White. I am actually quite shocked that you would be interested in coming to join such a small branch, given your already evident success. Having said that, I would be more than happy to welcome you on board and allow you to bring your flare and style to my growing brand. I will be in New York at the end of this week, and would love to meet you to discuss a start date.

Thank you again for your interest and I look very much forward to working with you in the near future.

Kind Regards,
David Masters"

I felt sick, I felt panicked and I felt shocked. I hadn't expected to hear back so quickly, and I definitely didn't expect a job offer. I couldn't do anything except stare at the screen. I hadn't mentioned this to anyone and I didn't quite know how to deal with what was happening. I had a new job! Confusion was taking over, my mind was going crazy and I really wasn't sure what to do, who to speak to, what to respond to the email. I had prayed to God to give me an answer on how to go forward with things, how to get passed this difficult stage in my life, and here it was, here was an answer and I was terrified of what that meant. Was this God's way of saying that Dale and I weren't meant to be together? That he wasn't my destiny? Or was it the opposite, that we needed this time apart. That this would allow things to settle down here and in eight years he would be mine. I really wasn't sure anymore. I had always put my faith in God, and I was willing to accept that he was making this happen for a reason. So I quickly typed a reply saying I was looking forward to meeting him and I was able to start with him as soon as he wanted me too. I hit send, and in typical Kier style, I burst out crying. This was all of a sudden very real; I was going back home, and this time for good, or at least for the foreseeable future. As strange as it was, the only person I could think to speak to was Louise, the other girl who worked in the office with Sasha. Over the last four weeks or so, we had been chatting a lot more, especially since Sasha was so wrapped up with Harry and I no longer saw her, and I knew it was almost a definite that Louise would still be awake at this time, she was a bit of a night owl like myself. I didn't want to risk waking her just in case, so I text and said needed to talk and to ring if she was up. I didn't have long to wait before my phone light up and showed Louise's name.

"Hey you, how ya doin?" I was trying to sound chirpy because I knew I was going to have to fake excitement of moving back home to Scotland.

"Hi Kier, I'm good, a little shocked to get a text off you at this time of night. Everything ok?" Louise sounded concerned which I felt bad about. I had obviously shocked her and she had instantly thought bad news.

I laughed a little, "Yeah everything is fine. Actually better than fine," I lied, "I, God I don't know how to say this, but I've been offered a new job and well, I'm leaving." I tried to fake the right amount of happiness and sound like this was something really amazing in my life.

I wasn't quite prepared for the scream that came down the phone, but Louise did tend to get over excited, I mean I hadn't even told her about the job, or where I was going.

"Kier, Wow. You must be so excited. Wait where is it, what is it, when are you leaving DB?" I didn't expect anything less from Louise, 101 questions was the norm for her.

"Ok, calm down, you're more excited than me." I giggled and noticed my voice was shaking. I had to pull it together. If I started to cry it would let the cat out the bag. "Ok, it's em, working for a Scottish designer, and it's doing a lot of the main designing for the brand, so I'd pretty much be head designer." I know I was lying through my teeth, but if I made this job out to be less than what I'm doing now people would guess instantly that something wasn't quite right about it, "I'm going to have complete control over my designs as well as helping a lot of others with theirs, and it's really an amazing opportunity for me to really get my teeth into something new. I mean obviously my work is coming to an end with Rory White, I've got gear designed for him until autumn, and well the rest of my work can easily be passed around to others, but this really is an opportunity I can't give up." The tears were stinging my eyes, and my chest hurt from holding back the urge to cry. I have to admit, Louise's excitement made me feel better and stopped the dull ache, if even for a minute.

"OMG Kier, that's phenomenal. You're going to be like a head designer. Oh man, everyone in there is gonna freak. Dale is gonna die, I mean we all know you're the best designer he has." And it was back, the very mention of his name and that aching in my chest suddenly felt like I was being stabbed by a million daggers. I composed myself enough to get the next words out, "He won't even notice I'm gone." The tears were stinging the skin on my face and I was broken. Louise couldn't see me, but I was lying curled up so tightly just trying to stop the pain in my chest.

"Of course he will. You're his buddy. Whose he gonna talk to now." I couldn't hide it, the tears grew and suddenly I sobbed down the phone, knowing I had to say something or else Louise would wonder what was going on.

"Louise stop, you're making me cry. I'm gonna miss everyone so much, even Dale and his boring Starbucks chats." I tried to laugh. Over the last few weeks Louise was always keen to know what Dale and I spoke about when we stood at Starbucks for elongated periods of time, and I simply said most of the time he bored me stupid talking about his son playing basketball, or mentioning something to do with his past as a football player, I tried to make it seem like he annoyed me more than anything else. "I can't believe I'm crying. I'm gonna get the chance to be so creative and it's going to be amazing." Louise butt in before I could add anymore,

"Yeah and you can still come and see us ALL the time."

Louise was so upbeat, but yet again I lost it.

"No I can't Louise. I doubt if I'll see many of you again." My words were broken, and I was shocked that she actually knew what I was saying.

"You're so dramatic Kier, you're not gonna be kept that busy that you can't come and grab lunch every now and then."

I breathed. I caught the breath that was creating the pain in my chest and push it out to allow me to talk.

"Louise, the job is back in Scotland. I'm moving home again."

Now it was her turn to be silent, her turn to gasp in shock and say nothing, well, for a few seconds anyway.

"Scotland? But Kier that's not your home, your home is here, in New York. You told me that yourself that you feel more like a New Yorker than a, what did you call it Wedgie?" Louise said the word like she was describing getting your underwear stuck up your butt. I have to admit it made me laugh and this time a real one.

"Louise, you're hilarious, I think you mean Weegie. You know like Glaswegian but shortened, and you're right. I've been a New Yorker for half my life, but sometimes I just miss home. And every time I go back for a visit I miss it more. I need to go back and see if I really am missing living there or not." I couldn't believe the lies coming from my mouth but I had to convince everyone that I was happy, and Louise was a good starting point. She was a bit of a gossip and tended to speak before thinking so I knew me and my new job would be all over the office by 10am tomorrow, which would save me the bother of trying to fight tears to tell anyone.

"Oh right. God Kier, I'm gonna miss you so much. I'm so use to your big bright smile coming into the office, and you just kind of brightening up everyone's day. The office is going to be so dull without you around it." I was actually touched. Louise sounded genuinely sad to hear I was leaving, though that almost made it worse. If she sounded like this, I didn't want to imagine Dale's reaction.

"Thanks Louise. It means a lot knowing you'll miss me. Listen I'm gonna go. I need to be in the office for 7am, got a lot to do before I head off to distant shores. But, hey, thanks for listening to me. I'm excited now that someone knows." I bite my lip hard, again holding back the tears.

"No probs Kier. See you later on. I'm gonna miss you. Night." I've never been so happy for someone to hang up in all my life, because the floods of tears that fell were ridiculous, and if Louise had stayed on the line she would've heard them all. I just let them fall. I wanted as much out of my system before I had to face everyone else later on. I knew I had to let Dale know as soon as possible, so I text the phone he saved for me, and just said, "Need to talk, ASAP, ring me please." I knew if I made it sound serious I would hear from him quicker.

CHAPTER TWENTY-FIVE

I went to bed, I stared at the ceiling, I listened to music, I wrote in my diary, I re-read the email from David Masters, I did everything except sleep, and when my alarm went off at 6am, I was already showered, had eaten breakfast and was getting ready to walk out the door. I planned to hit Starbucks as early as possible to get as many cups of coffee in as I could to keep me going for the rest of the day. Looking at my watch and seeing it was only 6:05am, I was wishing the minutes away, praying for Dale to get my message, wishing with everything I was worth that I could speak to him before I went into the office. And needless to say I was more than shocked when I walked through the doors at Starbucks at 6:21am and my phone started to ring, and Dale's number flashed on my screen.

"Hi Kier, that text sounded serious, are you ok?" He was panicking; I could hear the rush in his voice.

"Dale, I need to tell you something, and I don't want you to panic, or blame yourself, or think anything other than positive thoughts for me, promise?" I needed him to react ok. I needed him to understand.

"Ok, but Kier I'm already panicking. What's wrong?" He was breathing deeply down the phone, so I decided just to blurt it out.

"Dale I'm leaving." And it was done. I had said it.

Silence.

More silence.

More silence.

Dale was silent for over a minute before he spoke.

"What do you mean by leaving? And leaving to go where?" The tone was flat; no emotion was able to be portrayed in his voice.

"I got a new job Dale. I applied a while ago, knowing that you and I would have to come to an end one day and knowing what it felt like the last time, well I couldn't face working with you, dealing with having you there everyday and knowing I have to pretend I don't care about you, or I don't want to be with you every second of the day." I stopped short of telling him where I was going; I was going to let him process this information first. Unfortunately, Dale was unwilling to let it sink in.

"Where are you going Kier?" Dale had no emotion in his voice.

"Scotland" I whispered this so quietly I barely heard myself.

"Where?" I knew he had heard, because the way he quizzed and the tone of voice said so.

I cleared my throat, "Scotland. I'm going home." Of course I was crying, how could I not be. I was telling the man I loved that I was moving 3000 miles away because I could no longer handle being in the same room as him.

Dale didn't speak, I was wondering if he was even breathing. The phone line was completely silent; there was nothing, "Are you still there?"

"Yes." That was it, a one word answer.

"Is that all I'm getting? Nothing else?" I was starting to get a bit annoyed. I was telling him I was moving because of him and he wouldn't even give me a response. He wouldn't say how he felt, what he thought? This was ridiculous, "Jesus, Dale speak to me." The frustration rushed out of my body as the anger built at his unwillingness to respond to me.

"I'm sorry." He said this almost as quietly as I first whispered Scotland. "Why Scotland? Why so far away. Who are you working for?" Although he was slightly more animated in his response, he was still talking at a whisper.

"I just emailed David Masters, the CEO, and he got back to me saying it would be a pleasure to offer me a position. I'm meeting him at the end of the week to discuss details. I'm sorry I didn't tell you any of this, but I just needed to work with God on this one, and maybe this is his response. This is him telling me I have to leave your company because if we are ever going to be together, it certainly can't happen when we're still working together." It was difficult saying this to him, difficult accepting that I was saying we were over. But something in my heart was telling me this was the right answer, I had to leave. It's like that quote, "If you love something let it go, if it doesn't come back, it was never meant to be, but if it does it will stay there forever."

"But Kier, Scotland? Why so far away? You could've started your own line here in New York; you could've found another company here, close by." Dale was trying to speak more but I interrupted.

"No I couldn't Dale. I can't be here knowing you are. Sasha would still want to catch up and so would Louise and I would have to deal with hearing about you all the time, and I can't get my head into how to process that. If I'm in Scotland, I'm away from it all. I can move on with my life without feeling the need to have you there every step of the way. You have become such a massive part of my life and I almost feel like I lean on you now, I use you as a support and that's not fair on either of us. I need to be able to get through a day without craving to see you, without feeling a massive withdrawal because I can't be near you." I rushed the words out so my voice wouldn't break. I needed him to know that I loved him, but I couldn't be near him and love him, my heart and my head couldn't process those two parts together.

"So this is all my fault. You're giving up everything you have here because of me. Kier you can't do that, not because of me. We can find a way to work through it." Dale, much like myself, rushed the words from his mouth and I was no longer sure if he was doing it because he was fighting tears, or if he was fighting the guilt of thinking I was leaving because of him.

"Dale it's not like that. It's not your fault that I am choosing to leave. It's not your fault I have fallen so much in love with you and it is definitely not your fault that you have to stay with your family over being with me. The reason I fell in love with you, or one of the main reasons was because of how unselfish you are, how unwilling you are to think of your own happiness over your boys, and the love you have for those boys just escalates the love I have for you. They are your choice, and they are the right choice. They are only little and they need you to look after them; I can do that for myself." I was struggling to speak, struggling to make it through the next sentence.

"I really don't want you to go Kier. I really can't stand the thought of not seeing you everyday, not being with you everyday. Damn it." I could hear Dale was in the car and the steering wheel had just taken a beating. "This is so unfair. I love you. I want to be with you." I heard the strain in Dale's voice. The confusion that was in his mind was felt by both of us, but this was crunch time. We both knew what had to be done, and we both knew we couldn't go on like we were.

"Dale, if I could choose I would stay in your life forever, even just as the small part I am just now, but let's be serious here, how long is it going to be before someone clicks, or someone launches another set of accusations, and you don't need that. I love you too much to even consider allowing for that to maybe happen. Scotland is just another path along the road that I hope leads straight back to you, and if not, then I have to have enough faith to believe that this is all part of God's plan and you aren't my destiny." Yet again I could feel my heart crumble into a million pieces at the thought of no more Dale in my life. I needed all the strength I had not to break down, I had to believe my own words and put my faith in God. "This will all work out Dale, we have to believe that." I was completely unaware of the fact that I was sitting in Starbucks with tears streaming down my face and looking a complete mess. I didn't care. To be honest at that moment I didn't care about anything, my world was suddenly dark and empty and I felt completely alone. I tried to get lost in Dale's voice but even that wasn't of comfort, only a reminder that I was no longer going to be hearing that.

"Are you in our place just now? Are you walking to work? Where are you?" Dale quizzed me in a frantic fashion.

"I'm in Starbucks. I can meet you quickly but I need to be in control of myself before I go into the office. If I break down and cry in front of anyone they will know something is going on." I didn't even know if that's what he was going to ask, I just assumed he would want to see me.

"I'll pick you up. We'll talk, just for half an hour or so. I just need to see you." Dale wasn't asking, he was telling me. In a way it made me feel better, at least he cared.

"Broadway in five minutes. I'll wait at the corner." I was trying to compose myself, and at this moment words were not my friend.

"I'll be there in two. And Kier, remember, I love you." Dale hung up; I finished my coffee, grabbed my skateboard and took less than thirty seconds to reach our meeting point, and was completely surprised that he was already there.

As I slide in the car, Dale drew quickly round the corner, grabbed and kissed me like I was leaving today.

"Don't go Kier. Please, just stay. We can work this out." He continued to kiss me as he spoke, "I can't lose you. Not now. Please Kier, we can work it out, I promise we can." Dale was hysterical. His words were barely comprehensible, he was barely comprehensible.

I was holding it together, but only just. I had to. If I went into the office with swollen eyes and tear-stained skin everyone would know straight away that something was wrong when I announced I was leaving.

"Dale, don't do this. Don't do this." I was pleading with him, "We know this is the right thing to do. You and I can't stay us when we aren't just us. Loving you is the best part of my day, but worrying about people finding out, worrying that something will happen and you'll no longer be able to see your boys, that's the worst part of my day, and I would rather lose you now with the hope of getting you back, than risk losing you forever because I was the one who lost you your kids." I could barely look into his eyes.

The idea of looking at those eyes, and losing myself in them wasn't an ideal situation for me to be in. If I stared into his eyes I'd give in, I'd say ok, I won't go to Scotland, I'll stay here, but that wasn't the answer. I had been that girl long enough, the mistress, the bit on the side and I couldn't be her anymore. The love I felt for Dale was like nothing else on this Earth, but if people found out about us, it wouldn't be portrayed that way, we both knew that, and we had run the risk too long, it was time to give up, time to go our separate ways to see if eventually our paths would return to each other.

"I have to go Dale. This is the only answer."

He broke. He lost it completely. The realization of it all must have suddenly sunk in, because Dale just held me, tighter than he ever had before.

"You know you will always be my beautiful princess. Never forget that...promise me." Dale was just sobbing in my arms, but I had to focus on not breaking down.

"I'll never forget, even when I am 3000 miles away, it's still you that will be making my heart beat." Tears weren't an option just now; I allowed my eyebrows to drop, my jaw to clench and my eye gaze remain focused on everything except Dale's. I stared into his hands which were now laced round my own. He tried to speak through his tears.

"How can I let go of this." Dale looked completely destroyed, like his whole world had just collapsed around him. "You really are my soul-mate Kier, nothing will change that." He stopped talking, and just cupped his hand around my face.

"Dale let's not treat this like a goodbye. I'm not leaving today, ok." I smiled a little through my sadness, attempting in someway to look on the bright side.

"Ok. I just don't know how to say goodbye to you. Just please don't leave too soon." Now Dale half smiled. I wiped the tears from his face, and gently kissed him on the lips.

"Now you get yourself into that office and you're going to watch me perform an Oscar winning performance of my excitement over a new job." Again I kissed him lightly on the lips, gave him a quick hug and climbed out the car. I wasn't hanging a round for a big farewell, not when I was still here now.

I skated towards the office, and by the time I got there, I had a text from Dale,

I want you tonight...all night. If we don't have many left, I want as many as I can.

WOW. I smiled and for the first time in the last twelve hours, I felt genuinely happy. I can honestly say this is the first time in my life that I feel like someone does really care about me. Anyone else I've been with I've felt like a trophy, or like I had to be that "trophy" girlfriend, but with Dale, Kier, is enough. Just me, no acting, no pretending, just being goofy, quirky Kier. That's what made this hard, knowing that I would never meet anyone else like him. Someone who just makes me feel so good about myself, that all I want to do is smile, that person who doesn't see my flaws, but instead sees them as qualities, as more reasons to fall in love with me. But I couldn't focus on this. I had to go into the office with a big smile on my face and look happy to be going home to Bonny Scotland.

CHAPTER TWENTY-SIX

As I stared up at the office building, I composed myself, and went in. I was met straight away by Sasha, though I was shocked she was in the office considering it wasn't even 8am yet.

"Kier, hi. Why you in so early?" She looked slightly panicked, but was still smiling.

"I'm always in this early; I was going to ask you the same question though." I looked at her, and I have to admit I had a slightly accusing tone to my voice and look on my face.

"Well, I was, em, helping Harry with a few things." She started going red, but smiled all the same.

"Oh, I see. Things still going well there?" I smiled; she was still a little naive, I didn't have high hopes for her and Harry but it was nice to see her so happy.

She took a deep breath, widened her eye gaze, and allowed a massive grin to come across her face.

"Kier, Harry left his wife. He left her to be with me." Sasha was practically shaking with excitement. I was completely aware of the fact my face had gone from a smile to a look of confusion. I wanted to speak, say anything, but suddenly I felt sick, and almost angry. Not at Sasha, not at all, angry because she was getting him. She was getting to be with the man she wanted and what was I getting? Answer, nothing.

"Since when?" I tried not to sound mad, or look angry, but I have to admit it was a struggle.

"Since last weekend. I didn't want to say anything until he had actually moved out. But he did Kier." Sasha stopped in her tracks, and stared blankly at me, "Are you ok, you look mad at me?" I could see in Sasha's eyes she was worrying about me judging her, or she thought I was judging her. I felt bad because here was a girl, so overly happy, and I was being a bitch because she was getting the situation that I wanted.

"I'm sorry Sash, I'm just, well I'm in shock. I mean, I didn't even know he was thinking about leaving. I've hardly even heard how things are going with you two." I was trying to sound more upbeat and to be honest at least this was keeping my mind off of thinking about pretending to be happy about my imminent job move.

Sasha smiled again and got a little giggly like before, "I know, we really haven't seen each other. Well, obviously after Rome we've still been spending time together, in fact we've been together almost every night since then. Well Harry just decided that he couldn't picture life without me but he can picture it without her. He said he loves me too much for it all to end, and that was it. He had it out with her a few weeks ago and she begged him to stay but he's really just been searching for somewhere to live, and to get himself organised. But he got a place last week, moved out last weekend and well now he is just mine, and Kier I am so happy. Please don't be angry at me, I know I've split up a marriage, I know that makes me a horrible person, and I know you are all into God and you probably see me as some adulteress whore, but I love him, I honestly love him and I know we are going to work." Sasha had puppy dog eyes on, and it was like she was pleading with me to believe her, which I of course did. Or at least I believe she thought she loved him, which, when you're twenty-one is enough. When you're twenty-one, it's always true love.

"Sasha, I am honestly happy for you. I'm shocked is all, and well I've kind of got a lot on my mind, so hearing that at 8am has certainly thrown me. I mean, wow." I quickly hugged her to show my acceptance of the situation, "This is great Sash, you deserve to be happy." I was using every morsel of my self-worth to not fall apart. I was happy for her; I was just upset that I couldn't tell her the same thing.

"Thank you so much Kier. I can't believe this is actually happening. We're going to tell people as soon as possible, make it official. Harry is worried if it leaks out Dale and Steven will think he's been trying to be underhand, and hide something. So that's why I'm in so early. We were speaking to Steven, and hoping to see Dale too, but he isn't in yet." Sasha was completely beaming with joy. She was obviously living on cloud nine, and I hated that I couldn't just be 100% happy for her.

"So what did Steven say?" I was trying to be supportive, I was urging myself to be a good friend, and again, at least it kept me from having to speak about my own "good" news.

"He said it was our choice, that he had an inkling that something was going on and he respected us for coming to him and telling him the truth. He did say however we had to tell Dale straight away so he wasn't being left out. God knows where he is, is he not usually in here at the crack of dawn?" Sasha questioned me, not in an accusing way like Suranne would've but more just in a general, "have you seen him around" way.

"I haven't seen him. I usually see his car in the underground when I come in, but I didn't see any cars in there this morning. Maybe he has an early meeting or something?" I was good at playing it cool about Dale; unfortunately, thinking about him, or mentioning his name panged my heart and made my chest burn. It wouldn't be long before I wouldn't be seeing his car at all, stupid things like that seemed to break my heart a little more.

"Oh well, I'm sure we'll be able to tell him sooner or later. I'm just dying for everyone to know. Kier, I am so in love with him, I feel like I'm finally complete because I've got him. You have no idea how amazing it feels to find your soul-mate." Sasha beamed again.

Ouch! And I suddenly felt like I'd been kicked in the stomach. I have no idea? I have every idea. I met my soul-mate, he was mine and we were perfect and now I'm moving 3000 miles away because we can't be together and the thought of being in the same room as him, knowing I can't have him will destroy me even more than what I already am. That what I wanted to say but of course, I couldn't. So I simply said,

"Lucky you. Maybe one day I'll have that too." I smiled, but I knew the sadness in my eyes wasn't being hidden.

Sasha, being Sasha, just saw this as me being upset because I wasn't with anyone.

"Yeah you will Kier. You're a great girl, anyone would be lucky to have you." Sasha gave me a hug before adding, "And you've always got me." She kissed my cheek and skipped away, evidently in search of Harry again.

I had to almost laugh, you've got me. I had barely heard two words from Sasha since she started her great love affair with Harry, and evidently now they were a full on couple I'd probably hear from her less. Though I suppose that doesn't really matter given that in a month or less I won't even be anywhere near her. It's kind of gutting she didn't even ask what was wrong with me. There was no point in me over analysing everything, I had to find Suranne and drop the bombshell to her.

I wandered around the work room, looking at the place I had practically called home for the last six months and before I knew it would all be gone. That broke my heart almost as much as leaving Dale. This was my dream job, this was the one thing I had always wanted and it was gone. I would be stepping down a level, working for an unknown designer, someone less known by name than myself. It was demoralizing to say the least. And yeah I could've went out on my own, I could've launched my own label, but I would have to stay in New York to do that for the moment, and I didn't want to be too near Dale. Yeah LA was an option, yeah other places in the US were also options, but to be honest, I just needed a clean break. If I launched my career in the US I would still be too close to Dale, would still have to hear about him, and that wasn't what I needed at the moment. I needed to be far enough away from him that I could have a chance at being over him. I was hoping to spend some time in the workroom alone to get myself together, but unfortunately I forgot today was our team meeting so by 8:30, the rest of the girls were in and I was squirming in my seat awaiting the arrival of Suranne.

As her voice echoed down the corridor I felt the same chill run down my spine as I always did when she was nearby. The woman made me completely uneasy, though I had to admit I was looking forward to dropping the bombshell and watching her lose the best designer on her team. Ok, I was being big headed, but it was true. I sold the most designs, made the most money for the company and was the most requested by clients, the evidence was there for itself.

"Ok, team, let's not dilly dally, straight to business. We're coming up to spring which means you should be getting your Winter Collection together for viewing. So, what have we got?"

The girls started messing around with designs and

showing bits and pieces, but I held steady. My Winter Collection was already made up and on hangers ready to go be shot for press. It didn't take long before Suranne shot me a look.

"So Kier are you perhaps going to contribute?" She was so sarcastic it made me sick. What a complete bitch. I was going to take great please in saying my next sentence.

"Actually Suranne, I don't think I will." I paused, watched the look of horror spread across the other girls faces, and again, Suranne, looked disgusted at me.

"And can I ask why, I do assume you have some sort of collection pulled together?" Again with the sarcasm.

"Yeah I have my whole Winter Collection finished and made up ready for press photos; unfortunately, I'm not giving them to you." I was being so blunt. I wanted to see how far I could push Suranne before she would crack.

"Kier, this is not a game. You are part of this team and I need a Winter Collection from you, if not then I'm afraid we will need to have a serious talk." Suranne had a look of almost delight in her eyes at the thought that I hadn't done my work for once.

"You're right, we do need to have a chat, but not about my designs. You see, I don't have to hand over my Winter Collection because within the next month I will no longer be a member of staff within DB Designs." I smiled.

The other girls gasped in shock, and Ashleigh looked confused beyond belief. Suranne started to squirm in her chair, and much like Ashleigh the confusion in her face was priceless.

"I don't quite understand Kier. Are you leaving?" Suranne allowed the words to trickle off her tongue.

I had a look into each of their eyes. As I looked round at them all I suddenly felt, not relief, but a feeling of knowing I wasn't making a mistake by leaving. These girls, these women were all so involved in their own lives they didn't realise or take in anything that was going on round about them. This team was supposed to change the look of sportswear fashion, and to be honest, none of them had. Their designs were of mediocre standard and they had no real drive or desire to aspire to any real goals. This wasn't a team I wanted to be involved in, this was a mess. Plain and simple. As much as I loved working here, I wasn't willing to be the one who pulled the team through. We had quarterly sales figures to meet and I could almost guarantee it was my sales keeping the team afloat, in fact Dale had mentioned, only on the cuff, that this was the case. I took a deep breath and decided just to be honest.

"Well Suranne, I have been offered the job as head designer for David Masters, a new up-and-coming designer, who wants raw fresh talent to pave the way for his designs, and of course I jumped at the chance. It will allow me to really unleash my creativity and to finally work for a team that has actual goals. Suranne you have made me feel so uncomfortable working for you, made me feel like I was worthless, my designs were worthless. And as I look around this team, I realise just how much all this doesn't matter. None of you matter to me. I have been keeping the sales figures up because you all design to just get by, whereas me, I design to be the best, to put clothes out there that make people fall in love with fashion again. Now I'm going to apologise, not for sounding like I'm full of myself, but for not saying this sooner. You see I have the drive and the desire to be something, whereas all of you seem to be lacking that spark. I'm sure you are all lovely people, to be honest I've never taken much time to get to know you well enough, but fashion is about more than throwing a collection together for the sake of getting it done on time. You have all made these comments, these suggestions, questioning me, my talent, my integrity and I know deep down it's jealousy. I was the one who got to go to Rome, so you all made these accusations on my relationship with Dale, and to be honest I'm fed up with it. If I'm going to work within a team, I want them to be people I can trust, people I can respect, not people who at the slightest hint of someone doing well, throw around mindless hearsay and ridiculous rumours. So, I applied elsewhere and David Masters jumped at the chance to take me on board, so I accepted." I couldn't believe these words had just left my mouth. I had never in my life stood up for myself, I was usually the shrinking violet who didn't say anything and would let everyone walk over me. I suppose I realised I didn't have anything to lose. For all I knew I could be in

Scotland this time next week, and after the speech I just made, I was almost excited about it. I could make a difference to David Masters. People in New York were already aware of my name so the foundations were set. And after a few years of designing for someone else then maybe I would be ready to go out on my own.

The others just stared at me, obviously reeling from my outburst. I didn't intend on being so brash towards them all and I wasn't exactly sure where the strength had come from, but I didn't regret it at all. I had been working with these people for almost six months and not one of them had done anything that I thought was really outstanding. I know I sound like a bitch, and I know that running through their minds would be how highly I think of myself, but to be honest, I no longer cared. I was leaving, simple as that.

Suranne looked at me wide-eyed and in a state of complete shock.

"Well Kier it's good to see you think so highly of yourself." Sarcasm again, the lowest form of human intelligence, I wouldn't have expected anything less from her.

I kept my confidence high, I was holding myself together by a thread, but I couldn't allow them to see that. If I cracked in anyway at all it would be evident I wasn't as excited about my new job as I was making out. I still had to drop the biggest bombshell of where I was going, and if I allowed my emotions to take over now, trying to allow the words to leave my mouth that I was moving to Scotland wouldn't be impossible.

"Well, you know Suranne, if you don't have confidence in yourself then that's the first route to the self-destruction of your career. I believe in myself and in my ability, and I think the fact that I wrote to a company and got an offer of a job straight away shows me that I am as good as I think." I knew I had to mention Scotland soon, and there was a surge of power going through me, so I just said it, "So, in the next few weeks when I move to Scotland and start my new job, I know I will be great." God I sound like an idiot, 'bigging' myself up like this. I did have complete belief in my ability, but I wasn't this cocky, but if I didn't keep this level of cockiness up then I knew I would fall apart. I was aware of the gasps when I said the word "Scotland". They all, again, gave me a wide-eyed shocked look, Ashleigh again looked completely confused.

"Kier, you're moving to Scotland? I mean, Scotland. Why Scotland?" Every time Ashleigh said the word Scotland it was like she was saying some forbidden curse word and the world would end just by her mentioning it.

"Well, as you all know, I am originally from Scotland, and I guess I've been missing home a lot more over the last month or so. Aiden was the only thing really keeping me in New York and well obviously we ended so I don't have anything tying me here now. I just, well, I want to go home, simple as that. New York is great, but I'm not a New Yorker." I hated lying. I thought of myself as more of a New Yorker than I did Scottish; I had been here longer than I stayed in Scotland, and leaving would be one of the hardest things I have ever had to do.

"I can't believe you are leaving. What about all the contracts you have signed up, Keep Me Cupid, Rory White, those actresses that adore your designs, what will happen with them?" Ashleigh was quizzing me and I was unsure if she was concerned about my future or just hoping she could step in and take on my work. But as I said, Keep me Cupid were just launching, so everything had been done for the first wave of designs, and I had clothes designed and most of them made up for Rory White until early 2010 so I don't think he would struggle. Every one of their faces dropped as I explained all this.

"So I don't really have that workload, and the actresses I design for were all just one offs or two-offs if you want to put it that way." I smiled a little at my stupid joke. The conversation had gotten too serious, I needed to lighten it up and get away from the whole subject of me leaving, "And if they really want me to design something for them, they will be made aware of where I am, only difference is it will be under a different name this time. Anyway, none of this really matters, I just wanted you all to know what was happening, and well I suppose maybe hear someone say Good Luck?" I smiled, and this time, I allowed my cocky exterior to break for a moment and just go back to being me.

The girls all crowded round me and patted me on the back, hugged me, which was a little uncomfortable considering I didn't really regard them as friends and had slated them only a few minutes ago, but I appreciated the response. Suranne kept her same icy disposition and merely looked to continue with the team meeting, I was however, completely taken aback by her next sentence.

"Maybe it's best if you're not part of the meeting Kier. I mean, technically you are no longer part of this team, and the topics being discussed are for the Winter Collection and well, you will be long gone by then, so I would appreciate if you would find something else to do for the next hour. Thanks." Suranne turned to face the rest of the girls before I could give any response. To be honest I was quite happy to not be involved in her meeting. She was a big reason behind me applying elsewhere for work. Although my affair with Dale was the main reason, Suranne had made my working life miserable for too long now. Her jealousy towards me was almost going to break me down, and I was so unwilling to allow my talent to be compromised by someone else. So David Masters wasn't as big a designer as Dale Brenton, but I could help him build his company, I could be the head designer that he is looking for and I could propel him into new heights of the business, or at least that's what I had to tell myself.

CHAPTER TWENTY-SEVEN

As I picked up some paper and my sketching pencils, I decided to go and drop the news to everyone else. I went from office to office just rolling off the same story I had told my own team, the response from everyone else was a bit different, in fact when I spoke to Steven I welled up as he told me how big a loss I would be to the company. I appreciated that, Calvin gave a similar response. Obviously Louise knew, and had spent little time keeping it to herself, so by the time I got in Sasha was in tears saying she couldn't believe I hadn't told her this morning, and Arlene was looking slightly smug and happy at the knowledge I would no longer be coming in to the office. I had a temptress relationship with Arlene. She had a very big crush on Dale, which she wasn't very good at hiding, so my friendship with him annoyed her, and she didn't hide this fact either. She and Suranne had bonded over their mutual dislike for me, and Arlene was one of the ones that helped to launch Suranne's attack on me before Dale intervened. Needless to say Dale was quick to put her straight, and she was also in his line of fire alongside Suranne. He hadn't told me what he planned to do about their disloyalty and to be honest now I was leaving, I didn't really care. I had enough to worry about. Talking to the three girls, I just remained calm, and allowed a certain amount of "excitement" to be in my voice. When I was leaving the office Sasha got me on my own and apologised for not letting me speak this morning, and I said it was ok, I was happy for her getting on with her life, and knew she was dealing with a lot herself without me adding to the basket. Ok, I was annoyed at how self-involved she was, but she was still a young girl so I couldn't really blame her for being so focussed on herself. The only person's office left to go into was Dale's. I had to keep the pretence up that Louise and Suranne were first to know, so breathing deeply I walked into Dale's office and I could see in his face he wasn't holding it together as well as I was, which actually made me feel good knowing this was breaking his heart as much as mine.

"Hey you. I won't stay in for long, just trying to make people believe you don't know any of this. Most people know now, everyone is shocked. How are you holding up?" I wished I could embrace him, wished I could wrap my arms around him and hold him forever, but I tried to use that connection we had to show him I was still there.

"My heart won't process this Kier. I know you are doing this for the good of us, but how can you be leaving. How am I supposed to take the fact that because we fell in love you now have to leave? I'm the one who can sort any problem, and now the thing that matters the most is the one problem I can't resolve." Dale put his head into his hands, and I could see his eyes were bloodshot from holding back tears, "How has the reaction been?"

"Mixed. Suranne acted like she didn't care, Arlene could barely control her excitement at the prospect of me no longer being here. Steven and Calvin say I'll be a great loss, Sasha is too wrapped up in her own world to realise what is going on. I'm guessing they've spoken to you by now?" I searched his face, trying to see if the news about Harry and Sasha would spark anything in his own head.

"Yeah they came in, I gave them my blessing, they left and I had to punch the wall to stop myself from screaming that they get to be together, and we don't. I don't believe for a second they love each other like we do, and if the way you talk about them together is anything to go by, they definitely don't have the bond we do, they are not soul-mates like you and I." Dale's eyes were glazing over and I knew if anyone saw him like that they would click without trying.

"Come on, Dale. We can't do this. We can't make it seem like this is a big catastrophic disaster and you are falling to pieces because I'm leaving. We have worked too hard at keeping our bubble together; we can't let it burst at the last stop. So, show me that grin of yours, and look like a boss who is happy one of his employees is doing so well." I smiled at him, and allowed my eyes to say the words my heart was feeling. Dale, sensing this, gave me a similar look and simply added, "DTO."

The rest of the day in the office was a blur. I started to

pack up my work, prepare myself for the move. David Masters called three times to make sure I was still going to meet him for a late dinner on Friday night as soon as he arrived in New York. He said he couldn't believe that he was going to have me as an employee, which to be honest, made me feel good about everything. This whole situation felt like a dream, and every time I spoke to David Masters it became a little more real, and I allowed myself to believe this was happening. The way he spoke on the phone, he wanted me to start by the end of the month, which was fine by me, the quicker the move the better, like pulling off a Band-Aid I suppose. I told Dale on the phone that night all about my conversation with David Masters. He had wanted to meet up but his wife had arranged dinner for the two of them so he couldn't get out of it. I think for the first time ever I was glad I wouldn't be seeing him. My heart hurt, it felt like it had been smashed with a sledge hammer. I needed time to process everything that was going on. The last twenty-four hours had been a complete whirlwind and I needed to stop and breathe. I left the office early for the first time ever, clipped my skateboard to my backpack and walked towards the park. My iPod was locked in place in my ears and I lost myself in the words of Paramore, Within Temptation and Flyleaf. I couldn't believe this was all happening. A year ago I was just finishing up at Parson's; I was madly in love with Aiden and looking forward to the up-and-coming summer months of just lazing around the city. It's amazing how much can change in a year. Aiden and I managed the friend thing for about a day, but I think it was hard for both of us. It wasn't that I didn't still have feelings for Aiden, even now I still thought about him, but what I felt for Dale just completely overshadowed all my other emotions, and not in a bad way, in a way that made me feel like that's all I ever wanted to feel again. And now here I was, facing a future without him, an uncertain existence of not really knowing where I was heading or what I was going to be feeling. And all it made me think was, where would I be a year from now?

CHAPTER TWENTY-EIGHT

The next week flew by. My meeting with David Masters went better than I expected. He had so many new and fresh ideas that it was completely exhilarating to be sat speaking with him. He was going to give me free reign over what I designed and he seemed interested in the already growing number of contacts I had in the fashion world after only such a short time. He tried to bring Dale up a few times but I never allowed the conversation to stay on him too much. If I was starting a fresh, Dale couldn't be a factor in it. We set a date for me to start on the 1st of May, which was a little over three weeks away. I got excited sitting speaking to him, as long as the subject stayed on his work, his designs.

Dale had been almost attached to my hip since the news broke; we had spent almost every night together, including two over nights that he passed off as business meetings. He still wanted to go away for the weekend as planned, a final farewell I suppose you could call it. I had debated with myself over it, trying to decide if it was a good idea, but deep down I knew I would regret not having one last weekend feeling like his. I had already made my excuses for where I would be, and he told his wife he had to fly to California to speak about a new shop opening. It wasn't a complete lie; he was sending Sasha and Harry to deal with it, a slightly underhanded cover up and a way to make sure Sasha wouldn't get in the way of our plans by asking me to do something.

Easter arrived in the blink of an eye; I was struggling to get my head in gear to believe I was leaving New York in just under two weeks, and that I would have to give all of this up, nothing more so than Dale. I was trying to focus my attention on the upcoming weekend. Dale managed to swing it so we would be spending the whole weekend together, Friday – Monday. As excited as I was, and in general terms spending four days with someone would seem like a lot, but all my mind could focus on was knowing on the Monday we would be over. I knew for the weekend at least I would have to focus my attention on the hours we were spending together, on the time we still had. I had spent the last two weeks packing everything in the office, packing up my apartment and basically just getting organised for my move. My relatives in Scotland offered me a room in their house when I moved over, but I decided just to get my own place in the Merchant City area of Glasgow instead. It had a great view of the city, or as much of a city as you could call Glasgow, but it was homely and I knew the first few months were going to be difficult, so having my own world to escape into would be perfect. It was difficult looking at my apartment here, seeing it looking so bare and empty. I had been so happy finding the place, Greenwich Village and getting it at a fixed rate which meant I paid probably half of what everyone else in the area paid. I loved the little cafes, the jazz bars, and the other world I stepped into when I went home every night. I wasn't sure if Glasgow would have that same appeal.

I was still going in and out of the office, but really there wasn't much for me to do, so I spent a lot of time on the basketball court. My coach said in the last two weeks I was playing harder, faster and stronger than I ever had before. He was gutted about me leaving, saying he couldn't believe the talent in me and I was throwing it away to go to a country where they probably didn't know what a basketball was. I laughed; my coach was so old school in his approach that everything was so black and white. Dale worried about this, me loving a sport so much and having to drop that dream too. I assured him I would find somewhere to play in Scotland, and he seemed to know I wasn't convinced myself, but believe what I was saying anyway.

The Tuesday morning before our weekend away was one of the few I was actually going into the office. Sasha had decided we should have a mini office party to say bon voyage to me. It was also one of the few mornings I had come into the office with Sasha. She was still beaming with excitement over her relationship, not thinking for a moment to mention the fact I was leaving in little over a week. She was babbling on about going to California for the weekend and how great it would be, which was a relief because she didn't mention my plans. As we walked and talked, I sent Dale a text simply saying,

"Good morning handsome just thought I'd tell you how ridiculously good looking you are and hopefully put a smile on your face for the rest of the day. Lusm, ( )"

Our texts always finished with our brackets now. It was our special symbol that only we had, and the LUSM was, *love you so much*. We had a few other letters that we had accumulated into our own little language over the last few weeks. Sasha had been a little more interested than usual over the last few days regarding my love life and how I was coping from my break up with Aiden, and how she was sorry she hadn't really been there. I just said I was fine and I realised that some things just aren't meant to be no matter how much you want to try to hold on to them. I had told Louise that I had fallen for a man called Sean who played basketball on the court next to me on a Saturday and I also told her I had kissed him etc but he was married. She was shocked, but what shocked me more was how great she was. She always asked if I was holding it together, if I heard from him, all the things a friend should. I'm not really sure what made me open up to her, but something told me I could trust her, well enough to talk about the situation without mentioning the man in question was Dale. It made me laugh sometimes because she had made a lot of comments about the rumours regarding Dale and I, and always said how she didn't understand how people could believe any of it. She was quite naïve, but also just a really genuine person who could only see the best in people, and being able to open up a little, even if it wasn't about the person it really was, was a huge relief. Sasha was quite curious about how close Louise and I had gotten and I simply said we went for a drink after work one night and we just chatted and ever since we were just closer. I think she was slightly jealous in a way, not that she would show it, but I think to her I was her friend, full stop.

As we got closer to the office, Sasha went into detail about every item of clothing she was taking with her, what they had planned, what they wanted to do etc, and I have to admit I was actively listening, a lot of "yeah's" and "wicked" and "awesome's". And when my phone flashed up Sean I was even less aware of what she was saying. The message was a simple, Can you call? I smiled at the prospect of speaking to him, and was glad we were at the office. I gave Sasha a quick hug and said I had to dive to the 7/11 for some Red Bull and I'd be up in ten. I watched her disappear and quickly dialled Dale's number.

"Good morning you, and how's your handsome face this morning?" I was completely beaming as I always was when I spoke to Dale. Something about the sound of his voiced sent a wave of calm over me and just made me want to smile.

"Kier, something happened." Dale sounded terrible. My face dropped and my stomach sank. I knew whatever this 'something' was, it wasn't something I was going to be happy hearing about,

"What's wrong, Dale?" I was panicking. My heart was racing so fast I was afraid I would pass out.

"Kier, she knows." Dale's words were hardly audible, but I knew exactly what he had said. I felt like a bomb had gone off in my stomach, and my heart somehow managed to double in pace, and now I was really worried I would pass out.

"What? She, as in your wife? What does she know?" I couldn't breathe, I could feel the colour had drained from my skin, and I was shaking all over.

"She answered my mobile this morning and it was a call from the hotel in Vermont just to confirm the booking. I tried to cover up that I was going to surprise her, but she's not buying it. She said she knows I haven't arranged anyone to watch the kids because she called everyone we knew. I don't know what to do Kier; she said she's taking the kids away from me. This is a mess." I could hear just as much panic in his voice as was in mine. This was a disaster. How could this be happening, not now? Not when we were so close to the end.

"Ok, we need to calm down, be rationale." For some reason my head snapped into gear, and I was suddenly full of ideas, "Ok, can you not think of anyone that would say they were going to watch the kids, someone you can trust? What about your friend, Malcolm. You need to tell one person about us if you have any hope of staying where you are?" My mind was working on overtime, my body was being driven by an overload of adrenaline and I was convinced my heart was going to stop.

"Ok. I have kind of spoke to Malcolm regarding my attraction to you, especially after that day we bumped into you and he was trying to get me to set you up with him, so I can cover that. I just don't know if Sarah will believe I was getting him to look after the boys." Dale was rushing his words, searching for an answer in every syllable he was saying.

I was quiet for a few seconds. I was processing every bit of information in my head, searching through every detail to try to piece everything together to get some kind of solution. I switched off and just let my mind take over.

"Ok, just say you didn't want her to find out about the surprise away and you knew she would never suspect Malcolm of watching your kids. Say anything like that Dale. It doesn't sound farfetched." I couldn't believe I was making up solutions to allow his wife to believe he wasn't having an affair, finding a solution so she wouldn't leave him.

"I can do that. Yeah, she'll believe that. The only other thing is that she saw a few texts in my work phone from you because she wanted to check everything, nothing serious but she was aware that they were flirtier than other messages. And she knew I took Kaih to one of your basketball games. I didn't tell you we were there, was a spur of the moment Saturday afternoon and we were going by NYU gym and I saw your team's name so Kaih and I went in. I told him I knew you from work, and he told Sarah what we had been doing, and she has put two and two together. I don't know what to do Kier. I can't lose my boys. I can't not be in their lives." Dale was in tears, and not the usual tears he had, but he sounded hysterical.

Again my mind went into overdrive. As much as I wanted him to not be with his wife, I knew right now, he had to be. He had to be there for those boys and I had to do everything I could to make sure that happened. I had to make sure I done everything in my power to help him out. I knew exactly what I had to do, and as I took a deep breath I prepared myself for what I was about to say.

"Dale, give her my number. Tell her to call me if she doesn't believe nothing is going on between us and if worse comes to worse I'll say I had a crush on you and leaned on you a lot for support. I'll put the blame on me. I'll do whatever has to be done. Will that work?" I breathed heavily, I was crying silent tears, holding it together for him but secretly my heart was no longer just broken, it was shattered into a million pieces.

Dale didn't speak. I heard his breathing slow and sound less rushed, less strained. He was silent for a while before he finally broke the silence.

"You would do that for me? You would speak to her and make out it was all you?" I could feel the expression on his face, could picture his eyebrows dropped, biting his lip in his usual confused fashion.

"Dale I would do anything for you to make you happy. I know you have to be with your boys, so yeah, I'll speak to her." The tears still rolled down my face, but I managed to keep my voice calm, relaxed and almost frighteningly controlled.

"I can't believe you would do that for me. I can't believe you would do what you know will make her stay with me because you know I need to be with my boys. You do realise if you don't speak to her there is a very good chance of her leaving me, which leaves me open to be with you." Dale sounded confused, and I could tell in his mind he was trying to process if I was doing this as a way out, so I quickly jumped in.

"Don't think for a minute I'm trying to find a way out. I'm not. Believe me when I say my heart is completely broken in two saying this, and I know by doing this it will pretty much eliminate any chance I have of being with you, but I can't be selfish and just want you for myself, not just now anyway." I couldn't believe how strong I was being. I knew in my mind I could use this situation to my advantage, allow her to leave him and then come along and pick up the pieces and have him as my own but I couldn't. "I know I have to do this Dale. It's simple as that. This was a situation we both got ourselves into, and I'll sort it. I'll do whatever it takes to keep you safe."

"Wow." I could hear a break in his voice. "I can't believe you would sacrifice your happiness for mine. You have already done so much Kier. You really are the most unselfish person ever, and now I have to lose you." The shattered pieces of my heart dropped to my stomach as he said this. I could feel his love for me, I could hear his heart shatter too, and I think at that moment we both realised this really was the end. I just had one request.

"Dale, I'm not going to come back to work after today. It's too difficult, but can I ask one thing? Can you meet me this afternoon, leave the office for an hour, just to say goodbye?" I smiled thinking about kissing him one last time, at the same time wanting to scream at the thought of it being the last time.

Dale didn't speak. I didn't push him.

"Kier, I don't think that's a good idea. I'm going to have to give her your number this morning, and I imagine she will want to talk today. We're going to have to rebuild a foundation because I don't think she will fully believe everything, even after speaking to you. I just don't know if we can risk being seen together. Not now, after everything." Dale's voiced had calmed to an almost eerie level, and for the first time I felt anger towards him.

"Are you being serious? You won't come and say goodbye?" I was baffled at his answer. After everything I had just said, everything I was willing to do, everything I had already done, he wasn't going to say goodbye to me.

"Kier, after everything, is it worth ruining it all now. What if this is the one time that someone sees us. How do we cover that up?" I couldn't believe these were his words. I couldn't believe how selfish he sounded. Maybe I should've left it there, but I needed a goodbye, I needed him to do at least one thing for me.

"No Dale. This is unfair. I am doing everything I can to hold this together, to hold your life together, and I can't accept you saying you won't even say goodbye. After today I may never see you again, and you won't even give me an hour to try and let go?" I was shaking my head in disbelief, gritting my teeth with rage at how selfish he had become in the space of ten minutes.

He didn't speak again. I continued to grit my teeth and clench my jaw. My knuckles were white from squeezing two fists in sheer frustration. And finally he spoke.

"I'm sorry Kier." I was waiting on another reason behind

not wanting to say goodbye, preparing myself to feel more disappointment in the man I thought I knew. "You're right. I can't believe what I was saying. Are you in the office yet?" Dale sounded back to normal again, as though he had flicked a switch to stop him sounding like the selfish man I was listening to only a minute ago.

"I'm outside, but I haven't gone in as yet."

"Ok, forget meeting me for an hour; let's take sometime together this morning. That will be safer. Sarah knows I have a meeting with a fabrication company this morning, what she doesn't know is they called just before I text you to say they were unable to keep the meeting, so I have until 12:00 if you want to go a drive. And Kier believe me when I say, I wasn't saying I didn't want to meet to be selfish; my head is all over the place. I don't even know what I'm saying to be honest. I'll pick you up at Bailey's Bar in five."

I just said ok, and casually walked round. This was one meeting with Dale I wasn't prepared for. I had spent the last two weeks worrying about saying goodbye after four days together, now I had three hours to say my goodbyes, and under circumstances that weren't going to make it pleasant.

When I saw his Range Rover, I froze. My body started to ache from knowing what was about to happen. Every part of me was in pain, in agony, no one part more so than my heart. As I climbed in, for the first time ever I didn't smile, I didn't take his hand; I just stared at my feet and let the tears fall from my eyes.

"Kier please be ok. I can't handle making you feel like this. Please be ok." Dale didn't drive far; he pulled into the underground car park of the Plaza, swiped his member's card and pulled into a space. He had barely stopped the car before he reached over and pulled me into his arms.

"I can't believe this is how this is all ending. I am going to miss you so much and I don't even know how to go on without you. I know I say I need to be there for my boys, but Kier, I need you just as much, I want you just as much. But it's really no longer about me, is it?" His eyes were now as red as mine, and we were clinging to each other with sheer desperation, knowing we would have to let go forever.

I couldn't talk. Every part of me had given up and I was

just a broken doll. Nothing would function. Dale kissed me repeatedly but even my lips wouldn't respond. Dale pulled me closer, trying to get some reaction from me.

"Kier, please say something. Say you hate me; say you despise me for making this happen, say anything." Dale stared into my eyes, and emotionless I stared back. I slowly blinked my eyes, stared at the floor and then back to his eyes.

"I don't hate you Dale." I willed my hands to move to his cheek, "I will always love you. I'm just angry you weren't going to say goodbye to me. After everything Dale, you weren't going to give me one last chance to let you go?" I wiped the tears from my face and tried to breathe through my words. Every part of me felt like giving up. As I continued to wipe my eyes, Dale took over; he gently cleared the tears away and then kissed me gently.

"The truth is I didn't know how to let you go Kier. I am terrified of letting you walk out this car knowing that you may never come back into it. Knowing that when I let you walk away today I'm allowing the best thing I've ever had in my life to walk away." Dale mirrored my glance to the floor.

And suddenly I felt it. I felt his pain, how much this was hurting him too, how much he was risking by being with me, and how much it hurt him knowing he couldn't risk it anymore. I felt every ounce of his love as it ran from his fingers into my pores. And I smiled.

"I love you Dale Brenton. I love you like I love no one else. Maybe I will get out of this car and that will be it for us, maybe I will walk away today and in no time you will forget me. Or maybe, this is the only way that God can allow us to come back together. Maybe this is the only way that we can reunite when the time is right. Just never forget I love you, ok?" I couldn't believe I had suddenly calmed myself. I suddenly felt this force take over and make me feel like this was right. And as I looked at Dale I knew he felt the same. We knew the time had come to let go, to go our separate directions and to try to find a way to go on with life without one another, and as difficult as this goodbye was, it was happening for a reason, and whether we knew that reason or we didn't, we just had to have faith that we would know why soon enough.

"I'm going to go now Dale. I can't spend the next however long with you, knowing it will just lead to the same conclusion. We've said it all, and there aren't any words left to say that will make this any easier. So can I just say goodbye now?" I had nothing left to say, no more thoughts in my head he hadn't heard, no more words to express that hadn't been said 100 times. We were over.

Dale cupped my face, stared into my eyes and kissed me. I let go for one last time, allowing myself to be absorbed into his lips, to allow myself to fall in love with him one last time. It was the perfect goodbye. And as we pulled away, I pressed my fingers to Dale's lips, and simply whispered, "Let's not say anything more. Please. Let's leave it at that."

I climbed out the car, and without looking back I left the car park.

And that was it. That was my farewell to the love of my life. I was strong enough in the car, but I just cried all the way home. I called Sasha and made up some phoney excuse as to why I wasn't going into the office. She could evidently tell there was something wrong, but she didn't want to ask given the tone in my voice. I felt some form of relief knowing I wouldn't be going back to that office again. I would call Louise and ask her to pick up anything else I had left in the workroom, but I was pretty sure I had picked everything up. It was another relief knowing I wouldn't have to have the big farewell to everyone, or deal with any random gifts or anything like that. I didn't want to celebrate the fact I was leaving, I wasn't leaving because I wanted to, though no one knew that, except Dale. I just couldn't believe after nine months that was it all over, it was all done. No more DB Designs, no more laughing in the office with Louise and Sasha, no more getting excited over showing off my latest creations. No more Dale. It really was all over.

(Brackets)

CHAPTER TWENTY-NINE

I hadn't seen Dale in nearly two weeks. I think we both knew it would be a bad idea. We did have a few random texts messages and I spoke to him on the phone once. I think the hardest part was that he no longer sent me our symbol, he no longer sent ( ) which made me think we were no longer those two halves of the one whole. I tried to push that thought out my head. Over the last week my head had been taking over because my heart was too broken to be able to commute any information. I just prayed one day it would be easier.

I couldn't believe in two days I would be heading to Scotland. My start date got pushed back to the 5th, so I had some extra time to get organised. I just couldn't believe I would be leaving the place I loved more than anywhere in the world, the place I truly called home. I hadn't given up my apartment yet; it was too hard to let it go and was hoping more to sublet it instead. I had a few people view it and had left my own landlord in charge if I didn't find anyone before I left. I didn't realise how much stuff I had until I started packing it all. My life had suddenly become nothing more than cardboard boxes. For the first time in my life I had carefully organised everything so I could easily settle in quickly when I got to Glasgow. It frightened me even the thought of it. Glasgow suddenly seemed like a million miles away, it could've been the moon. I'm not going to lie, there were moments when I would get excited about the move, I would look forward to being away from New York, from the constant reminders of everything that had happened over the last nine months, from everything that made me think of Dale and everything I had lost by losing him from my life. I just had to focus on that thought and not allow myself to let any sort of feelings of how much I was going to miss New York enter my head.

As I wandered around my apartment, I felt like all I did was check my emails, make a start on fresh designs and occasionally text friends. I had become a recluse over the last two weeks; I just had no drive to speak to anyone, no drive to explain why I was a broken shell. I was shocked as I walked into the sofa room and my phone was ringing. Picking it up I noticed the international dialling number and knew instantly it would be David Masters, or someone from the company.

"Hi, Kier Scott speaking."

"Kier, hi there, how are you?" I knew instantly it was David's PA Therese. I guessed she was calling to finalise details of when I would be arriving in Scotland.

"I'm good, thank you, and yourself?" I was trying to sound upbeat; it wouldn't go down too well if I sounded completely depressed to my new employer.

"Good. Ok, Mr Masters has asked me to give you a call Kier, are you ok to talk?" Therese was a very delicate sounding woman, and every time I spoke to her she sounded like was about to burst into tears.

"Yes, of course, fire away." I was acting the part of the excited new recruit, well I thought.

"I wish you hadn't used those words." I was confused by this statement and back tracked to what I had just said.

"I'm sorry, I don't understand." I guessed maybe this was some kind of Scottish humour I wasn't familiar with.

"Kier, I wish I was calling on better terms, but you see, things haven't been going too well here over the last two weeks, Mr Masters has lost three contracts, and he has been reviewing his options, and well, at this time, he isn't in the position to bring you over here to work. I'm so sorry Kier, I know how excited you were about moving here, and that you had already given up your position with DB Designs, and Mr Masters can only apologise for this. I am so sorry, honestly, so sorry." Now she actually sounded in tears, and me, I couldn't even open my mouth. I wasn't sure what had just happened, or what I was supposed to be feeling. Had she really just said I now no longer had a job? Is that what this whole phone call was about?

"Kier, are you there?" I must've been silent for longer than I realised.

"Yes, I'm just, well, I'm in shock to be honest. I don't understand how things so dramatically changed in such a short period of time. Everything was fine when I spoke to Mr Masters last week." I was urging her to give me an answer of what the hell had happened and how I had gone from having two jobs to having none.

"Kier, I don't know what to say. Mr Masters was hoping that by signing you it would boost his appeal, but unfortunately he couldn't meet the demand of what clients wanted, he got snowed under and so people cancelled orders, then the fabric company wouldn't release any more fabric until he came forward with the money, and well, to be honest he is going under and that's the long and short of it. I'm really sorry to have to be the one to tell you this, and well, I'm just sorry. Hope things work out for you, I have to go." And that was it, the line went dead.

What on earth had just happened in the last fifteen minutes? I had gone from convincing myself Scotland was the best idea for me, and now I didn't have a job at all? This was insane. I didn't know whether to laugh or cry. In one hand this massive air of relief swept over me as I realised I could stay in New York, but on the other hand, I didn't have a job to support myself. I couldn't believe this. I picked up my phone and scrolled through the endless lists of names three or four times before I realised I was fixated on the one person I knew would know what to say to me.

"Hi, it's me. Sorry to call, but can you talk?" I tried to breathe but yet again my body had gone into shut down and didn't know how to process any of the information I had just received in the last fifteen minutes.

"Yeah of course I can talk. How you doing? Is everything ok?" Just hearing their voice allowed me to calm myself a little.

"Are you free? I really need to speak to you, in person if possible?" I needed some sort of comfort and a casual conversation down the phone wasn't going to help.

"Sure. Are you at home? I can meet you half way? Maybe the coffee shop on Bleaker Street?" I smiled, thank God.

"Great. See you in ten minutes?"

I practically ran all the way to Bleaker Street in anticipation of being able to speak to someone to make sense of this situation that seemed to have fallen on my lap. And as I saw them standing outside the coffee shop I got an instant rush of excitement and couldn't help but kind of shout out towards them.

"Hi." For the first time in two weeks I found myself with a smile on my face that was real, it wasn't false or fake, but 100% real.

As I got towards them I got a little awkward and wasn't sure how to react but couldn't resist throwing my arms around their neck and hugging them.

"You have no idea how good it is to see you." I smile again, and was aware of how happy I felt, something that had all but faded away from me.

"Wow Kier, you're a little over excited are you not?" He smiled, and I couldn't help but grin back. He looked great.

"Yeah I guess I am. You look great. I like your hair, it's different." Without thinking I reached up and softly touched it, and then stared into his eyes, "I've missed you."

"I've missed you too. I'm actually shocked you called, but happy at the same time. Everything ok?" He kind of took my hand in his and again I felt a little rush of happiness.

"Not really. I didn't know who to call. The truth is I scrolled through my phone book at least six times and every time the only name I got to that I wanted to speak to was you." I stared up at him, and tried my best to show him I was meaning every word of what I was saying.

"I wasn't really expecting that comment, but let's go inside, I'll buy you a coffee and you can explain all." And with that Aiden turned and opened the door and lead me inside.

After two hours of sitting in the coffee house, I had explained everything, not leaving out any details. I opened up about the affair, Suranne, the job, everything. I decided to just be honest with Aiden; he was the one person in the world who had never tried to hurt me so he deserved the truth. He laughed with me; we cried together, he was shocked, surprised, taken aback, in fact I think he went through every emotion imaginable, but when I finished telling him the whole story, he pulled me towards him, hugged me and then ever so gently kissed me. At first I wasn't sure how to respond. I had been so wrapped up in Dale that the thought of kissing someone else didn't really cross my mind, but it felt nice. Aiden always made me feel so safe, and I think more than anything, that's what I needed at that time. Just to feel safe.

"So what now Kier?" Aiden obviously needed an answer. Knowing I had just kissed him back, he obviously sensed some kind of feelings still there and considering what happened between us it wouldn't have been fair for me to leave him hanging. So I just said the one thing that seemed rationale.

"Let's go back to the start. Let's forget everything that has happened, wipe the slate clean and just go back to being us again Aiden, well as long as you don't mind having an unemployed bum for a girlfriend." I wasn't sure what response he would have, if I would want to hear it, but I looked straight into his eyes and willed an answer from him.

"Are you nuts, you're my girl. Even when we were apart you were still my girl. I love you Kier. Always have, always will." I was thrown by the proclamation of love, and I wasn't ready to say it back, so I merely reached over and kissed him, hoping that would be enough.

"Good, that's exactly what I wanted to hear." And as I kissed him again, I convinced myself I was telling the truth.

It didn't take long for us to be Kier and Aiden again. Within a month we were completely normal again, I quickly fitted back into the group we were once a part of and acted like nothing had ever happened or changed between us. We never mentioned DB Designs. We never mentioned that I was no longer designing clothes; instead I was working at the Ice Bar, just trying to get by. I missed fashion, but I wasn't ready to fully commit to it again, not until I knew Aiden and I were good once more. I don't think our relationship could handle any twists of fate at the moment, and me going back to fashion design could definitely throw a spanner in the works. The only reminder of the DB Designs was Louise, who surprisingly had become my closest friends. She was relieved when I said I was staying, and we started hanging out a lot more. She was also dating Aiden's friend Todd, whom she met at a party she attended with me and she couldn't have been happier.

Over the course of the year, life seemed to settle down. The four of us spent an amazing summer together in

California where Aiden had been offered some work for a few months, and since Todd worked alongside him a lot of the time, he managed to get him in on the act too, so Louise and I took extended leave from both of our jobs and joined them. We sunbathed all day, they worked hard and at night we hit the town and lived it up LA style, clubbing, dinners and a lot of rebuilding of a relationship for Aiden and I.

Aiden never mentioned Dale, and whenever I was with Louise or we were together as a foursome I tried to keep the topic away from DB Designs. I had given Louise some story about how hard it was hearing about everything so she never mentioned it. I would love to say I had been strong enough to erase Dale from my memory, but I wasn't and we would occasionally drop each other a text of some sort. I'm not sure if that was making it harder or easier, but I wasn't quite ready to cut him away completely. He was still interested in my career and although fashion wasn't a big part of my life anymore, he was happy to hear basketball was. I was back playing point guard harder and stronger than ever and had been scouted for the national team. I wasn't sure how far it was going to go, but I was having more fun than ever, and working in the Bar freed up a lot of time for me to put in extra practise. Aiden still hated my competitiveness, hated how much I put into basketball, but I think he was just happy in the knowledge knowing I was with girls most of the day. He still had some issues, obviously after everything that happened, but I think we were stronger now than ever before, although I was evidently aware he would never fully trust me again. I suppose he has a right to considering I still think about Dale, still miss him all the time. I tried to block him out but I guess that was one part of me that was going to stay there. I still liked the random messages, liked knowing he was there to hear about my achievements. I didn't mention work, more because I felt like a bit of a failure having given up on fashion but at least I was surviving. We never spoke on the phone now, but the texts were enough. Nothing would make me forget him. Not even how wonderful Aiden was. 2009 had been mine and Dale's year and as it drew to a close it was difficult to imagine that just being a memory now.

CHAPTER THIRTY
New Year's Eve 2009

As it hit midnight 2010, I knew that would be it for Dale Brenton and I. He hadn't said he wouldn't text me in the New Year, and I should've been filled with hope following his TBUBT text (thinking bout you big time, yet another of our own little creations) but a part of me almost knew that I wouldn't hear from him again. As that clock hit for the New Year I tried not to focus on the negative. I tried to push myself to not focus on Dale. It was almost a pleasure to know I was working in the morning because it gave me an excuse to not have to put on false smiles for the next few hours. And it was a guarantee that if I got drunk I would cry and then Aiden and I would be caught in yet another fight, and that's not how I wanted to start the New Year, not after telling him the truth about everything else. He couldn't know how gutted I really was about losing Dale, about giving up my career. He couldn't ever find out that every time I hear the initial DB my heart broke, every time I smelled Cool Waters my world felt empty, every time Hallelujah blared in my ears I wanted to rip my heart out my chest so I wouldn't have to feel it anymore. I wanted to be over Dale. I wanted to forget the way he looked at me, the way my hand felt in his, the way everything stopped when I was with him. I wanted all that, but again, as that clock struck midnight something told me the answer to that would always be a no.

I only stayed at Aiden's for less than an hour that night. I felt I owed him my presence beside him on New Year's Eve. I don't know if he sensed my feelings anymore, I was getting very good at acting one way and feeling another. I put every bit of my mind into wanting to be with him, wanting to be there cuddled into his arms and giving him my first kiss of 2010, but my heart would never fully be there. As much as I tried to resist, Dale always held that part.

The week after New Year, as I walked home, I had my iPod

attached to my ears as always, and was shocked when a playlist came on of a CD I had given Dale. He had never been a big music fan, so now and again I would make a mix CD and he always said the song choices blew him away. As I allowed the music to play, and listened to the words of *The Climb* and *God Blessed This Broken Road* as they blared through my ears, and felt the tears as they streamed down my face. The realisation of the last year was only too clear at the front of my mind. I had been through a rollercoaster of emotions and now as I cried my heart out, I realised what I had lost and gained in the last year. I had felt a love for someone that was truly like a fairytale. A love that was indescribable, that I knew would never be repeated again with anyone else. Aiden was a great guy and I did miss him, at times when I was working, or away at basketball tournaments, but we never had that connection that Dale and I had. We had gelled together. Regardless of all the good memories that I replayed in my mind, the negative thoughts had also started to creep in. I thought about everything I had gone through with him, and it wasn't just the good thoughts that stayed in my head. I thought about everything that had happened, everything I had given up to protect him, to make things easier for him. To make him happy. I had asked him after I didn't move to Scotland if we could speak on the phone once a week, but he rejected the offer, not giving me a reason. He doesn't really text me to tell me how he's doing, just merely to say he's thinking about me, or some closed off comment. It's like suddenly he has realised how great his 2.4 life was and now I don't mean anything to him. I tried to convince myself I was being stupid, and irrational or that I was worrying about nothing and he thought about me as much as I thought about him, but I couldn't shake the feeling now that he was happier without me. I had just spent three months working at a job that had nothing to do with my passion. I had to sacrifice my friends and everything for him. I was even going to move back to Scotland, alone, just to make him happy. I would never hate Dale, nothing could make me hate him, in actual fact nothing could stop me loving him, but when I thought hard in my head, there were moments where I disliked him. I couldn't have been more right when I said I wouldn't hear from him. I had sent him a text on New Year's Eve just saying I knew 2010 wouldn't really include him but I would always love him etc, and I know he got it on New Year's Day, but I got no response. No response saying he would always love me, nothing to say he wouldn't be in touch a lot. Nothing. This is what hurt. This is what made me feel like I meant nothing to him. It made me angry at myself. Angry for believing he did love me. Angry for believing he was thinking about me as much as I was thinking about him. Angry for allowing myself to be so heartbroken and feel like my world was empty because he was no longer there. And more than anything, I was angry at myself for still being in love with someone who obviously didn't care as much about me as they say they did. Someone who made me make all the hard decisions and they just watched me walk out of their lives. Someone who, now, I wasn't sure whether they were lying to me the whole time about how they felt, and they made me fall in love with them out of some ego trip. The one conversation that sticks in my mind that Dale and I had is when I said, "You've ruined me for everyone else." And his response was, "No I've just made you perfect for me." And he was right. I was perfect for him. I was only perfect for him. He was the only person I wanted to be perfect with, but I couldn't be, so compared to him, everyone else meant nothing. No one else made my heart skip a beat like him. No one else made me feel my world was spinning every time he spoke. Even now, if my phone rang and it came up his name I wouldn't be able to control the butterflies. He has ruined me. That was the only way to describe it. I wanted to believe so badly that he was in as much pain as me, that his heart was hurting as much as mine was, but I just couldn't get my head to process that as being true. My heart was hurting too much to think he could love me, because if he did he would still want to speak once a week. He would still want me to be included in his life. For so long he had been my best friend, the person I turned to when things weren't going right, or when something was bothering me. He was the person who said no matter what he would always be there for me if I needed help. He was the person who made me smile when I was

227

feeling down, the person who helped me get through even the toughest day. And now, during the toughest time of my life, when I needed him most, he was the one person who couldn't be there. He was the person who could stop me crying, but he was also the person that was causing the tears. It just hurt that he hadn't even mentioned not wanting to have any contact after the New Year. If he had said that was what he was planning I could've prepared myself for not hearing from him, I could've gotten myself ready for the time hitting 12:00 midnight and me having to deal with not hearing from him anymore, instead I had made the assumption myself, though deep down not 100% believing it. Dale had been everything to me over the last year. He had been every breath I took; every beat my heart made, every second that passed me by was dominated by him, even now that he wasn't in my life, my heart was still dominated by him. Every time I was training it was still his face I pictured, imagining it was his arms I would fall into after I won Gold at some event. He was still my driving force to succeed, he was still my everything and he was still the only person who I wanted to spend my life with. But suddenly I was faced with him not there at all; I was faced with him not being a part of my life in anyway. I had been dealing with not seeing him for eight months now, but the thought I'd at least always hear from him, even if it was just a text message once a week, that still seemed enough. I'm not going to lie, I was lost. I wandered around in a complete haze all the time and just tried to make it through one more day. Thank God for Louise, without her I honestly don't know how I would've gotten through the last few months. Dale had been so adamant that I didn't reveal anything about him and I to anyone, but if I had kept this locked inside I would've gone crazy. It was so unfair of him to expect me to deal with this alone, especially when he was so unwilling to be there when I wasn't feeling strong enough to cope. Louise still didn't know it was him, but she was aware of my love for *Sean* and she helped me through some of the toughest days. I prayed to God to make me stronger, but there were moments when even his power wasn't able to pull me through. I needed the support of Louise's words telling me he wasn't worth my tears. Telling me he wasn't worth all the pain my heart had to deal with. God gave me the strength to stay breathing, but Louise gave me the support to want to keep breathing. I had never felt so heartbroken over someone before, had never felt so lost or so unlike myself. Without Dale I felt like half a person, felt like I was wandering around, passing life by not really caring what was going on. Of course I tried to put every effort into making things work with Aiden again, I genuinely hoped that one day I would wake up and feel the same way about him that I had before, would see him as being as amazing as Dale, if not more so. But I was kidding myself. I knew it in my heart that there wasn't another person in the world who would compare to Dale. No one else could make me get butterflies for them after a year. Every single time I went to meet Dale I was so excited, looked forward to it so much that I would rush myself to meet him and smile the whole way there. With Aiden I didn't get that. In fact it didn't bother me if days went by and I didn't see him. With Dale if an hour passed without his face it felt like years. Aiden and I had a relationship that everyone saw as perfect, a great match, destined to be together. My heart knew who my destiny was and his name certainly wasn't Aiden and what was worse was how guilty I felt being with this man who to everyone else was perfect for me. He loved me like no one else; he looked at me like he would do anything for me. He was completely infatuated with every part of me, and I couldn't even force myself to tell him I loved him. Even after eight months, the words had never once escaped my mouth. I felt like if I told Aiden I loved him it would take away what I felt for Dale. To God it would show I wasn't as serious about Dale as I made out. To be honest I didn't even know if I did love Aiden. There were times when I thought maybe I do, but then I thought about how I loved Dale, how there was no question in my mind about how I felt about him. I knew I loved him, it seeped from my pores how much I loved him, how much I desired to be near him and to have him in my life. But he didn't want me. He couldn't even stay in touch as a friend. It made me feel sick thinking I had opened my heart to him, I expressed every emotion to him about how I felt, held nothing back, and by him not responding in anyway I just felt like he never really felt any true feelings towards, like he never felt anything. Anyway, I could go round in circles talking about how much I love and feel betrayed by him but it won't change anything. Dale was gone and I just had to realise that.

Sat in work on the Friday after New Year, I was having a new lease of life on things. It had been over a week since I last text Dale, a week since I knew he had received it, so my heart had finally caught up with my brain and realised that he wasn't going to be in touch. That day in work had been good fun; I had been having a carry on with two of my work colleagues James and Ally, and had pretty much been just focussing on myself.

"You guys crack me up. Seriously. Anyway, I could completely destroy you both in any fitness challenge so don't start." I was laughing hard and actually feeling like myself. Suddenly my phone started to vibrate in my pocket. As I took it out, I felt sick as the name flashed up in front of me.

1 new message from Sean

I didn't know what to do. I wanted so much to just delete it. Wanted so much to be strong enough to not look at it, but I couldn't. I couldn't *not* see what he was saying.

Hope ur doin good. TBU.

I didn't know how to react. I didn't know whether to be annoyed or relieved. I wasn't sure whether to smile or cry. He had text. He was thinking about me. And regardless of the fact it had taken him a week, he had text. He had gotten in touch. He was thinking about me. I took a few deep breaths and looked at the clock. 16:55pm...I had five min until I finished work so I decided to wait. I had waited seven days so Dale could wait seven minutes, and were those seven minutes long. I couldn't wait to send back something, anything. As I walked out of the bar I stared at the phone, I had to remain calm and composed. I had to remember it wasn't Dale's fault any of this had happened and I had to keep that in mind when I replied. So I kept it simple.

I'm doing good. TBU too. Hope ur smiling.

And that was it. Nothing more. Nothing less. Simple. I did hope he was happy. As much as I went round in circles, thinking he felt nothing, didn't miss me, my heart still believed he did, it always would, I realised that now more than ever. As long as Dale was ok, then so was I. I had to keep it in my head everything he said. I had to keep my brain switched on to everything he had said to me before, every word he had made me promise to believe. It was because of how much I missed him that I switched my brain off to all the good and focussed on every part that could be negative in this whole situation. As I walked home I played Kate Voegale singing Lift Me Up, and I smiled to myself. The words seemed to fit perfectly in with everything I was feeling and thinking. Maybe the day for the fight to be won was just happening. I was willing to wait forever for Dale, and had told him this on numerous occasions, and I still meant that. Dale had only made me one promise and it was to meet on the 17th of October, like we had always said, and I really hope he meant it. Listening to the amazing lyrics of this song were filling me with hope, real hope that my lips would one day again touch his, and when that happened I wouldn't have to say goodbye to him again. He would be mine.

It was amazing how much better I felt in the space of a few hours, all because he had text me. He just seemed to have a knack to make me feel like me again, even with just a text message. As I walked into the house and began sorting out my clothes for training my phone beeped again, and yet again it said his name on my screen.

Can you call for a quick word?

I didn't even hesitate.

"Hey you." I was already smiling as soon as I heard his voice.

"Hi, wow you sound great. I just had to speak to you, especially after that amazing text you sent last week. I've been so busy and just had no time to reply. That really was a fantastic text. In fact every time you text it is fantastic." I could tell he was smiling, and thinking about it made me smile.

"Well you know me; I tend to get caught in the moment and can't help myself. I just needed you to know that last year was something I never want to forget, a time I wouldn't give up or change in any way."

"Well, I mean you know how I feel. I am still completely crazy about you. In fact, we had a lot of new starts and I was going around doing my introductions and none of them compare to you. No one has your flare, your style. Nothing. No one makes my heart race the minute I look at them. No one makes me want to cancel all my plans just so I can sit and chat to them all night. It's just so difficult sometimes. I mean I don't know how you feel about everything, but I miss you every minute of the day. I get so many reminders of you, so many times that make me ache to see you or speak to you, but I know I have to resist. I mean, even just now I'm sure I'm not helping matters speaking to you."

"Truthfully Dale, nothing could make this harder. Nothing could stop me feeling like a part of my world is missing. Nothing could stop me knowing still, that you are the one I would do anything for, the one I want to do anything for. So many things happen and I just wish I could tell you about it, or I'll do something at training and be thinking why you are not there seeing it happen. I just miss you I guess, and the constant reminders of you are so hard to deal with sometimes." I sighed. I wasn't sure what else to say.

"DTO. I've never felt so lost without someone. I was closer to you than I've ever been to any other person in my life, so having to deal with everyday being without you is tough. I hear someone laugh in the office and imagine hearing your voice straight after. Someone runs by with black hair and I pray it's you. I stand at Starbucks and I hope that one time I'll turn round and see you standing. But then at the same time, I have to try and switch you off in my head because I can't be with you. I can't just expect you to be there and to wait around. And I have to focus on my boys and not on myself. You know I will always feel the way about you that I do. I will always love you, and whether it was a day, a week, a month, a year, ten years, it would always be the same with us." I could hear the hope in Dale's voice, as though he was almost convincing himself what he was saying was true.

"Of course it would. It's you and me. Nothing would ever change between us. I know I'll never stop feeling the way I do about you. I know no-one else will ever compare to you. And whether I try and convince myself otherwise, it really won't happen. You changed my whole outlook on life, and that's just one of the reasons why I love you so much." I wanted him to know how crazy I was about him still, how much he had given to my life, just by being him.

"You know I feel exactly the same Kier. I am praying so hard to know the outcome of all this, to know if we will get that happy ending, if I'll get to feel complete again, like I did the whole time I was with you. You are the most amazing person I have come across, you are the most beautiful person inside and out and I can't believe I had to give you up. But I honestly pray that it's God's Will for us to be together again, for us to be united as one." I could hear his voice break slightly, not that I could talk, the tears had been running down my face from the first moment he started speaking.

"Thanks for that Dale." I had taken a few deep breaths and managed to get the words to come back. "I pray for that too. I pray for some sort of resolve. To wake up one day and not feel like I'm fighting against the world to feel like myself again, and I know one day it will happen. I just don't know if that means I'll be with someone else or if I'll get the answer I want, you." I sobbed a little as I said the you.

"Please don't get upset. One day you will get the answer. Just keep praying. Keep hoping and keep believing that one day it will happen. And whether that answer is me or not, nothing will ever change about the way I feel about you. And if it's meant to be, we still have our whole lives to spend with each other." I could feel Dale smiling down the phone. I could feel that he was happy thinking about a life with me and that made me feel better about everything.

"You know I will always pray. If we aren't meant to be together I just have to realise how lucky I am that I was blessed to get the time I had with you. It's just something that will take time to get used to. I've known you for less time than most people in my life, but you have become a bigger part of my life than anyone, so losing that is just difficult to comprehend." I tried not to get upset, instead, in my head I just thought of the word to *Lift Me Up* again. For some reason that song gave me strength, made me feel like I could do this without him, made me realise that suddenly I didn't need the reassurance of him being there, because if he really was meant to be mine, God would make him be mine, no amount of tears or hurt would change that. "As I said, I will always love you Dale, that's the one thing in this whole situation that I can say is a definite. But I also know that being with you isn't a guarantee, so I have to try and get on with my life like it was before I met you. As much as Aiden doesn't give me the same feeling in my heart that you do, and in all honesty, I doubt anyone ever will, he is a great guy. He is everything I should want, and before I knew what it was like to be with my soul-mate, I thought he was the one for me, and I'm determined to try to make it work with him. Compared to you, anyone is going to be second best, at least with Aiden I don't have to go through getting to know someone else, with him, he was a factor in my life before you, so by being with him, it's almost a way of erasing the last year and resetting my memory, if that makes any sense. I don't mean for a minute I'll forget you, but it just seems easier to try to love someone I did before, than try and love someone new. I know it probably sounds a bit of a stupid reasoning, but for some reason it makes sense to me." I realised I was babbling on, but I kept going anyway. "And before you worry I won't be happy, or I'm settling or anything negative like that, I'm honestly not. Aiden and I are getting on great, and there may not be the connection I had with you, but really am I ever going to get that with anyone?" He tried to speak but I just continued, "It's not your fault I fell in love with you, it's not anyone's fault. I realise it was just one of those things that happened and nothing could've stopped it, but for the moment, I have to push me and you out of my head until l find out what the answer is going to be between you and I." I breathed and as I was about to continue, Dale spoke.

"What do you mean then Kier?" Dale sounded panicked.

I breathed again. It was taking every inch of my willpower to say what I was about to say, my head and heart hit that eternal contradiction, but for once I was going to allow my head to win.

"For the moment, I have to get use to a life without you

there. To be honest, I didn't expect to hear from you after New Year and I was getting use to not hearing from you after this week. And now I have to be able to get through a day, a week and more without thinking about whether you are going to text me, or call me. I need to get use to the fact I won't see your name flash up on the screen, or I won't hear your ringtone go off. I'm not doing this because I feel any less for you than I ever have; I'm doing this because of how much I feel for you. I love you that much that I need to let you go to see if you will come back because if you do, then I know we are meant to be." My eyes were filled with tears, my heart was broken in two yet again and I wanted to scream that I needed him in my life to make me feel whole, but I couldn't do it. I couldn't keep him in my life if I wanted things to work with Aiden. And if he loved me like he said he did, one day we would work. One day he would come back to me.

"You mean it this time, don't you? You want no contact at all? What about Louise talking to you, or hearing from Sasha, I mean will you ask them about me? Can I ask them about you?" Dale again, sounding panicked, rushed out everything again, in fact so fast that I could barely make out what he was saying.

"I don't expect you to pretend I don't exist, and don't for a second think I am going to forget you. I will still mention your name to Louise and well, I don't really see Sasha now, but you can ask them anything about me if you need to. I just mean no direct contact anymore. We have to find a way forward, and you said yourself, you need to focus on being where you are just now. You need to concentrate on making that work, and well I need to focus on me and Aiden and making us work. I'm not saying this won't be hard. My heart will be breaking all over again, and I'll want nothing more than to text you, but I know I'm strong enough to fight through until it gets easier not having you. And I'm sure you feel the same." I felt strong, even with the tears rolling down my face I knew I was doing the right thing.

"Ok." Dale paused for almost ten seconds. "So this will be it? No more talking? No more texting? No more anything?"

"I think it has to be Dale. At least until you know if what

you want is me, or until you know if you can actually be with me."

"Ok. I understand where you're coming from. I just, I can't believe this is our final goodbye." Dale's voice broke and I quickly picked up the conversation.

"It's only goodbye if you never plan on saying hello again. And I honestly pray that one day you will. I would love nothing more than to end up with you by my side. It's always going to be you Dale. Always. But for just now, let's just say, ciao for now?" It was my turn to break. I covered the mouth piece so Dale didn't hear me cry. I didn't want him to know I was hurting. I wasn't ready to let him feel how much I was aching inside. I wanted him to think I was being strong and this is exactly what I wanted to happen, when really I still just wanted to say let's just try and talk everyday, let's just try and be friends, stay in each other's lives some way or another.

"Ok." This had suddenly become his favourite word. "Just before I say it, just remember Kier, I do love you, more than I have anyone. No matter what happens from here forward, I need you to remember everything between us. Please never forget anything I told you, because I meant every single word of what I felt for you, what I feel for you. That will never change. Even if I don't see you, I don't hear from you, I will always love you. You are my soul-mate, Kier Scott."

My heart hurt so badly. My body was shaking as I fought against the urge to break down and sob. I wanted to believe him. I wanted to believe he loved me and that he meant all those amazing text messages, all those amazing conversations were real, everything was real. I just had to try and not believe it for the moment; I had to find a way to not remember them. So I lied,

"I promise I won't forget anything. You and I are locked in there tight, both in my head and in my heart. Ciao for now Dale, I'll speak to you soon." I wanted to close the conversation, but I wasn't willing to say goodbye. Not to him.

"Yeah, I'll speak to you soon. Take care." And just before he hung up, he whispered faintly, "I love you."

I was glad he had hung up because I couldn't hold it in

anymore. I broke completely. I cried so hard my whole body was shaking, I couldn't catch my breath and I knew once and for all that would be it until we could be together. Saying goodbye to Dale was like saying goodbye to myself, because without him there was no me. He was still a part of my life; he would always be a part of my life, even if he was never present with me again. I had said my goodbyes to him so many times, but it was still hard. Every other time I knew we would end up still having some kind of connection to each other, be that an occasional text or a random phone call, but now, it was just over. We were done. It was time for me to focus on myself, focus on Aiden and lead my life as though Dale Brenton had never been a part of it.

CHAPTER THIRTY-ONE
7 years later...

Thirty-two. I couldn't actually believe I was thirty-two. Life had passed by quickly over the last seven years and it was hard to believe that my life had taken the path it had. I should be going on to describe the falls, the crashes, the times when my life hit those black moments and I was at rock button, but truthfully, things had actually gone well for me over the last few years. There may have been dark times, but I couldn't recall them as memories. Life was good.

It didn't take me long to get myself back on track. I was now designing my own line that had been adorned by so many celebrities I lost count. It hadn't been easy allowing myself to fall back into fashion, I suppose I was scared I would be haunted by my past memories and they would impede on my designs, but after a chance meeting with Micah Kayel when I worked in the Ice Bar my career kicked itself off and I finally got to show my work, under my name at numerous fashion weeks. I had been working in the Ice Bar for just short of a year when he came in with a few other people that he worked alongside. He had made a comment about some clothes I was wearing, asking who the designer was and where I had purchased them from and when I said I designed them myself he went nuts. He couldn't believe I had this 'talent' and was working as a barmaid. One thing lead to another, and within a year I was showing at New York Fashion Week. I couldn't believe I got there so quickly. I still had a few contacts from when I worked at DB, a few actresses, the rap group I had designed for, so I made a few calls, asked if they wanted to see some of my new work and it went from there. Everything seemed to fall into place naturally, and I was finally back doing what I loved. Everyday I would wake up, smile and just be happy I was finally feeling like me again.

Aiden and I however didn't go the distance. We split up just over a year after getting back together. He asked me to marry him and I just couldn't do it. I had still never uttered those three words you're supposed to and well to be honest I wasn't ready to be his wife. He said he understood that but could we at least consider having a baby, and of course that wasn't me, kids were never part of the plan with me, I wasn't ever supposed to be a mum; I was too focussed on myself for that to happen. My career meant everything to me, and it wouldn't have been fair for me to try and hide that from Aiden. I had learned not to change myself for others, and as much as Aiden meant to me, he didn't mean enough for me to be someone I'm not. Basketball was still a massive factor in my life too; in fact I had played in the Olympics as part of team USA, believe it or not. So with the mix of fashion and basketball, Aiden became second choice, and he wasn't willing to accept that anymore, and I didn't expect him too. We hadn't spoken since. Last time I heard he had gotten married and was doing well at his job and had become a dad twice over. I didn't feel any regret at missing out on a life with him, I felt more relieved that I hadn't let my guard down and just done what he wanted. My life was where I wanted it to be, my career couldn't have been better, and I had an Olympic Gold under my belt. The years had flown by and as much as I hate to admit it, Dale hadn't quite become as distant a memory as I had hoped. I still thought about him every day. Every fashion show I attended I prayed he would be there. We had bumped into each other a few times over the last seven years, but to be honest we didn't really speak too much. He congratulated me on my career, said he admired my designs, general chit chat but nothing that would engross us in one of our usual conversations. We seemed to cut each other off before it went that far. I often expected to leave the show and receive a text message asking me to call him, or just saying TBU or anything like that but it never happened, and as much as I wanted to, I never once gave in and sent anything to him. I still saw Louise of course, in fact I was maid of honour at her wedding to Todd, luckily him and Aiden had parted friendship beforehand so it saved for an awkward moment. They did go the distance and on occasion I would ask about Dale in a round about way. I had all but lost touch with Sasha. She married Harry, though from what I hear from Louise, it's not the best of relationships: fighting, adultery, and all the rest. Sasha was still working as a creative designer, doing photo shoots, runways shows and anything else that she could, and her career was progressing as well as mine. Louise had been stepped up to manage the main office of DB Designs after Arlene was let go following on from the backlash of me leaving. Dale finally just fired Arlene and Suranne saying he felt he couldn't trust them within his company after they made such a harsh judgement on his integrity. I tried to feel guilty over it but I really didn't have any remorse for either woman. Between her and Suranne my life was almost over, they had pushed me to almost breaking point and I couldn't feel sorry for either of them. Although I had been happy with Aiden, and my job in the Ice Bar kept me going, in the first month or so after leaving DB Designs I was a wreck. I cried all the time, I was a broken shell, and to be honest without Louise I really don't know where I would've ended up. I'm just glad I had people to stop me wanting to give up. I had bumped into Suranne a few times; she was back doing behind the scenes work for a model company called Volt. When she left DB Designs she was back to square one because she hadn't really done anything that was recognised as brilliant since way back in 2000. Again, I tried to feel sorry for her, and was almost tempted to give her name to a few friends of mine to get a better job, but she had broke me down to nothing, made me feel like I was worthless, and granted the whole time something was happening between Dale and I, it was none of her business and she just ruined her own career trying to ruin mine. As much as I had hated her for doing it, and as much as I had sunk into that depression over not having a job, I had come out on top. If I had stayed at DB's I would possibly still be designing for him and wouldn't have ended up with my own shows all over the world. I could hardly believe sometimes that eight years had passed me by since first meeting him. I checked up on occasion as to what Dale was doing, and I was pleased to discover his two boys were doing well. Both professional athletes now, in fact I had met Kiah at the Olympics. He played basketball for the male team USA, and had proven to be a useful tool. He was still young so he wasn't lined up for every game but it was a learning opportunity for him. He was very like Dale, but I had tried not to get too close. It was too difficult to imagine bumping into Dale and his wife, and seeing him play happy families. I couldn't deal with that. Even after all the time that had passed, my heart still beat only for him, and even the very mention of his name still made me go weak, though I have to admit hearing the name Brenton mentioned during the Olympics made me more determined, maybe leading to such a big success for myself. His other son had joined the New England Patriots and was the best Quarterback they had ever had, as well as the youngest. I have to admit, I didn't know his kids, but I was so proud of them both, which may seem strange, but I guess my love for him made me love everything he did, and I knew how proud he would be. This was the times it was most difficult, when I wanted to be by Dale's side, seeing him beaming with joy over his boys, or seeing him be so happy. It made me crave seeing his smile, that cheeky grin that made me melt every time he flashed it at me. Nothing over the last seven years had made me stop being in love with him. No other person had ever come into my life that gave me the same feeling he did. Yes there had been other men, but I didn't get that connection with them, and they found it difficult to comprehend how much I was involved in my work or how much time I dedicated to training. Dale got that about me, he was the only one who got that about me.

I couldn't believe it was fall already. I had been busy every season this year and the coming months were looking to prove very similar. I made the conscious decision to buy an apartment with another apartment across from it to use as my work room. It meant never having to travel too far and if I got inspired at anytime I had everything at my fingers tips, and with my success over the last few years, money was no longer a problem for me. As I prepared my spring collection in my work room, minutes turned to hours, to days, to months. I was completely unaware of anything except getting my designs finished. I didn't really rely on having a staff too much; I did all the designs myself, and would only really employ casual staff to make up the designs. Work distracted me. Work soothed me. So much in fact that I hadn't even realised it was October. In particular October 16th...2016. I couldn't believe I had forgotten. Tomorrow was the day Dale and I had always said we would meet again. The day we were finally supposed to be able to be a real couple. Suddenly I panicked. I wasn't sure what to do. I think half of me had always expected to hear from him before now, for him to tell me that he was happy at home, or for him to already be back in my life. We had agreed to meet tomorrow at midday at the top of the Empire State Building, the place we had spent that amazing day all those years ago. But now, I wasn't sure if I should go. I hadn't been back up there since that day. In fact I do everything I can to avoid being anywhere near it. The sight of it was too painful...even from my apartment view I tried not to look over at it too much. But now I was faced with the reality of whether tomorrow I should go. I should see if fate was going to take me back to Dale, if I would find out he still loved me. I had tried not to think too much about how he would have felt over these last seven years. To be honest it was all a little too difficult. My heart wanted to remember everything he said as fact but my mind felt too hurt to believe any of it was true. I doubted how much I had crossed his mind, instead could only imagine him being happy at home. Imagining her being with him; loving him. It was those exact thoughts that made me not want to go tomorrow, that made me think I would stand up there alone and then I would be back to square one. But then I thought well at least if he doesn't show up then it's closure on all of this. It would be closure on the last seven years of my life; it's over once and for all. Confusion set in, and I tried to let my mind go blank, and focus on designing, but for the first time in a long time, that didn't happen. He was there, imprinted on the front of my memory and he wasn't going to leave. I had to go. I had to see that I wasn't part of his world, his life. At least then I could get him out of my head. I looked at my watch, 1:03am. Again time had passed me by, and I was aware that in 10 hours and 57 min I would be standing at the top of the Empire State Building awaiting my fate. Nervous didn't even describe the way I was feeling.

CHAPTER THIRTY-TWO
11:46am

I was early as always. I couldn't remember how long the elevator ride took. I couldn't remember how long it took to get into the building. I couldn't remember anything about it. My mind was so focussed on Dale that day back in December, 2008, that everything else blurred in my mind. I looked at my watch, the same watch he had given me all those years ago in Rome. I had passed security, and it was now 11:53am. Seven minutes to go. I checked my watch every second. I checked my phone every other second. I still expected a call, and the fact I didn't have one didn't fill me with confidence. Instead it made me realise this was a wasted journey. At least if nothing else I could reminisce and finally say goodbye, once and for all.

Exiting the elevator at the top, I felt the cold blast of air and I could see the skyline of New York before me. If nothing else, I was getting to experience this amazing view again. I had my iPod, as always blaring in my ear. *Lift Me Up* had become my song of choice over the last few years, and every time I heard it I pulled from the power of the words that seemed to give me strength to deal with any situation. Today was going to be a hard one, a final farewell to something that had never really been mine to let go of. Over the last eight years he had been always in my mind, always locked on in my thoughts, but I knew after today I was going to have to forget him completely. I wondered what he was doing just now. I wondered if he even realised the date? I wondered if he debated over whether to go, or if it was simply just another day to him. I knew he wasn't going to show up, but I just wondered if he even thought about it. If he got to Oct 17th every year and thought about me, and thought about everything we had together, or if it was just another date to him. I can honestly say no day has gone by in the last few years that I haven't thought about him. A day when there wasn't some kind of reminder of him, but I didn't know if he felt that way too. When I was at the Olympic in London, I saw him from a distance with his wife. Although he wasn't looking loving into her eyes, he was standing next to her, hand in hand. I was so glad by that time that my events had finished, because seeing that broke me. I had had to imagine him with her so many times, but seeing it, there in front of me, made me feel like my whole world had just come away from me and I was left standing in front of the gates of hell. He didn't see me, and I was sort of glad, because I could at least see how he acted with her on a regular basis. The look on his face that day was focussed and he seemed to ignore everything else around him, but still, seeing him hold her hand, seeing him have that connection with her that he had with me, was like a nightmare come true. I think that's the reason I knew he wouldn't be here today. He had his life. He had an existence that I really couldn't be a part of, that I'm guessing he didn't want me to be a part of. Today would just give me closure on the whole situation. As I walked towards the edge of the observation deck, I almost smiled as Hallelujah came on my iPod. That was the song, the first song I had ever had with him. The song I had given him on that first CD, and now here it was, as though it was a confirmation of a goodbye. I leaned my hands on the railing, looked out at New York and breathed deeply. As I released the breath I couldn't tell if it was a sign of relief that this was all over, or if I was breathing to stop the tears falling down my face. I thought all the way here I was ready for this goodbye; I thought I was ready to completely let go. Like every other time with him, I was still struggling to say that word, but now was the time. I breathed again, and this time I didn't fight it. I let the tears well in my eyes and splash down my cheeks. *"It's a cold and it's a broken Hallelujah"* the words were perfect. He was my moment of hallelujah, and now nothing. I was falling into a daze and as I listened to Jeff Buckley move onto the third verse, I glanced at my watch. 12:00pm. If he was coming he would be late, if he was coming. I don't know why I was fooling myself. It had been seven years since our goodbye. Seven years of looking at my phone 100 times a day and praying I would see his name. Seven years of wanting to be with him, and hoping he was going to appear. Seven years of trying to make myself believe in my heart what my head had always known. Seven years of feeling like I was only half a person. Looking at it that way I didn't even know why I was standing here, why I was tormenting myself, why I even thought for a second that I would come up and he would be here was now beyond me. As Hallelujah came to a close, I wandered around the observation deck looking out at the sights on New York. I could hardly believe that eight years ago I had met the man of my dreams, had a year-long love affair that was like nothing else I had ever experienced. No-one else that had entered my life in the last eight years had given me the same emotional connection that Dale Benton had; no one had touched my heart in a way that made me not forget them. It was difficult to comprehend that now I really had to let all this go. I had to realise that fairytales don't come true, that is why they are always based on the imagination of others and not real-life events. I was one of the lucky ones, I had at least been aware of what it felt like to be with my soul-mate. Even if Dale didn't believe I was his, I know he was mine. In the year I had been with Dale nothing had been sour between us, aside from the drama related to us, me and him were always great, always perfect. We had never argued, never had cross words. Even when I felt like my world had abandoned me and I hit rock bottom, I never felt harsh feelings towards Dale. None of it, really, was his fault. And even now, I think he made the right choice staying with his family, I'm not selfish enough a person to think he should've gone with his heart and chose me. I still have a belief that people come into your life for different reasons, and well, maybe if I hadn't met Dale I would still be stuck in a rut with old friends who dragged me down, and I would've never thought of myself as being anything special. It was just hard to try and comprehend that this was the final goodbye, farewell, whatever way I wanted to put it, we were over. It was no longer ciao for now, it was simply, done.

I looked at my watch...half an hour had passed, 12:30pm lit up on my watch. It was actually over. A part of me didn't want to believe it, there had been a part in my brain that always thought he would show up, and now, being faced with the reality of it was a little overwhelming. The tears started in my eyes, and my heart sunk in my chest. I had been so strong for the last few years, and today, as everything hit me, it was a lot to take on board. I knew when I saw him in London with his wife that he was back on track with his life. I knew that for him to be with me, it would mean giving up a lot more than he would gain. I mean, I'm just me. Just Kier. When we were together I wasn't successful, I was still living in a loft apartment and getting around on a skateboard. His wife was one of the most sought-after psychiatrist, successful, and I had to admit she was attractive, maybe not what I would've imagined him being with, but attractive none the less. No wonder he chose her, it was obvious that was what was going to happen. As much as my heart was breaking at this moment, I had to admit, I was still glad I had come. I get my resolution and granted, it wasn't the resolution I wanted, or I had dreamed about, but now my heart and brain were working from the same page, and I could finally move myself on. I looked at my watch again, undone the strap and walked to the observation viewers. The last eight years I had stared at that watch everyday as a constant reminder of Dale and I and what we had. It was the only real connection I still had with him now, but suddenly, it no longer seemed right holding on to that. Another chapter of my life was over, and it was time to move on. Dale gave me up because he had to do the right thing, and I was ready to fully accept that. He gave up the fight for us and left me behind, but at least he wasn't toying with my emotions. He hadn't shown today because him and I weren't meant to be. I placed the watch on the observation ledge, about turned and walked towards the elevators. I wanted to look back, to go back and pick it up, but I knew this was a better option, a clean break, a new beginning for myself. And while I stood in the elevator, I pulled my mobile phone from my pocket, and went to Dale and hit delete, then I went to Sean and hit delete. And finally, I opened my MTL folder, I read through a few of the messages I had sent and received from him, but it was too hard, was breaking my heart too much, so I marked them all, and again hit delete, and as 657 messages emptied from the folder, I fell to my knees and let it all out. When the elevator reached the bottom, I stood up, took a deep breath and as the door opened I looked at it as me exiting my past and beginning my future. The story of Dale and Kier had been a long road, it was filled with love, true love, but also hurt and heartbreak that I was ready to stamp out. The cold rush of the October New York air rushed through my whole body. As I stepped through the door and I smiled as I heard *Breakaway* by Kelly Clarkson blare through my ears. My life was just beginning, and as much as I know Dale would always be present in my thoughts and in my memories, I had to let go. I had to breakaway. I believed that Dale had come into my life for a reason, and as much as my heart broke at the very mention of his name, I still felt it was all good that came from me meeting him. I loved every ounce of him, and loving him had made me love myself a lot more. I would never have pushed myself to design the way I did when I was with him, and that had led to me having my own company and my name being recognised among the best. From 2008 – 2009 I had the best time of my life, I fell in love with my soul-mate and even now I wouldn't change that, I will remember that year and smile because I got that year, I got the fairytale even if it was short. Regret will never enter my mind, not with Dale. There is nothing about the time I had with him that I would give up. Yes it was difficult at the end, and yes my heart was in so many pieces I wasn't sure if it would ever feel whole again without Dale in my life, but the love I felt, that surge of electricity between me and another human being could never be replaced, it would never be erased from my mind.

I walked all the way back to my apartment that night. Stopping off at Starbucks, going to Zabar's for some food, basically just trying to take my mind off everything else that was in my life. Walking around in New York, no matter how long you have lived there, feels like a different world every single time. I never got bored of the smell of the city, the sounds, or the look on tourist's face as they ooh'ed and aahh'd at the skyscrapers. I was happy to forget the rest of the world and just focus on me and New York. I wanted to call Louise, but I wasn't quite ready to open up about it all yet. She knew there was a date we would've met, a time but she didn't know when, and now, well I just needed to try and get my head around this before deciding if I wanted to let anyone in. I stared down at my empty wrist, sure I had done the right thing, but at the same time, missing the feeling of him still being with me. But, I wasn't going to dwell, I had gone for seven years without Dale, I was just going to have to learn to get use to that. This was the last landmark date that had anything to do with us, and I realised now, more than ever it was time to move on and stop allowing myself to live a lie that he was still mine.

It was 19:42pm by the time I got home, the air temperature was feeling more and more like winter, and I couldn't wait to get into my apartment, and get lost in some mindless TV.

As I got in, I pulled on my grey sweats and my favourite navy blue FDNY hooded top, and walked towards my wardrobe. I had been keeping a diary almost religiously since I was eighteen, and all of them were in a locked case on the bottom of my storage unit. I went in and took out the first diary I had that ever mentioned Dale.

I still can't get Dale off my brain. Ha!

I had to almost laugh. Nothing had even happened between us when I wrote that. With Dale it had been an instant attraction from that first fashion event that I laid eyes on him, and reading back my diary made me realise that even more. Love at first sight? Lust at first sight? I was no longer sure what it was, but I knew how special that year with him had been. Irreplaceable is the only word I can use to describe the whole event. But I realise now that when things aren't meant to be, then they just won't happen. I remember reading that quote by Bernard Shaw, the one I had spoken to Dale about, the one that said, "There are two great tragedies in life, one is losing your great love and the other is finding them." I don't know what frame of mind Mr Shaw was in when he wrote this, but I'm guessing he had just had his heart broken and his mind wasn't dealing with it very well. The way I see it, when related to my own situation, Dale was my great love, and what happened between us was a tragedy, and like all tragedies, they aren't meant to have a happy ending. In life, does anyone really ever get the happy ending? In all honestly, if you even get some sort of ending you should think of yourself as lucky. And I have my ending. I have a fashion label that is known all over the world, people know my name and recognise my face, and I have everything I want, well everything except the man I love, so really, all I can say is, give me tragedy. I know even now he is my soul-mate, and just because he didn't show up today doesn't make him any less of my soul-mate, it just means that the year we had was all we were ever supposed to have. I know I will move on, but I doubt I will ever meet anyone who makes my pulse race by the very mention of their name, who makes my knees go weak, or who makes me feel whole again, but I can deal with that. In my life at the moment men are always going to have to be 2nd place. By remaining single for the moment, I can focus the energy wasted on building a new relationship, into something that really means something to me and that is fashion; designing, working on creativity and making other people happy with my clothing. And I still have basketball, which takes up a lot of time. I'm still playing as much as possible and loving every second of it, so my days were full. I hoped one day I would wake up and Dale wouldn't be my first thought, and even though after eight years he still is, I am still in the belief it will happen. I will always love Dale, but sometimes love just isn't enough to make things right. All I know is for that moment in my life I have never been happier, never felt more content, and never felt more whole. Dale will always be in my heart, and I will never regret my decision to be with him or start an affair with him because I mean it, with my right hand held high to God, it was the most wonderful and amazing time I have ever experienced and even now I can't get it out of my head. Dale made his choice, he chose the life he had and I couldn't hold that against him. He done exactly what he thought and felt was right, all I hoped was he was happy in his decision. I'm not going to lie and say I don't care, because I do and I will still miss him, the way I always have, but at least now I have some closure, and I can face the future knowing where I stand. All I know is to me, Dale Brenton was MTL and nothing will change that. He will forever be my other half, the one who completes me...*My Bracket* ( )

( )

Brackets by Joanne K Jardine
Published by SHN Publishing
www.shnpublishing.com

(Brackets)

Lightning Source UK Ltd.
Milton Keynes UK
UKOW051834121211

183641UK00001B/150/P